THE ESCAPERS

BOOK ONE OF THE ALIEN HARVESTER
SERIES

L. J. MONAHAN

CONTENTS

Book design by Autumn Raven

Cover design by Autumn Raven

For Parker and Jack,
your love of reading inspired me.

PROLOGUE

THE ALIEN SPACESHIP smelled of the sea.

Bryce had been trapped in this tiny cell for hours. Hardly bigger than a school locker, it had just enough space for someone of modest size to sit down with an inch to spare on each side. The seat was crafted without padding, no thought to comfort, just two sheets of blue alien metal meeting at a right angle. It was dead-dark in the cell; Bryce couldn't even see his hand in front of his face. There was a hole in the seat in case he needed to go to the bathroom, but thankfully he didn't, even though it had been hours. Or at least he thought it had.

He knew his cell adjoined others of the same size and shape, as if humans only came in one size. The other cells had been sealed shut when he boarded the ship, so he didn't know how many were occupied. But he guessed there were others on the ship, many others.

He could hear whimpering from the cell on his left. He felt for her, but he could do nothing to help.

The ship moved noisily. The engine rumbled, and he could feel shifting as the ship hit turbulence from time to time.

Strangely, he felt calm. Perhaps it was shock. Today started out just like any other: chores, a shower, breakfast, school. Yet now he found himself locked in an alien spaceship on his way to God-knows-where.

Actually, in the back of his mind, he knew where the ship was headed. Even though his aunt and uncle had tried to keep the news from him, turning off the TV whenever an unpleasant story came on and refusing to talk about anything upsetting or controversial, he still knew. Information seeps in, like water finding the leaky spots in a roof. The kids at school had told Bryce everything that his aunt and uncle had tried to keep from him. Not that he let them know; he appreciated the effort to shield him, even if it didn't work.

No, Bryce knew where he was going. The ship was heading toward an Imjac work camp. He had been harvested.

CHAPTER
ONE

CREAK!

Uncle Kyle really needs to fix the barn door.

Bryce sat up on his bed and rubbed the sleep out of his eyes. He didn't need a clock to know the time: five o'clock in the morning, on the dot. His uncle was as reliable as a Swiss watch.

Bryce pulled on his pants and slid into a sweatshirt, shivering in the cold. He crept down the hallway, passing the closed bedroom doors, then ambled down the stairs. He opened the door to the mudroom and tucked the end of his pant legs into his boots. He paused at the front entrance; he could hear his aunt stirring in the bedroom above him, but the house was otherwise quiet.

I beat her.

He pushed open the front door and let it close softly behind him. It had rained the night before, and the soggy ground gripped his boots as he walked. The barn loomed in front of him, a long building with a peaked roof. A crescent moon hung just above its eaves. He loved this time in the morning—the stillness of the air, the absolute silence. Even the creatures of the night lay dormant in this in-between time.

He slid the barn door open, and the pungent odor of fifty cows cooped up in a building overnight struck his nostrils like a brick. He blinked to adjust to the lights. Uncle Kyle waved from the milking machine on the other side of the barn, where cows stood patiently waiting their turn. Cows, like humans, were creatures of habit.

Nearby, one of the cows lifted her head above the stall walls, staring at him placidly. He strode over to her and rubbed her head.

"Morning, Dottie," he said, scratching each of the four black dots at the crown of her head for which she was named. "Ready for your milking?"

He walked along the stalls, greeting each of the animals. It surprised him when he moved here that the cows, like people, had their own personalities. Some were outgoing, like Dottie. Others were shy and didn't like to be touched. A few were downright grumpy.

"You beat me here again," a voice rang out behind him.

Bryce turned and saw his cousin Amanda smiling at him. She was dressed in her work jeans, boots, and a loose Alhambra High School sweatshirt. Her brown curls just touched the tops of her shoulders. She had dark brown eyes like her mother, but pale skin and freckles like Uncle Kyle. Other than the freckles, Bryce and Amanda looked enough alike to pass as brother and sister.

"Well, maybe you should stop sleeping in," Bryce said with a smile. Sleeping in on a dairy farm meant waking up at 5:05 a.m. instead of 5:00.

Amanda grabbed a shovel that had been leaning against the wall and tossed it to him. "Your turn to clean out the stalls, Mr. Early Bird."

Bryce took the shovel from her and grimaced. She was right—she had cleaned out the barn the day before.

Scooping manure off the barn floor was by far the worst job on the farm. Uncle Kyle called it the best part of having kids. Bryce didn't think he was joking.

As he made his way from stall to stall, loading the cow pies into a wheelbarrow, Bryce thought about what the kids back home in San Diego would think if they saw him now. Living on a farm. Getting up before the sunrise. Scooping cow poop off the floor. It was a far cry from the sun-loving, beach life he had in San Diego. It had only been three years, but in some ways it felt like his San Diego self was a completely different person than who he was today.

Of course, the world was a completely different place than it was three years ago. Before then, aliens were figments of imagination, little green men in cartoons and movies.

Turns out they were blue, not green. And now they ruled the earth.

———

At seven, they all sat down for breakfast.

"Easy on the sugar, Bryce," Aunt Sammie said as Bryce covered his oatmeal with the sweet stuff. "That bag has to last us until December."

"Sorry." It was easy to forget how limited they were on supplies. Since the invasion, getting products from other places on the globe had become difficult, if not impossible. Everyday luxuries like sugar were hard to get. Luckily, they could trade milk, butter, and Aunt Sammie's homemade cheese with other farmers for food, so they had plenty to eat.

"It's okay." His aunt smiled at him. "Living the way we do now isn't easy."

"Mom, the only reason that he uses so much sugar is he hates oatmeal," Amanda said.

Aunt Sammie's eyebrows rose in surprise. "Is that true, Bryce?"

Bryce felt his face flush. He did hate the oatmeal—it reminded him of the paste in kindergarten. But he couldn't complain, not after his aunt and uncle had opened their home to him and treated him like a son. He would eat paste every day if it made them happy.

"No, I like it," he said, taking a big spoonful and shoving it in his mouth. "Mmm." He rubbed his stomach for effect.

"He's just saying that," Amanda said.

Bryce shot Amanda a dark look. She stuck her tongue out at him in return.

"Bryce, I can make you something else," Aunt Sammie said. "It's no big deal."

Bryce shook his head. "Please don't go to any trouble. Amanda's wrong—I like the oatmeal."

Aunt Sammie shrugged. "If you say so."

Uncle Kyle cleared his throat. "I was talking to Big Jim in town," he said. "There was a harvesting yesterday."

"Do we have to talk about this with the kids here?" Aunt Sammie protested.

Uncle Kyle set his spoon down. "I think we do," he said. "They need to know what's going on. It affects them, after all."

"Fine," Aunt Sammie relented. "Where was it?"

"Santa Rosa."

Aunt Sammie's jaw dropped. "Santa Rosa," she repeated. "So close?"

Bryce shrugged. "What's the big deal? Santa Rosa is not *that* close, right?"

Amanda shook her head. "Not too close. Twenty-five miles away."

"Close enough," Aunt Sammie said. "*Too* close for my comfort."

Bryce felt his insides tighten. The blueskins' raids were getting nearer and nearer.

"That's not the worst of it," Uncle Kyle continued. "This time the blueskins went after kids about Amanda and Bryce's age."

A knot formed in Bryce's stomach. The only harvesting the aliens had done so far had been of young, able-bodied adults. Now that they were after kids, he and Amanda could be targets. Hadn't the blueskins done enough to him already?

"Why are we talking about this?" Aunt Sammie questioned tersely.

"They need to know the truth," Uncle Kyle said. "And they need to be prepared. You two know what to do if you see an Imjac ship?"

"Run," Amanda said. "Run back here."

"And hide," Bryce added.

"Right. Run right back here and go straight toward the barn. We can hide you there for weeks if we need to, long enough for the blueskins to get bored and go away."

"What if we're not near home?" Bryce asked.

"Then take shelter somewhere safe. Every farmhouse has someplace you can hide, and farmers around here would take you in without a second thought."

"Can we please change the subject?" Aunt Sammie said, rising to clear her bowl.

Uncle Kyle reverted to his familiar smile. "We can do that. Bryce, can you look at the milk machine for me after school? It's acting a bit funny lately."

"Sure," Bryce answered. But inside, he felt anything but sure. The blueskins were close and getting closer every day.

———

Though Bryce had his sweatshirt zipped up tight, his ears burned from the cold. He hadn't gotten use to the falls and winters of NorCal. He spotted Amanda on her bike, waiting for him on the road. His biked bumped down the steep gravel driveway. Then Bryce made a sharp right at the Hubbard Dairy sign as he hit the main drag. Amanda punched her pedals behind him. Soon they were off at a good clip.

Amanda pulled up next to him, and they rode side by side. At this time of the morning, the only traffic was the occasional pickup truck. The road was flat and wide, so they would have lots of warning of any traffic coming their way.

The sun peeked over the hills to the east. Knotty oaks dotted the golden hillsides, providing shade to cows and sheep. It was beautiful country, but Bryce still missed the ocean.

"Do you think they'll come here?" he asked Amanda as they rode. "The blueskins, I mean."

"I don't know," she said. "I guess it's possible…I never would have thought that they'd have stopped in Santa Rosa. You escapers must be hard to find."

"I'm not an escaper," he answered, even though he knew she was joking. She knew why he ended up on this farm, more than five hundred miles from his old home. He wasn't like the other kids, whose families moved to Alhambra to get away from the alien Imjac. His aunt and uncle's farm was the only home he had now.

"I know, Bryce. I just wish everyone else did."

Bryce remembered his first day in Alhambra, when the army bus dropped him off at the end of the long driveway. He stared at the farm and felt he had been left in another world, an eleven-year-old alone with a duffle bag that held all his belongings.

Aunt Sammie and Uncle Kyle came down the driveway

to greet him with Amanda at their side. They had met before at family gatherings, but it had been a few years, and Bryce was struck by how much they seemed like strangers to him.

"Hello, Bryce," Aunt Sammie said, a hand on each of his shoulders. "Welcome." With her dark curls and deep brown eyes, she looked so much like his mother that Bryce felt his eyes well up. He bit his lip to stop the tears.

Uncle Kyle reached for his bag. "Let me take that for you," he said with a friendly grin.

Bryce held on to his duffle for a moment, then relented and handed it to his uncle.

The two adults started up the driveway toward the house, leaving Bryce and Amanda alone. They gaped at each other for a silent moment.

Suddenly Amanda broke into a smile. "C'mon," she said, grabbing Bryce by the arm. "I'll show you your room. When you're done unpacking, there's a newborn calf in the barn. You can help me feed her."

And just like that, Bryce had felt at ease.

But most of the town had no idea about the circumstances that led him to Alhambra. To the locals, he was just another escaper, another invader in their small town.

And most locals hated the escapers; it didn't matter to them that the escapers moved to Alhambra to avoid the blueskin harvests. As far as they were concerned, the newcomers should head back to where they came from.

He gripped his handlebars firmly and pumped his legs, shooting out ahead of Amanda.

"You're not going to get away from me with those little chicken legs," Amanda said, laughing as she pumped her legs hard and caught up to him. A serious look crossed her face. "Look, I wouldn't worry about the harvesting. They probably got everyone they needed in Santa Rosa, so they won't bother to come here. I mean, who has even heard of Alhambra?"

"Yeah, you're probably right. I sure hadn't heard of this cowtown before I got shipped here," Bryce said playfully and raced ahead for good.

They pulled up at the entrance to the school and stopped. Funded by a 1920's robber baron, Alhambra High School was built in the classical style, with tall columns that supported a peaked roof. Wide, grand steps led up to the main entrance, and even though the building had seen better days on the inside, the groundskeeper kept the hedges in the front perfectly manicured.

"Come through the front doors today," Amanda pleaded. "You don't have to go back there."

"Yes, I do. You know I do," Bryce insisted. "But don't worry about it—I don't care. It doesn't bother me at all."

Amanda furrowed her brow. "Okay, see you later." She rode to the bike racks in front of the school and hitched her bike to the rack. Halfway up the walkway to the main quad, she turned back to Bryce and waved.

At the start of the school year, the local kids made it clear that the main hallway and quad were not for escapers. A few of the escapers rebelled, boldly venturing into the hallway and quad. They paid the price in bruises. Bryce quickly saw that the escapers were outmanned. He wasn't afraid to stand up for himself, but taking on all of the locals alone was foolhardy.

So today, like every day, Bryce steered his bike around the main building of the school to join the escapers in the back. He locked his bike to one of the smelly dumpsters and entered the school through the door the custodians used to take out the trash.

———

He saw Amanda later in the halls during passing period, standing at her open locker.

"What's new, cousin?" he said, sidling up to her.

Amanda sighed. "Nothing, other than the fact that Mr. Lorry just gave us about two hours of homework tonight! I hate math."

"I'll help you," Bryce said, confidently. "We'll get it done in a half-hour."

Amanda seemed a little relieved. "I wish I was as good as you at math."

"Well, you can help me with my English. Mrs. Garcia assigned an essay that's due on Friday," he said, "on a book that I hardly understand."

"Is this escaper bothering you, Mandy?" a voice rang out.

Bryce turned around to find himself staring into the narrow-set eyes of Max Peaks. Tall and broad-shouldered, Max and his minions led the anti-escaper movement, thinking it was his personal duty to hound escapers in the hall. To make matters worse, Max had a thing for Amanda.

As usual, with him were his two flunkies, Darla and Dwayne, known behind their backs as Dumb and Dumber. They were supposedly cousins with Max, but the only resemblance Bryce could see was that they were all the same shape, rectangular, six feet tall and four feet wide.

Amanda slammed her locker door shut. "Max, you know this is my cousin. He's no escaper—not that you should be bothering them anyway."

"It doesn't matter that he's your cousin," Max said, swiping his bangs from his long, wide forehead. "His parents sent him here to hide from the blueskins. And now look what's happening? The blueskins came to Santa Rosa just the other day. All because of guys like him." He jabbed one of his fat fingers in Bryce's chest.

Bryce grabbed Max's hand and pushed it away. "My

parents didn't send me here—they died in the war against the blueskins. I'm here because I have nowhere else to go."

Max laughed. "Am I supposed to feel bad because your parents suck at fighting?"

Dumb and Dumber guffawed behind him.

Bryce felt his face warm and his hands curl into fists. "Leave my parents out of it. At least they aren't stealing from the whole town."

Max's parents owned the only grocery store in town. And while most businesses had suffered since the war, somehow the Peaks were getting richer and richer. Most suspected it had to do with price gouging, as the other markets had to close their doors for lack of supplies. There just wasn't another place in town to get your everyday groceries. The Peaks knew this and charged accordingly.

Max's already-narrow eyes moved even closer together. "What did you say?" He grabbed Bryce by the sweatshirt, lifted him off the ground, and slammed him into the bank of lockers. "You take that back."

Bryce felt the air escape from his lungs as Max's sturdy arms pressed into his chest. He looked around, but there were no teachers nearby to come to his rescue. "Fine," he huffed. "You take back what you said about my parents first."

"No way," Max spat. "I don't apologize to escapers."

Amanda grabbed Max's shoulder. "Let him down, Max."

"Or what?"

"Or I'll scream."

He laughed, and Dumb made a move to put her hand over Amanda's mouth. She was too slow, though, and Amanda slipped out of her grasp and let loose with her loudest horror-movie scream.

All eyes in the hallway snapped onto them. Mr. Lorry

poked his head out of his classroom and trudged in their direction.

Max dropped Bryce, who landed on his feet awkwardly.

"This isn't over," Max said, and stomped away with his friends in his wake.

———

Later that afternoon, Bryce lay on his back under the milking machine. He made one last adjustment with his wrench and stood up. "That should do it," he said, handing the wrench to Uncle Kyle.

"Let's give it a whirl then," his uncle said. He flipped a couple of switches and pressed the start button. The machine fired up smoothly.

"All right!" Uncle Kyle said, clapping Bryce across the back. "I don't know what I'd do without you."

Bryce flushed under his uncle's praise. "It was no big deal."

"No," Uncle Kyle said. "It is a big deal. In normal times, I could get parts in from the factory." He lifted his cap and pushed his hair back. "But these aren't normal times. The factory is closed. Without you, we would be back to milking by hand."

Bryce shoved his hands into his front pockets and shrugged. He had always had a knack with technology that he couldn't explain. From a young age, he loved to take things apart and put them back together. Alarm clocks, toy robots, old computers. His room in San Diego more resembled a machine shop than a bedroom. His mother would complain constantly about not being able to go in his room without risking breaking her neck. "This is going to sound weird, but sometimes it feels like the machines are talking to me."

Uncle Kyle laughed. "That's not weird. Sometimes I think the cows are talking to me. Especially Dottie."

They gathered up the tools to bring back to the shed.

"Can I ask you a question, Uncle Kyle?"

Uncle Kyle tossed a wrench in the toolbox. "Shoot."

"Why do the people around here hate escapers?"

Uncle Kyle stopped putting the tools away and looked Bryce in the eyes. "Is something going on at school I should know about?"

"No, no," Bryce lied. "It's just a feeling I get sometimes."

Uncle Kyle opened the shed and held the door for Bryce. "People are scared. The whole world just got turned upside down, and all of a sudden a bunch of new people come moving into town. They're just lashing out—I don't think they mean it."

"That makes sense, I guess," Bryce said. "It isn't right, though."

Uncle Kyle put his hand on Bryce's shoulder. "You're not an escaper, Bryce. This is your home. Remember that."

CHAPTER
TWO

BRYCE AND AMANDA rode home that next afternoon from school in perfect fall weather. The locals called it the Indian summer, but it wasn't sticky hot like summer could be. There were cool mornings, and long, warm afternoons. Not quite as good as the weather in San Diego, but pretty close.

It had been a perfect day at school too. Bryce had avoided Max and Dumb and Dumber in the halls. He aced his math test. Best of all, he had no English homework because Mrs. Garcia was out sick. Bryce was looking forward to a free afternoon after he finished his chores. He might be able to go fishing at the pond.

As they steered their bikes up the driveway, Aunt Sammie sat in shadow under the covered porch. "Come in, quick," she said, waving them in urgently.

"What is it, Mom?" Amanda asked.

She gestured toward the house. "I'll tell you inside."

Bryce was about to object; he wanted to get his chores done. But the look on his aunt's face told him that he shouldn't argue.

"There was another harvesting," Aunt Sammie said

inside as she put a plate of cheese and crackers on the kitchen table.

"Where?" Bryce asked.

"Petaluma," she said. "About five miles away."

Five miles.

"Why are they coming here?" Amanda said, her eyes welling with tears. "Why not San Francisco or Los Angeles?"

Bryce thought that he knew. "It's probably easier to find people. Think about it: in a big city, there are plenty of places to hide. Kids can go into skyscrapers or down into subway tunnels. Besides, the cities were hit hard after the invasion. Most of the kids have gone other places by now."

Aunt Sammie nodded. "That makes sense. I want you two to stick around here for a few days—I don't like you skipping school, but we can't take a chance with the harvesting so close to us."

"I can't skip school this week," Amanda argued. "I have two quizzes and a project due."

Amanda was one of those strange kids who lived for school. To Bryce, a couple of days away from the books sounded like a vacation. He liked helping Uncle Kyle on the farm; it felt good to move around instead of sitting at a desk all day.

"Well, I'm okay with it," Bryce said, swiping a cracker and a slab of cheese from the plate.

"I thought you might be," Aunt Sammie said, smiling. "It'll just be a few days. I'll call the school and explain. I'm sure that we're not the only family doing this."

Bryce and Amanda finished their snack in silence, then set to work on their afternoon chores.

Later that evening, Bryce, Amanda, and Uncle Kyle were in the barn working on the tractor. Actually, Bryce and Uncle

Kyle were working, while Amanda complained to them about her mom's decision.

"We have to be able to go to school, Dad," Amanda insisted. "We can't live our lives being afraid of the blueskins. Right, Bryce?"

Bryce grunted. He lay on his back underneath the tractor, screwing the oil pan back into place.

"Now, Amanda, your mom has a good reason to keep you close to home," Uncle Kyle said. "Do you want to end up on a blueskin ship on your way to who-knows-where? I don't think that you do."

Amanda huffed. "Bryce, can you help me out here?"

Bryce slid himself out from under the tractor and stood up. "I think we should give it a few more days. You can't be too careful."

Amanda groaned with frustration.

Bryce wasn't missing school at all. Why would he be? Most of the students and at least some of the teachers resented him. Here on the farm, he felt wanted and useful. Part of a family.

"Try it now," Bryce said, gesturing toward the motor.

Uncle Kyle turned the ignition, and the engine whirred to life.

Uncle Kyle looked at Bryce with admiration. "It's like you're part machine yourself."

"That would explain a lot," Amanda said. "Like his lack of ability to talk to girls."

Bryce felt his face redden and playfully punched Amanda in the arm. "And I thought it was the cow stench," he said, laughing.

Uncle Kyle leaned against the milking machine. "There's no hurry. I was thirty when I met your aunt. Someday you'll meet a girl who doesn't mind the fine smell of bovine."

"Speaking of Mom, can you please talk to her about

school?" Amanda said. "We're too smart to get caught by the blueskins."

Uncle Kyle pushed his hair back under his worn tractor hat. "I'll see what I can do. But you know that your mom is pretty stubborn sometimes."

"So am I," Amanda answered.

———

As it turned out, Aunt Sammie's stubbornness outlasted Amanda's. Bryce and Amanda stayed home for three days. Bryce gladly spent his days working with Uncle Kyle, tuning up the truck. The amount of work on the farm amazed Bryce—there were always broken sections of fence, supplies that needed to be picked up, or animals that needed care. But it felt a lot less like work than the assignments from school.

Amanda, on the other hand, spent her time poring over her books so she didn't fall behind. When she wasn't studying, she pestered Aunt Sammie about going back to school.

Finally, after the third day without news of a harvesting, Aunt Sammie relented. They could go back to school the next day. Bryce felt disappointed. He realized that school meant different things to Amanda and him. For Amanda, it was an opportunity to see her friends. To Bryce, school was just another reminder that he was an outsider. Amanda was his only friend, but as his cousin, she had to be. And at school they rarely socialized. She had her friends, and he had, well, the other escapers.

Fall in Sonoma Valley dressed in its finest as they left for school that morning. Vibrant reds, oranges, yellows, and greens painted the hillsides. The air was crisp and clean as a fresh-picked apple, and just a few clouds lingered in the sky. Aunt Sammie liked to call this tourist weather—the kind of day that, before the invasion, sent many people to the vineyards for wine tastings and picnics. That is, before the Great War. Now people had a lot more on their minds than tasting wine.

Amanda spent the bike ride to school complaining about all the work that she missed.

"It's going to take me a week to catch up," she said. "It's not like they stop teaching just because we're gone."

"Relax," Bryce said. "If your grade percentage drops to 97 for a week, I don't think that's a big deal." Bryce remembered when he took his studies this seriously. He had always been the top student in his class. But since the war, school didn't matter as much to him.

They reached the edge of town when an engine roared behind them. "Uh-oh," Bryce said, looking back. "Knuckle-head alert."

Amanda saw the car too. "And I was already having such a great morning."

Max pulled his car next to them, with Dumb and Dumber in the back seat. He drove an old '60s muscle car that was black in most places, aside from the occasional primer marks from when Max bumped into things. Judging from the amount of primer on the car, Max bumped into things a lot.

Max slowed next to them. "You need a ride?" he yelled.

"No, we're good, Max," Bryce said. "Just trying to stay in shape."

"I wasn't talking to you, escaper. I wouldn't give you a ride if your life depended on it."

"Why don't you take off, Max? I don't want a ride with you," Amanda said.

"Suit yourself, loser," Max said and took off in a cloud of exhaust. They could hear Dumb and Dumber guffawing as they rode off.

———

By third period, Bryce was reeling from the amount of work that he had to make up. Two papers. Four math assignments, not including that night's assignment. A science lab that he would have to complete during lunch the next day.

He met up with Amanda outside the gym after school. The throng of students spilling into the quad provided cover for Bryce, but he kept a wary eye open for Max and his cousins.

"I hate to say it, but you were right," Bryce said with a grim smile. "They didn't stop school because we weren't here."

"I told you. Are you bummed that we stayed home now?" Amanda asked.

"Not really. But I might change my mind tonight after my fifth hour of homework."

Amanda's brow furrowed. "Bryce, what's that?" she asked, pointing toward the sky.

Framed by afternoon sun, a blue box buzzed along the horizon. Like many things far away, it was hard to judge its size, but as it moved closer, Bryce could vaguely make out the blueskin logo on the side of the long rectangular ship. Mesmerized, they watched as the ship dropped in altitude and flew slowly from one side of town to the other in looping paths.

"That's no fighter," Bryce said. "Way too big. And it's not flying like one of their scout ships."

"That's a harvester!" Amanda exclaimed. "They're here for us."

Suddenly, the ship was two hundred yards out and closing.

By then, other students noticed the ship, and it was as if all the noise, the everyday chatter, had been sucked away, leaving a dreadful silence. Then, like a glass shattering on the ground, shouts and screams punctured the hush, and students scrambled in all directions.

Bryce grabbed Amanda's arm. "We need to go."

"Let's go home!" she said frantically.

Bryce hesitated. The bikes were still at the racks, his at the back of the school and hers at the front. If they could make it to the bikes, they might be able to get away. Getting home on foot would be impossible. They would be out in the open, miles away from home—the Imjac would find them.

Bryce said, "Let's find someplace to hide on campus."

Amanda stared at him in disbelief. "The blueskins are going to get us. You know why they're here. Let's get our bikes. We need to make it home."

"I don't think we can," Bryce argued. "We need to hide here—they can't take everyone. C'mon."

Amanda relented. "Okay."

Bryce heard his father's voice in his mind: *Stop. Observe before you act.*

He paused, pulling Amanda back from the fray. Kids were moving in all directions, wide-eyed looks of terror painted across their faces as they dove into open classrooms. Others ran off campus.

The alien ship now hovered over the school football field, preparing to land. They didn't have much time.

He saw Mr. Green, the PE teacher, holding the gym door open and waving kids in.

Might as well. I always liked Mr. Green.

"This way!" Bryce screamed and pulled Amanda toward the gym.

"Get in! Get in!" Mr. Green urged, his trademark grin absent from his goateed face. After Bryce and Amanda entered, Mr. Green slammed the door behind them.

They joined a group of about twenty kids in the center of the gym. Some students stood in small groups, huddled together. Sam LaPell skulked around the corner of the gym looking for a hiding place behind a garbage can.

Amanda held her hands to the sides of her head. "Oh my God," she said. "My mom was right—we should have stayed home. She's going to kill me."

"No, she isn't," Bryce answered, placing a hand on his cousin's shoulder. "She'll just be happy to see you when we get home."

Bryce felt less sure about the decision to stay at school. He wondered if they had made a mistake. Maybe they should have gone home. Now it was too late. A large open room might not have been the best choice to find refuge. If the blueskins came into the gym, there would be no place to hide.

Mr. Green blew a whistle. "Alright, listen up. We're not going to be able to fight these guys, so our best shot is to get out of sight and stay quiet." He pointed to a couple of upper classmen. "Can you guys pull the stands out? We can hide behind them."

A girl Bryce didn't recognize stalked off toward the door. "I'm going home!"

Mr. Green caught her by the arm. "If you go outside, you won't make it home. They'll catch you and load you on that ship. Your best chance is to hide here."

Her wide eyes scanned the other students, who hadn't moved. She thought it over for a minute and returned to the center of the gym with the others.

There were no more rebellions after that.

While the bigger boys pulled the stands from the wall, Bryce and a few of the other students helped Mr. Green push tables and wrestling mats in front of the doors.

"This won't hold them, but it might stall them for a bit," Mr. Green said. He was trying to remain calm, but Bryce noticed streams of sweat pooling on the teacher's forehead.

With the fortifications in place, Mr. Green clicked off the gym lights. "Okay, everybody keep it down. If we're lucky, they'll move right past us."

I don't think we're going to be lucky. Unless the blueskins are a whole lot dumber than I've heard.

Behind the stands, Bryce stood between Amanda and Jason Park, who Bryce knew from algebra class. Jason was a Korean American from Los Angeles and was on the JV basketball team. Despite the chilly weather today, Jason wore an Alhambra Basketball T-shirt over shorts.

"Bro, it's getting noisy out there," Jason said, his knees visibly shaking.

Bryce heard it too. The high-pitched whirring of the ship reminded Bryce of his aunt's hair dryer. An occasional scream accented the engine noise.

The hair-dryer noise became louder and louder until it seemed the ship was hovering right above them. The walls of the gym began to vibrate, and the stands shook like they did when five hundred people stomped their feet during basketball games.

"Oh my God!" someone squealed.

"Shhh!" Mr. Green admonished.

Suddenly, the noise from the ship stopped completely, and there was a dreadful silence. Bryce could hear his own heavy breathing, and his heart rattled in his chest.

"What happened?" Amanda whispered. "Did they go away?"

"I don't think so."

It was quiet for a minute more, and a glimmer of hope hatched in Bryce's mind.

Maybe they're gone. Maybe they couldn't find us and took off. Maybe they'll catch their quota before they reach here.

"Did they go? Did they leave?" a boy's voice called out.

"Keep it down. They're still here," Mr. Green answered.

A loud, hollow pop shook the walls. A minute later came a cacophony of sounds from outside: glass breaking, doors crashing open, people screaming. Voices speaking in a tongue that Bryce had never heard. The sounds of destruction.

"Let's go," Amanda said, her eyes like a wild animal's. "Let's get out of here."

"No," Bryce answered. "Hang tight. If we go out, we'll run right into them."

There was no point in staying quiet any longer. The bedlam outside surely hid any noise they might have made in the gym. Bryce could hear someone nearby weeping and whimpering. He tried to ignore the fear swelling up inside of him.

"They're going to get us, bro," Jason said.

Through the slats of the bleachers, Bryce peered at the gym doors. *Don't search here. Keep moving. Find someone else.* He felt shame in these thoughts, but he knew they were likely the thoughts that everyone around him shared.

Then the gym doors blew open, scattering the tables and wrestling mats across the gym. Sunlight burst through the entryway, and a sulfurous smell filled the room. Five figures marched through the doorway. Blueskins. They had the shape of people, but their movements were different, herky-jerky, mechanical. Four of the figures were smaller, just over five feet tall. A slightly larger alien stood behind them assessing the scene. He uttered something in the alien tongue, and the four smaller aliens fanned out across the gym.

Bryce tried to stop his knees from shaking.

"They're going to find us," Jason whispered, a little too loudly. Bryce could hear the desperation in his voice. He was feeling the same fear but didn't see the point in talking about it. He closed his eyes for a moment. *If I can't see them, they can't see me.* It was a stupid, childlike thought, but it made him feel safe. Well, safer.

Blueskin footsteps rattled across the gym floor. Bryce held his breath, afraid it would give him away. If not, the beat of his throbbing heart would. He opened his eyes and looked at Amanda: her eyelids were stretched wide, her body perfectly still. She was the embodiment of a prey animal.

Suddenly Bryce heard loud shouting in an alien language. They found someone. Bryce angled around toward the edge of the stands and saw Sam LaPell near the garbage can holding his hands in the air in the universal sign of surrender. Two aliens stood by him, pointing blasters at him. Apparently, the aliens didn't recognize the sign of peace because when Sam stood, one of them shot him. He crumpled to the ground in agony.

Did they kill him? He should have been hiding with the rest of us.

Sam lay unmoving for a minute. Finally, he woke with a start and pointed toward the stands. "Don't shoot me again! They're over there," he said. "They're all over there."

"That jerk," Amanda commented.

The aliens rushed behind the stands. Bryce found himself face to face with a blueskin soldier, who held a blaster at Bryce's chest.

"Come," it hissed.

"Oh my God," Amanda cried. "Oh my God, oh my God, oh my God."

Bryce put his hands on her shoulders and looked her in the eye. "We'll be okay." He didn't know that, didn't feel that, but he somehow knew his cousin needed to hear it.

She gulped and nodded.

Cries broke out around them. Rough hands pushed them as they marched past, arms in the air. A girl planted her feet and refused to move with the others. An alien blasted her into unconsciousness, and then dragged her out by her arms.

Even with the language barrier, the aliens made themselves clear: they were to line up and be quiet. Two soldiers brought a large light that illuminated the gym like a second sun. Guards surrounded them—escape would be impossible.

From the far end of the line, Bryce stared at the aliens. Along with their short stature, they were stocky with thick chests and arms. They wore black uniforms that covered their entire bodies except for their heads. Their exposed skin was a brilliant cobalt blue, set off by large, intense yellow eyes. They hardly had noses at all, just two small holes in the center of their faces that sat right above their small, round mouths. The blueskins' eyes shifted quickly back and forth, never seeming to settle on one thing. The guard nearest Bryce gave off a pungent, briny odor.

With the kids lined up, another blueskin strode into the gym. He was much larger than the others, over a foot taller, and even the other aliens eyed him cautiously.

He walks like he's in charge.

As he came closer, Bryce noticed a maroon scimitar-shaped scar that ran from the large alien's mouth to his left eye.

I'll call you Red Scar.

Red Scar looked at the line of students and said something to one of the alien guards. He walked to one end of the line and started examining the students. An air of malice hung around the enormous alien.

"What's he doing?" Amanda whispered.

"He's choosing us," Bryce said.

"Silence," the nearest guard hissed.

They speak some English. Good to know.

Slowly, Red Scar marched down the line of students, pausing before each one, his glowing amber eyes staring unblinkingly into each face. Those he wanted, he poked with a long, black finger in their chest. Those that he didn't want, he simply walked away from. Each student Red Scar passed let out a sigh of relief; those that were chosen had different reactions.

Bryce found it strange that the alien passed by Hunter Davis, the biggest and strongest among them, as well as two other tall, athletic girls. In fact, the alien skipped all the large kids. The ones that were chosen were of average height or smaller. Bryce was medium height and thin. So was Amanda.

Not good.

Red Scar stopped in front of Amanda. Her knees shook uncontrollably, and tears poured down her cheeks.

"It'll be okay," Bryce whispered out of the side of his mouth. "Stay strong."

"Silence," said one of the blueskins who stood at Red Scar's side. Red Scar himself glanced at Bryce, and Bryce felt his own knees begin to quiver.

The big alien fixed his glare back at Amanda.

Then he pointed at her.

"No," she cried. A guard grabbed Amanda's wrists and started to pull her away. She looked at Bryce, who nodded.

I'll be joining you soon. Stay strong.

Then Bryce stood face to face with the Imjac leader. Though he had seen the aliens before on TV, in real life the blueskin's appearance caused his stomach to turn and his hands to coil into fists. Red Scar's eyes were a brilliant yellow, with a dark pupil the shape of a poisonous viper's. The skin of the alien captain who stood before him was completely different than that of the two guards by his side. Lines of black mottled the giant alien's skin like granite veins, with dark lines waving in and out along the side of his face. Most shocking was the blueskin's mouth. It hinged open to reveal row after row of small, dagger-sharp teeth. The blueskin's breath reeked strongly of rotten fish.

Here was the face of the creature that had killed his parents. The face of the breed that killed millions and changed the order of the world. The face of the being that would determine his future.

The Imjac captain studied Bryce, looking at his arms and legs. The alien's stare felt like it bore beneath his skin. At one point the alien grabbed the top of Bryce's arm and gave it a mechanical, forceful squeeze. Bryce remembered what his parents always told him: when you meet someone new, look them in the eye and give a firm handshake. He thought that a handshake would be out of order, but he returned the alien's stare, trying to ignore his quaking knees.

Satisfied with what he saw, he poked a finger into Bryce's chest and then pointed toward the exit. He issued a command, and a guard materialized by Bryce's side. Bryce felt both dread and relief. He had been chosen, as expected. But at least it meant he would be able to protect Amanda.

Stay calm. I'm going to survive.

He walked willingly with the guards, his head held high. He wasn't going to give them the satisfaction of breaking him.

Devastation awaited outside the gym. Classroom doors had been blasted off their hinges. Several unattended bodies of teachers and students lay on the ground. The glitter of shattered glass blinded him. A group of students, the unchosen, huddled in a mass in the quad, watching silently as he passed.

Bryce saw Amanda marching ahead of him with her head down, a guard at her side.

A group of parents had gathered in the school parking lot. They looked on as Bryce and the others marched toward the ship. He scanned the crowd for Aunt Sammie or Uncle Kyle, but they weren't there.

Probably for the better.

He continued his march with the aliens.

"Amanda! Bryce!" a voice screamed. "No!"

Bryce turned and saw Aunt Sammie sprinting across the parking lot, her arms stretched out in front of her as if she were reaching for the string of a balloon. She must have just arrived.

Amanda fell to her knees as she saw her mother. The guards yanked her to her feet and shoved her along.

Aunt Sammie continued running toward them, only stopping when a blueskin guard leveled a blaster at her.

"Amanda, Bryce, stay strong," Aunt Sammie cried out. "We'll find you guys. Help each other," she added. Another mother came over and placed her arm around Aunt Sammie's shoulder.

Bryce waved. "We'll be okay," he yelled. "I'll take care of her."

"Move!" One of the guards slammed him in the back with the end of a blaster, nearly knocking him to the ground. They marched toward the football field, which the harvester ship now dominated, its ramp down like an open mouth. Several guards stood in front of the walkway that led to the body of the ship. The two escorts left him at the walkway and turned back.

Halfway up the ramp, Amanda looked over her shoulder at Bryce.

Bryce gave her a reassuring smile.

"Walk," a guard grunted, pressing a blaster in his back. Bryce marched up the ramp and into the ship. It was dimly lit and smelled of metal, oil, and the sea.

Not just the sea, but washed-up seaweed.

Long rows of metal containers, each a little larger than a school locker, lined both sides of the ship. Most of the doors to the containers were open, but some were shut. Bryce couldn't see Amanda—she must have already been tucked into one of the cells.

When they reached the open door, the alien pointed inside.

"Sit."

Bryce ducked his head into the cell and sat on the hard metal bench.

"Drink," the blueskin said and handed him a sack of green liquid with a straw.

He stared at the sack. Should he drink it? Was it a poison of some kind? Probably not. If the aliens wanted him dead, they would have killed him already. He was obviously valuable to them alive.

Bryce put the straw to his lips and drank the sweet tangy liquid. He immediately began to feel sleepy, like he had stayed up all night. The alien waved his hand over a sensor, and the cell door closed. Bryce drifted off to sleep.

CHAPTER
THREE

BRYCE WOKE with a start and stood up, smashing his head against the top of the cell.

It wasn't a dream after all.

He wondered how long he had slept. Hours, probably. Which meant he could be hundreds, if not thousands of miles from home. Questions swirled in his mind. Where was Amanda? Was she in the cell next to him? Would Aunt Sammie and Uncle Kyle find them and bring them home?

Hope of a rescue glimmered for a second, but reality quickly snuffed it out. How would they even know where to look?

He knocked on the wall to his left, but it didn't give off the satisfying hollow ring he expected. It was more like a dull thud, and he doubted that anyone heard his knock over the roar of the ship. He had been to Niagara Falls once, and the noises emanating from the ship reminded him of the sound of the falls, the howl of millions of gallons of water shooting over a waterfall.

After a while, he felt the ship slow and descend. It rocked and bumped through the air, and Bryce thought that the liquid he'd drunk might be coming back up. The ship rattled and shifted, shook and banked. How strong were the alien ships? *Strong enough to defeat our ships in the Great War, true.* So, probably strong enough to handle a little turbulence.

Despite the rocky approach, the ship landed smoothly, descending straight down slowly like a helicopter. He heard the whirring of the engines die, then a loud metallic grating noise that he figured was the walkway rolling out. Alien chatter--clicks, grunts, and hisses-- followed.

Why did they take us? Why kids and not adults?

He had heard many rumors about the Imjac, commonly called the blueskins. Their brutality and singlemindedness in the two years since they invaded Earth was legendary. What could a skinny fourteen-year-old offer them? They were here to harvest the earth of her resources, and if the humans got in their way, they would be removed or destroyed. The Imjac set up mining stations all over the world. Ruthless in their pursuit of Earth's minerals, the blueskins had no hesitation to level a forest or flatten a mountain if needed.

With all of that power, why did the aliens need him, Amanda, and the others?

A few minutes later, the door to his cell opened. Bryce held up a hand to block the light pouring in from the outside. Four rough hands dragged him to his feet, his legs wobbly after sitting for so long. Holding each of his arms, the aliens steered him outside to a line of the captured. Bryce took his place in line beside Amanda, who looked green from the flight.

"You okay?" Bryce whispered.

Amanda shook her head, the crust of dried tears still on her cheeks. "Too dark. Too cramped," she said.

She must be talking about the cell in the ship.

"Si...lence," hissed a guard.

The blueskins unloaded the ship with ruthless efficiency

until a long line of kids stood side by side facing a cliff. Water stretched in front of them toward a stunning pink sunset. Sea birds rode the wind in search of food, and white breakers crashed on the rocky beach below. On any other day of his life, it would have been one of the most beautiful vistas that Bryce had ever seen. Today it was just a reminder of how far he was from home.

But where were they? The aliens surely didn't kidnap a ship full of teenagers to take them on vacation. Horrific thoughts thrust themselves into the void of unknowing. Were the blueskins going to eat them? Did the blueskins see torturing humans as some sort of sport? He felt himself becoming sick and tried to think of something else.

He glanced up and down the line. Many of the kids weren't from Alhambra High—the aliens must have made several stops to fill the ship. One of the last to leave the ship, a boy about Bryce's age, refused to stand up and lay on the ground in a heap crying. A guard tried to prop him to his feet, but the boy immediately fell to the ground again. After a couple of attempts, to Bryce's surprise, the guard gave up and walked away.

With the sun behind him, the alien Bryce named Red Scar loomed in front of them.

This is their leader.

Not only was he taller than the other Imjac, but he stood much taller than an average man, like an NBA center. The enormous alien stared up and down the line of kids, watching them with his menacing yellow eyes. The red scar beneath his eyes glowed in the dying light.

Next to him stood a small, thin Asian man in tattered clothes and bare feet. The large alien turned to the man and said something in staccato rhythm of grunts and hisses. The man nodded and faced the students.

"Welcome to the Imjac work camp," he said in a voice that he might have used to tell them the weather or the time of day. "Our hosts want you to know that provided you work hard and do not cause trouble, you will not be harmed."

Amanda sighed in relief. "A work camp? It's going to be okay," she said to Bryce.

Bryce shook his head. *It is not going to be okay. Not even close to okay.*

Red Scar uttered something else in his language.

"Tonight, you are free to rest," the man in the tattered clothes said. "Tomorrow, you will be instructed on your—" He paused and searched for the right word. "—tasks. Remember, so long as you follow the rules, you can live peaceably. If you violate the rules, there will be consequences."

He had no sooner finished this sentence than Red Scar strode over to the boy who refused to stand. The alien wrenched him off the ground with one arm and marched over to the edge of the cliff. The boy struggled frantically, kicking at the alien, but Red Scar held fast, dangling the boy over the edge. A girl down the line from Bryce started screaming and was promptly shushed by others in line.

"Okay, okay. I'll stand, I'll walk, I'll do whatever you want," the boy pleaded.

Red Scar said something to the man in the tattered clothes.

"Consequences will be severe and immediate," the man translated.

Red Scar released the boy over the cliff. He hung suspended in midair for a fraction of a second and then plummeted from sight, his frantic wails becoming fainter and fainter until ceasing.

Bryce stared at his feet. The boy's screams echoed in his head. He could hear Amanda sobbing beside him.

Be strong, Amanda.

"Follow your handlers—they will show you to your new home," the interpreter said.

And so they walked, wordlessly, with their captors. Bryce took careful steps; he wondered if the others were as afraid as he was. Their path wound from the landing spot along the cliff edge and then moved away from the water. Bryce could see that they were on an island. But where? They had flown for hours, and the air felt cool and refreshing. Something told him that they weren't in the tropics. He had been to Hawaii once before the war, and the air had a different feel.

A series of metal doors had been dug into a hillside and glittered like dozens of metal teeth. The guard stopped at the first one. He passed his hand in front of a sensor on the door, and it slid open. From the front of the line, he counted off six kids, who obediently marched inside the cell. The blueskin waved his hand again, and the door closed.

Two more doors opened and closed, and Bryce neared the front of the line. When they reached the next door, the guard shook his black-gloved hand over a sensor and again it opened. He turned to the side and counted off six students, Amanda the fourth, Bryce the fifth, Jason the sixth. Amanda paused and looked back at Bryce before she walked in. He nodded at her.

They stepped into a dim room half the size of his bedroom at Aunt Sammie's house. The walls, floor, and ceiling were hard-packed black dirt. Metal supports had been placed along the ceiling and walls to prevent collapse, and a dull orange light shone from a single bulb embedded in the ceiling.

The door closed behind them, and the six of them stood there together, facing the door in silence, absorbing their new surroundings. All six were students from Alhambra High. Bryce wondered if the aliens grouped them together on purpose so they would be calm and more likely to follow orders. Nothing like having a few friends to suffer with.

Stop. Look. Listen.

His dad's survival advice echoed in his ears. He backed up till he touched the wall, pressed his back against it, and slid down to his haunches, the rocks in the walls scratching his back. In contrast to the cool air outside, the room was stuffy and warm.

Amanda slid down next to him. "What are we going to do?" Her normally neat hair stuck out in all directions, and he could see that she had been chewing at her fingernails.

He placed an arm around her shoulders. "It'll be okay. We'll take care of each other."

"How can you be so calm about this?" she asked. "Aren't you worried?"

"Worrying doesn't help," he said. In truth he had been near panic since they arrived on the island—he just didn't want to show it.

He knew most of the kids in the room. Alhambra High was a small school, even with the influx of escapers. Jamal and Cherie Pitts, twins from Oakland, relocated to Alhambra about the same time that Bryce had. They shared the same medium-brown skin and curly, black hair. Jamal wore his hair short, while Cherie's flowed to her shoulders. They sat close to each other against the wall, talking in soft voices. Jason Park lay on the ground, spread-eagle, like he was making snow angels. A boy he didn't know sat slumped against the opposite wall. He had a large, blocky head and tangled blond hair. Bryce remembered passing him in the halls before and, worse, had seen him hanging out with Max and the Dumbers.

Just my luck to be stuck with an escaper-hater. But he's outnumbered now. Way outnumbered.

So why them? What did they have that made them all so special?

He thought about the students that the blueskins had taken from Alhambra High. What did they have in common? Why would the aliens pass up larger, stronger kids? It didn't make sense to him. Bigger kids would be able to get more done, to carry larger loads, to work harder.

Too tired to think, Bryce lay his head in his arms and allowed his eyes to close.

———

The door opened a while later, letting in a welcome gust of fresh air.

A girl with fiery red hair and pale skin entered, her arms full of supplies. She wore a black uniform like the aliens. A black bracelet with a large face, like that of an oversized watch, encircled her wrist.

Without speaking, the girl worked quickly, handing each of them a thin square made from soft material, along with a juice bag like the one Bryce had drunk before his flight. She plopped a bucket of water in the back of the cell.

"What's that?" Bryce asked the girl, pointing to her bracelet.

She stared at him through enormous green eyes, seemingly surprised that he had spoken to her. "You'll find out soon enough." She gave him a pitying smile and turned toward the door.

"Thanks for the juice," he said. "And the square. What is this?" He held up the square.

"You sleep on it. It's a mat," she said, turning back.

"Thank you," Bryce said.

The girl nodded and started to move away.

"Wait, one more thing," Bryce said. "Where are we?"

The girl looked back and gave him a sympathetic stare. "You're in hell."

Amanda soon woke and looked around the cell in disbelief, then buried her head in her hands. Bryce sidled up next to her.

"You wanna talk?" he said, elbowing her gently.

She just shook her head.

He wondered why he was able to stand this while Amanda struggled. Maybe Bryce was taking this better because of what happened to his parents—he had already been to hell and back. Amanda was experiencing her first taste of tragedy. He imagined life hadn't changed much on the farm for Amanda, even after the war. Sure, they had lost a few conveniences, like sugar, but life had gone on. Nothing like dealing with the death of two parents and being shuttled across the state to live with people you hardly knew.

He picked up Amanda's juice and handed it to her.

"Drink," he said.

She didn't move.

"Drink," he insisted, but she ignored him.

Jason scooted next to Bryce.

"What do we do now, bro?" he asked.

Bryce just shrugged. "Eat and sleep?"

He put the straw into the green bag and took a long swig. The liquid was sweet and syrupy, like what he had in the ship.

"Yeah, I'm starving," Jason said and punched his straw into the bag. He took a long drink and let out a satisfied sigh. "So why do you think we're here?"

"Dunno. I'm trying to figure that out." He surveyed the room. No furnishings of any kind, just dirt and rock everywhere. He touched the smooth rock walls behind him. They were cool to the touch. Bryce rose to his feet and walked over to the door. He passed his hand in front of the door's sensor.

Someone cackled behind him.

It was Cherie, one of the twins. "Do you think they would make it that easy?"

Bryce smiled. No use taking offense. "Always worth a try. Maybe they were dumb enough to leave it unlocked."

"Yeah, right," she said.

Bryce continued his search around the room.

Jamal, Cherie's brother, watched him appraisingly as he walked by. "What are you looking for?"

"Not sure. Just looking around."

Jamal shrugged. "Not much to look at."

His sister chuckled at his remark. The blond boy sat in one corner, his hands resting on his knees, his eyes focused on the floor. Judging by his flannel shirt and worn jeans, Bryce guessed that he was a farm boy. Definitely a local who hated escapers and was now trapped with five of them.

Amanda piped up, "This is where we're supposed to live? I thought this was a bad dream." She gestured around the room. "There's nothing—not even a place to go to the bathroom."

"That's not true," Bryce said from the corner of the room. "I think that's what this big hole is for." He pointed down toward the ground.

"Oh, gross! I can't go to the bathroom in front of everybody! In a hole!" Amanda exclaimed.

Soon the room filled with loud, chaotic chatter.

Jason leapt from his seat and started pounding on the door. "Let us out! Let us go home!"

Soon Cherie joined him, screaming at the top of her lungs.

The blocky-headed blond boy suddenly stood up. "Move out of the way. I'm going to knock it down." He pointed his shoulder in the direction of the door.

"I wouldn't do that," Jamal said levelly.

The blond boy ignored him and took three quick steps

and slammed his shoulder into the door. The door held steady, repelling him to the ground.

"Uh," the blond boy groaned, holding his shoulder. "I think I broke something."

"As I was saying, I wouldn't do that," Jamal stated calmly. "That door is made of the same alien material that the Imjac make their ships from. It's almost indestructible. It definitely can stand up to a one-hundred-and-thirty-pound dude smashing into it."

"One forty-seven," the blond boy muttered, lying in a heap on the floor.

Bryce stood up. "That's enough!" he roared. The room quieted, and all eyes turned toward him. "You're just wasting energy. We need to start thinking about how to stay alive."

"We *are* trying to stay alive," Cherie said. "We're going to bust this door down and go home."

"You're not thinking...I want to go home too," Bryce said. "But making a lot of noise and yelling is not going to do any good against the blueskins. It's just going to get us attention that we don't want."

"If we get this door down, we're out of here," Jason said and began shoving into the door again. "There, I just felt it move a little."

Bryce shook his head. "Look, you heard what Jamal said about the door. Even if we break it down—which is a long shot—the blueskins will be waiting for us. Remember what happened to that kid who didn't cooperate. They're ruthless."

Jamal nodded from his spot on the floor. "Besides, we don't even know where we are. We flew for hours. We could be anywhere."

"We could be on the other side of the world," Amanda whimpered.

Defeated, Jason and Cherie moved away from the door.

The blond boy picked himself off the ground and limped to the corner. Amanda remained where she was, her hands still wrapped around her knees. Bryce unfolded his mat next to hers and sat down. On a smooth portion of the wall, someone had carved, "Ryan was here." As Bryce ran his fingers over the lettering, two questions popped into his mind: who was in the cells before them and where are they now?

CHAPTER
FOUR

BRYCE SAT up on his mat and tried to remember where he was. His body felt stiff from sleeping on the thin mat. The air in the room was sticky and stale. The dim orange light from the night before glowed as before, giving no indication of morning or night. He ran his fingers through his hair and pushed it out of his face.

Nothing would feel better than a hot shower right now.

He looked over at Amanda. She lay asleep on her mat, curled into a fetal position.

Jason snored heavily on his other side.

Bryce heard someone else stir. It was the boy with the shaggy blond hair. He saw that Bryce was awake and quietly crept over to him.

"I'm Reese," he whispered. He held out his hand, blackened by the dirt that made up their floor, walls, and ceiling.

Bryce hesitated a second then shook the boy's hand. "I'm Bryce."

I guess we're all friends now, escapers or not.

"What you said last night was right," Reese said. "We were all getting a little crazy. We're in enough trouble as it is without stirring up more. My mom likes to say, 'When the bees are buzzing, don't bother the hive.'"

Bryce nodded at the logic. "I'm as scared as anyone, but I don't think crossing the blueskins is the way to survive."

Reese shook his head. "Me neither. What do you think they want with us?"

"I have no idea," Bryce said. "But whatever it is, I don't think we're going to like it."

Suddenly, the door to the room slid open. A patch of sunlight fell on the floor near the entrance. The girl with the big green eyes walked in, her arms laden with supplies. Two alien guards lingered outside the door.

The girl gave a drink bag to each of them and refreshed their water. If someone was still sleeping, she just placed the drink next to them. Reese accepted his bag wordlessly, but when Bryce got his bag, he tried to engage with her again.

"What's going to happen to us today?"

The girl shook her head sadly and nodded toward the guards by the door. She moved on without saying a word. After she left, the two guards came in, looming with their blasters in their hands. They were followed by the interpreter, the Asian man with the tattered clothes.

The others started to wake. Amanda's bloodshot eyes left evidence of crying through the night. Jamal and Cherie huddled together on a mat, ready to brave whatever came their way together. Jason sat with his back against the wall, looking uneasy. Reese simply sat on his mat with his head down and eyes closed.

The Asian man pushed his glasses up the bridge of his nose. "Our Imjac host have graciously given you a few minutes to wake and eat. Get yourselves ready for the day. When the doors open again, you will come out in an orderly fashion."

They drank their breakfast in silence. With each pull of

the straw, Bryce felt a surge of energy. Looking around, he could see the drinks were having the same effect on the others. They sat up straight, their eyes wide open, and began to talk more. When the door opened again a few minutes later, Bryce took the last sip of his drink and stood up, revived.

Strange, he thought. *I should be exhausted considering the travel, and where I slept last night. And yet I feel great.*

"I guess that door is for us," he said. He brushed himself off, ran his fingers through his hair one more time. He turned to Amanda.

"On your feet," he said.

She shook her head. "What's the point?"

"The point is we need to survive. And keeping the blue-skins happy for now is a good first step. Now give me your hands."

She held her hands up, and he pulled her to her feet.

The air was cool but not cold. The sky above them was clear and blue, but a bank of thick gray clouds hung on the horizon. Bryce could hear the faint calls of seabirds. A breeze blew in from the ocean, welcome after a night in the stuffy cell.

He and Amanda fell in line with the others. Some of them were from Alhambra, but many of them he didn't recognize. Most were built like him, short and thin, a few a bit taller. Slowly, the other kids from his cell emerged and took their place in line.

Bryce assessed his cousin. She seemed stronger than she had last night. But would she be able to hold up for the long haul? How could she be so strong at home and so fragile here? He would do everything that he could to help her, he promised Aunt Sammie that; would it be enough?

When all the cells in this area were emptied of new arrivals, the man with the tattered clothes assessed them.

Two alien guards stood at his side, their weapons at the ready.

"Follow me," he said simply, and began marching up a hillside on a well-worn path. An alien guard marched in front of the line behind the man, while the other marched at the rear.

Bryce guessed that there were nearly thirty new kids but only two guards. But after what they witnessed the night before, he was sure no one was willing to test the aliens.

Yet.

Amanda looked back over her shoulder at Bryce. "Why do you think we're here?" she asked.

"To do whatever they flew us across the world to do, I guess."

The man with the tattered clothes must have heard them because he turned around and stopped.

"No talking," he chided. "And please stay on the path. The guards are instructed to shoot any prisoner who so much as takes a step off the path, accidental or not."

The march continued. They stopped periodically at other cells and waited while other groups of kids joined the line. Soon more than fifty kids marched single file behind the man.

Bryce took in the surroundings as they walked. Gray-blue water flowed endlessly into the horizon on all sides. Low-lying shrubs, punctuated with the occasional tree, covered the land around them. He saw no furry creatures as he walked, but the sky was alive with birds of all sizes and colors. Lizards skittered across the path in front of them as they walked.

The man in the tattered pants led them inland, away from the sea. They crested a tall hill, then began a steep decline into a large, artificial basin. On one side of the basin loomed the tallest mountain Bryce had ever seen in person. Its sides sloped gently at first, then rose sharply to a towering peak. Greenery blanketed the sides of the mountain, and its peak was encircled by a ring of clouds. But there was something odd about the top of the mountain—instead of the two sides of the ridge meeting at the peak, they formed a semicircle.

"That's not a mountain. That's a volcano," Jamal said behind him.

Two enormous, alien-metal silos stood at one end of the basin. Bryce guessed that they were over two hundred feet tall. Two alien vehicles with large drilling apparatuses lay idle nearby, while in the distance, another made its way to the base of the volcano. "This place is huge—you could fit our football field in here five times," Bryce said aloud to no one in particular.

They were headed to the center of the worksite, where Red Scar stood near the silos. Two guards on hovering scooters buzzed around him, ostensibly for protection, as if the children were a threat to the alien giant. When they reached the silos, the man with the tattered pants stopped, and motioned for everyone to do the same. The kids lined up, facing Red Scar and his guards. The interpreter walked up to Red Scar and said something, then stood beside the giant alien.

Immediately, Red Scar spoke to them in his language.

The man immediately translated. "This morning you will begin your crucial work at the Imjac work camp. It is important that you follow directions closely. Do exactly as you are told, if only for your own safety."

Red Scar glared at them with his viper's eyes to make sure they were listening. Most kids nodded obediently under his intimidating stare. He spoke, and again the man in the tattered clothes translated.

"Your job will be to look in the tunnels for a very specific material. You will be divided into teams of two, a searcher and a digger. The searcher will use this"—he held up a dark metal cylinder with two metal prongs that extended from the top—"to find traces of the element. The digger will retrieve the element with this." He held up another metal cylinder with a claw at the end of it. "Each day your task will be to fill one bag full of the element. When your bag is full, you may go back to your room and rest." He held up a bag about the size of a plastic grocery bag.

"Easy peasy," Jason said out of the side of his mouth.

Bryce shook his head. *There has got to be a catch.*

A girl in line held up her hand like she was in class. "That's it? You just need us to fill a little bag every day?"

The man in the tattered clothes looked flabbergasted for a moment. Apparently, people didn't usually ask any questions. He turned and said something to the large alien, who grunted something in response. The interpreter broke into a smile. "Of course. That's all the Imjac would require—fill one small bag every day."

A sigh of relief broke out among the captured. Bryce could tell that many of them thought that this wasn't going to be so bad after all.

"Please hold your right arm in front of you," the small man said.

Everyone complied. Guards came by and attached a bracelet to each wrist, a black band with an opalescent top. When the guard attached the bracelet to Bryce's wrist, it gripped his skin with what felt like thousands of tiny teeth. Bryce could see now that the top was actually a screen like one on a cell phone or tablet.

This is how they'll communicate with us. How they'll track us too.

When everyone had received their bracelets, Red Scar made a gesture that was unmistakable: follow me. He led them to the edge of the basin near the volcano. Hundreds of tunnels no larger than five feet in diameter had been dug into the side of the large peak. Dim light emanated from some of the tunnels.

The interpreter spoke again. "This is where you will find the element that the Imjac need. Each of you will be partnered up and given a sample of the mineral, tools, and a bag. You will not be allowed to go back to your cells until you have completed your assignment."

An alien guard walked by and grouped them into twos. Bryce was matched up with Jason. Jamal and Reese partnered up, as did Cherie and Amanda, who looked terrified.

"I'm glad we're teamed up, bro! We should knock this out in no time," Jason said.

Bryce nodded but watched his cousin with concern.

When the guards handed out the tools, Bryce grabbed a searcher and Jason took the digger, the cylinder with the claw hand, and the bag. Then the group was led up the embankment toward the tunnels. Bryce could hear someone sobbing behind him; he thought it was Amanda but resisted the urge to turn around. An alien symbol had been carved above each of the tunnel entrances. Rather than letters, the alien writing reminded Bryce of star constellations, bursts of bright colors in irregular patterns.

Bryce and Jason reached the front of the line and were shoved into their tunnel.

"Dig," a guard hissed.

Bryce took a few steps inside. The tunnel was pitch black and smelled of bad eggs.

"Aw, dude, we've got to work in this stink!" Jason complained.

"We'll get used to it," Bryce said, pulling his shirt up over his nose. "I hope."

The tunnel narrowed as he walked further in, and Bryce couldn't stand completely upright. Jason, who was taller, had it worse—he had to nearly bend over at the waist. As they moved away from the entrance, the bracelet screens began to glow, providing a dim light.

"This sucks," Jason complained after they had gone fifty feet in. He waved his hand in front of his face. "And I am *not* getting used to the smell."

"I don't think this is the worst of it," said Bryce.

And it wasn't. The tunnel narrowed further, and soon they had to crawl soldier-style, on their elbows and knees. Rocks cut into Bryce's arms and legs. Both boys were huffing and puffing when they reached the end of the tunnel. The temperature rose as they moved deeper down the shaft, and by the end, sweat dripped off Bryce's brow.

"I guess this is it," Jason said as they reached a rock wall.

"Let's get to it. Hopefully, we can fill our bag quickly," Bryce said.

Bryce pointed the searcher in front of him, toward the wall of rock and earth. It looked a lot like a tool you'd buy in a hardware store, but he could tell there was more to it. He dug the tongs into the earth, and they began to grind through the rock. There was something organic about the searcher, something almost living that sensed him in the same way that his hands and eyes felt the machine. He could feel the tool engage with his mind, almost as if it were a part of him. As he turned it on, he felt it moving through the rock, as if there was a magnetic attraction to the mineral. It moved up and down the sides of the tunnel, guiding Bryce's hands. Finally, the ends of the prods glowed, and the machine lurched forward out of Bryce's hand and stuck itself into the rock.

"I guess we dig there," Bryce said, dumbfounded.

They switched places, and Jason manned the claw, which began to spin slowly to chip away at the dirt and rock. Bryce collected the sample of the element from his pocket; even in the meager light of the tunnel, the blue mineral gleamed.

"I wonder why the blueskins need this so badly," Bryce said aloud.

Jason stopped digging with the tool. "Hmm, I hadn't thought of that." He pondered that for a minute. "Beats me. I just know if we fill the bag, we get to relax." He started digging again.

But the question nagged at Bryce, though he knew it wouldn't be answered right now.

Jason used both hands to hold the alien trowel in place, and after a while, his arms shook from the effort. "Let's switch," Bryce said, taking the claw from Jason.

Jason, sweat beading on his forehead, just nodded, and the boys maneuvered around each other.

Bryce held the claw as it ate through rock and dirt. Again he felt as if he held something living; the tool seemed to be feeding off his energy. He only needed one hand to hold it upright and steady, and it ate through the rock at a much faster pace than when Jason held it.

"How are you doing that?" Jason asked, astounded.

Bryce shrugged. After a few minutes, the cylinder shut off on its own. Bryce sifted through the pile of rock and dirt that lay in front of him and found a glittering blue chunk the size of a marble.

"Here it is," he said, holding up the bright blue rock for Jason to inspect.

"Are you kidding me, bro?" Jason said. "That's it?" He looked at the rock and then at the bag that they were supposed to fill. "This is going to take us forever."

"I think that was the point."

"The point of what?"

"The point of kidnapping us. The blueskins need the element and want us to mine for it."

"We're helping them screw up the world more. That

sucks, bro," Jason said. "I wonder how much of this stuff they need?"

"I don't know." Bryce picked up the searcher and returned to the tunnel wall. "But we'd better get to it, or we're going to be in here all day."

They made steady progress after that. In truth, Bryce did most of the work. He couldn't explain why the alien tools worked so much better in his hands than in Jason's. He watched the other boy's technique and didn't see any faults. He had an inkling that it had to do with the connection he made when he touched the tools.

Just when Bryce thought he couldn't take another minute in the dark tunnel, a message flashed across the screen on his wrist.

"Return." His stomach growled. Time for lunch. The aliens clearly realized that in order to work, they would need to eat.

As they emerged from the tunnel into the sunlight, Bryce was amazed to see hundreds of kids sitting in the main basin area near the silos. Bryce navigated through the crowd with Jason and plopped down next to the other Alhambra kids, who seemed just as tired as he was. Jamal and Cherie Pitts leaned against each other back-to-back. Amanda sat with her knees pulled up to her chest. Her eyes were red and puffy, and streaks of black dust formed rivulets along her cheeks.

"Everything go alright?" Bryce asked her.

She shook her head.

"What happened?" he asked.

"I...can't...do...this."

"You have to," he said. "We don't have a choice." He sat next to her and put his arm around her shoulders.

The sun poked through the clouds and warmed his face. Bryce closed his eyes. He tried to imagine that he was back in San Diego, sitting on a beach with his parents. Or on the farm in Alhambra. Anywhere but here.

"Better keep your eyes open around here," a voice said. Bryce found himself staring at a boy in a Specials uniform carrying a basket of green drinks. A baseball hat advertising auto parts sat crookedly on top of his head, and one of his front teeth was missing. "If you want to stay alive, that is. Ready for lunch? Cooked up by your friendly alien over-lords." He tossed Bryce a drink bag.

"She needs one too." He pointed to Amanda.

"Here's one for her then," the boy said, tossing another. "Drink up if you know what's good for you."

Despite his callous words, Bryce thought that he saw sympathy in the boy's gaze. "Thanks," he said and plugged his straw into the drink bag. His back and shoulders ached from being hunched over. His elbows and knees oozed blood from crawling. He wasn't sure how he would last more hours in the tunnel.

Amanda finally lifted her head. "You look like crud."

Bryce had to laugh. "You don't look so great yourself."

"Well," Jason said. "You both look a whole lot better than the kids that have been here a while."

It was easy to spot them—their limbs were thin, with scars and scabbing, their hair dirty and mangled, their clothes simply rags hanging on bones. Bryce thought it strange that not one of them even looked at them since they emerged from the tunnels. There was no greeting from the others, not even an acknowledgement of existence. They sat down for lunch as a silent, sullen mass.

"They're zombies, bro. Zombies." Jason shook his head.

They are zombies now, but what were they before? Bryce thought.

A call emerged from the crowd. "Thief! Thief!"

Bryce looked up. A large group of workers stood and pointed in unison at one person. Bryce jumped to his feet.

He saw Sam LaPell at the center of the arms, a panicked look on his face. He held an element bag in his hands, which was obviously not his. As the zombies moved toward him, he dropped the bag and lifted his hands up, the sign of surrender.

"Thief! Thief!" the workers continued shouting and swarmed around him.

"Looks like Sam got caught cheatin'," Jason said. "He never could stay out of trouble."

"What are they going to do to him?" Amanda asked.

"Looks like they're going to beat the snot out of him," Jason said.

"Or kill him," Jamal added.

Bryce looked around for Imjac guards, but they just stood by and watched impassively.

Sam scrambled and tried to break through the crowd, but a sea of arms tossed him back to the center. The zombies moved toward him in a wave, their arms outstretched and thrashing. Sam disappeared from view.

Bryce jumped to his feet and raced toward the mob. "No," Bryce shouted. "Stop it!"

Jason grabbed him by the arm. "Don't, bro. He deserves it."

"No, he doesn't. No one asked for this."

He moved toward the horde, pushing and pulling the kids out of the way as he passed. "Stop! Stop this!"

He finally reached Sam and shielded him with his body. The thrashing arms pounded his back and legs.

"Quit!" he screamed. "You'll kill him."

All at once, as if turned off by a switch, the pounding stopped. The workers drifted off and marched back to the tunnels.

"That's what happens to thieves," one girl said over her shoulder as she walked away.

"Why did they stop?" Jason asked.

Bryce pointed to his wristband, which flashed "Work." "I guess they listen to orders."

Bryce looked down at Sam, who lay motionless on the ground. His mouth was bloodied and his face bruised. Bryce kneeled down next to him.

"He's still breathing," Bryce said.

"That's good," Jason said. "I doubt they have a hospital. How do they take care of sick people around here?"

As if in answer to his question, two blueskin guards walked up and grabbed Sam by the arms. They dragged his limp body toward the cells, his feet bobbing on the ground behind him.

The bracelet on Bryce's wrist flashed again. "Work." Nearly all the zombies had disappeared into the tunnels.

"Back to the tunnel for us, bro," Jason said.

After finishing his drink, Bryce felt energized again, just like he had after breakfast.

Strange, he thought. *I should be exhausted.* He couldn't remember ever working this hard, yet he felt as if he just woke from a peaceful slumber.

The work dragged on after lunch. Once, the boys found a fist-sized stone. But the other rocks they found were smaller, like peas, and did little to fill the bag. Finally, when it seemed like Bryce wouldn't be able to spend another minute in the tunnel, Jason added one last piece of element. The bag sealed itself automatically, and their bracelets began flashing "Return."

"We did it," Jason said, holding up a fist.

Bryce bumped his fist. "Yeah, we did it. Day one finished."

Bryce blinked at the afternoon sun as they exited the tunnel. Two guards met them at the entrance and walked them to the silos. A boy that was not much older than Bryce took the full bag from them and their tools, then the guards escorted them to their room. Entering the empty cell, they realized they were the first to finish.

Bryce stumbled to his mat and lay down.

Well, that wasn't so bad.

But something told him it was about to get a lot worse.

CHAPTER
FIVE

A GENTLE TAP on his shoulder interrupted Bryce's slumber.

"Leave me alone," he said, brushing off the hand, his eyes still closed.

But the hand didn't stop. In fact, if anything, it tapped more urgently.

He opened one eye to find he lay on the mat in the cell. The girl with the bright red hair stood over him, one of her green drinks in her hand, her eyebrows knotted with concern.

"You have to drink. Otherwise, you won't make it," she said.

Fighting the urge to lie down and ignore her, Bryce sat up and palmed the drink.

"Thanks," he said.

"It's nothing," she replied and turned away.

"Wait," he called after her. "What's your name?"

She took a moment, and Bryce wondered if it had been so long since she thought about her own name that she might have forgotten. "Merry," she said. "Like Merry Christmas."

"Thanks, Merry."

She nodded. "You had better drink that if you want to survive here. Most don't."

Bryce held up the green bag. "Drink these?"

"Survive." The cell door closed behind her.

Jason, Jamal, and Reese sat on their mats, drinking their dinner. Cherie and Amanda were missing.

Jason came over and sat down next to Bryce. "Who's your girlfriend?"

Bryce smiled. "Not my girlfriend, but her name is Merry. Where are Cherie and Amanda?"

Jason shrugged. "Haven't come back yet."

Bryce shook his head at the news. *That's not good.*

Bryce sipped his drink slowly and found that familiar sleepy feeling come over him again. He stopped.

"Don't finish your drink," he said to Jason.

"Why not? I'm starting to dig this stuff. The color's a little weird, kind of like blended-up frog, but the taste is legit."

"Look at the others."

Jamal and Reese, who had finished their drinks already, lay on their mats like wilted flowers, their eyes glassy and eyelids droopy.

"Yeah, they looked zoned. But, hey, we just did some crazy-hard work out there. I'm pretty pooped myself."

Bryce nodded. "I agree, but did you notice that when you drank this last night you felt really, really sleepy. I mean, think about it: when you go to bed for the first time in a new place, especially a strange place like this, you're going to be on edge, right? Especially on a thin mat. But I slept like a log."

Jason rubbed his chin. "Come to think of it, I did sleep pretty soundly last night."

"And didn't you feel super-hyped when you had the drink in the morning and again at lunch?"

"Yes. What are you getting at?"

"I think these drinks are drugged. The blueskins want to make us easier to control. They want us sleepy in our caves and hyped up when we have to dig. I bet, in the long run, that these drinks rot your brain. I bet that's what happened to the zombies."

Jason nodded. "That makes sense. But what are we going to do? If we don't drink this stuff, we're going to die."

"You're right. There's nothing we can do now. We need the energy to survive. But we need to come up with a plan."

"I'm with you, bro. I want to survive."

Bryce left his drink unfinished and lay back on his mat. Despite his growling stomach, sleep came quickly.

Much later, Bryce woke as the cell door opened. Cherie limped in, followed by two Imjac guards, who dragged Amanda in by her arms and plopped her on her mat.

Bryce pried himself off his mat. The muscles in his shoulders and back burned with the effort. His mind was cloudy, probably from the green drink. He shook his head and crawled over to where Amanda lay. She was covered in black dirt from head to toe.

"Amanda?" He gently patted her shoulder. "Amanda, are you okay?"

Amanda groaned.

"Amanda, you need to sit up. You need to eat." He turned her over onto her back. Bryce was shocked at her appearance. Dirt and rocks coated her hair. She had a large red gash on her forehead and her eyes were red and puffy.

He grabbed her by her arms and pulled her to an upright position.

"Leave me alone," she said and lay back down.

"I'll leave you alone if you eat first," Bryce said. "But you have to sit up."

He pulled her up to a seated position again. Picking up the drink next to her mat, he plugged the straw into it and held it up to Amanda's lips. She refused at first, but finally relented. "You'll leave me alone if I drink?" she rasped.

"Yep."

She took a long drink from the straw and then another.

"What happened today?" Bryce asked.

Tears immediately welled in her eyes. "Tunnels. I can't do tunnels." She took one more long drink and flopped back down to her mat.

————

The boy in the auto parts hat delivered breakfast the next morning. "Good morning, all," he said cheerily.

He was met with groans and grumbles.

"Not much for talkin' today, eh?" he said. "Not that I can blame you. I remember my first days in the tunnels." He reached into his bag and began handing out the drinks. "A little breakfast will do you right."

Bryce seized on his comment. "You were in the tunnels?"

The boy smiled, showing his missing tooth. "Yep, just about everyone was at one time." He passed out all the drinks like he was a waiter serving meals in a restaurant. "Now I'm a Special, though."

"What's a Special?" Jamal asked.

"A Special," the boy said, "is anyone who is not a digger. Any human, of course."

"How'd you get to be a Special?" Bryce said.

"Just hard work and a little luck. Now enjoy your breakfast—it gets better as you get used to it. And then it gets a lot worse. Cheers!"

And with that he swept out of the cell.

"That guy was too darn happy," Jamal complained. "Doesn't he know that we're in a death camp?"

"It must not be too bad for him," Cherie said. "'Cause he's a Special, whatever that means."

"I wonder what he meant by that last comment, about the drinks getting worse," Reese said. Bryce noticed that the farm boy didn't say much, but when he did, it was likely insightful.

Bryce thought he knew but made sure to down his drink. He would have to drink the green juice until he figured out a plan to stop taking it. He would need all the energy he could get for the tunnels. He looked over at Amanda. She sat facing the wall as she sipped at her breakfast.

He sidled over to his cousin. "Hey, Amanda. Time to wake up," he said as cheerily as possible.

Amanda just grunted in return. Bryce slid back to his mat.

She'll come around. She'll have to. Or else.

He thought about his promise to Aunt Sammie, to take care of Amanda. Of course, he would take care of his cousin no matter what.

When the guards called, everyone rose, except Amanda. She just lay, unmoving. Bryce began to panic. He saw what happened to the boy who refused to get up when they arrived. The Imjac would not tolerate someone not listening to orders. They would pitch her off the cliff.

Bryce raced over to her. "Amanda, we need to go."

"I'm not going back," she said firmly.

"Amanda, they'll kill you. You saw what they did to that kid on the first day."

She pounded her fist into the ground beside her. "I don't care. I don't care what they do to me. I won't go back in their tunnels."

Jason popped his head back in the cell from outside.

"Yo, Bryce! You had better get out here pronto. The blue dudes look a little antsy."

Bryce knelt down beside Amanda. "I'll work beside you today. I promise that I'll help you. All you need to do is stand up right now and come with me outside. Do you think you can do that?"

She held his gaze with his mother's brown eyes and then nodded. She held up her arms, and he pulled her to her feet. Then they walked outside together.

A beautiful pink sunrise greeted them as they emerged from the cell. Songbirds trilled in the nearby trees, and a gentle breeze filled the air.

Torture in paradise.

After one day, the trip to the tunnels felt strangely routine. There was no introduction from the man in the tattered pants today. Instead, two blueskins led the way directly to the worksite. Along the way, they stopped to pick up the other newbies. Finally, fifty strong, they hiked to the basin.

The kids who manned the silos were already at work, feeding the mineral that was mined yesterday into large maws at the bottom of the towers. It looked like easier work than tunneling, but it seemed to require some knowledge of alien technology. Some of the kids stood at monitors and pressed buttons. They all wore the same bracelets, like the other Specials Bryce had seen, and looked healthier than the zombies.

How do you become a Special? It was a question worth investigating.

Bryce stood next to Amanda and held onto her arm. When Bryce reached the front of the line, the guard first pointed to Jason, then to Bryce, then to the tunnel, even though Amanda was right behind Bryce.

Bryce shook his head. "I want to work with her." He gestured toward Amanda.

The guard pointed at Bryce and then at the tunnel. "Go," it hissed.

Bryce was about to protest again when Amanda grabbed his hand and squeezed. "It's okay. Go."

"You can do this," Bryce said to her and then ducked into the tunnel.

Then he and Jason began their descent into the stuffy, smelly mountain.

"Here we go again," Jason said.

"Into the darkness," Bryce said.

Into hell.

Surprisingly, the digging went easier today. Bryce adjusted to the darkness quickly, and the tools felt familiar, almost as if they remembered him. He manned the searcher but also took turns with the digger when Jason tired. By the time the return notice went off on their bracelets, they had nearly filled the bag.

The burning sun seemed impossibly bright after the dim light in the tunnel. Squinting and covering his eyes with his hands, Bryce felt like a mole seeing sun for the first time.

"Where are the others?" Bryce asked, looking around the crowded basin.

"There," Jason said, pointing to Jamal and Reese.

They made their way over and plopped down.

"How was your morning at the office, gentlemen?" Jason asked.

"Fantastic," Reese said, playing along. "As pleasant as could be. And yours?"

"Couldn't have been better."

Jamal shook his head. "You guys need to stop. I don't have the energy to laugh."

Bryce looked around for Amanda and Cherie.

"Where are the girls?" he asked Jamal.

Jamal just shrugged.

Bryce noticed Merry coming by with the lunchtime

drinks. He quickly scratched a message in the dirt in front of him. *Real food?*

As she came by, Merry stopped to read his message, shook her head sadly, and rubbed it out with her foot.

"Nice try, bro," said Jason, who saw his message.

Bryce shrugged. "It was worth a try."

As they sipped their lunch, Bryce watched the zombies carefully. They sat next to each other in silent rows. They weren't that different from the cows he cared for on Aunt Sammie's farm. He contrasted that with the new workers, who sat in groups and talked as they ate. That looked more like lunchtime at Alhambra High. Was it just the juice that warped the zombies' minds? Or was it that digging in the tunnels robbed you of your sanity too?

Finally, Amanda and Cherie emerged from the tunnels. Judging from the look on Cherie's face, digging hadn't gone well.

Amanda gently sat down next to Bryce and exhaled deeply. Her usual pale skin looked translucent, and her long hair was now a tangled, filthy mess.

"I know that it's tough here," Bryce said, looking her in the eye. "Can I help you?"

She just shook her head. Her eyes started to well up with tears, and she stood up and walked away.

Bryce turned to Cherie. "What's wrong? What's happening in the tunnels?"

She frowned. "I don't know...we get halfway down the tunnel, and she totally freaks out," Cherie said. "I basically do all the work. Today she just lay on the floor of the cave, crying."

"That's not like Amanda," Bryce said. "She works hard. I'll talk to her."

"Thanks. I don't know how much more I can take."

Jamal crumpled up his empty juice bag. "It's sad, man. One day, you're going to school like it's a normal day. The next, you're working yourself to death in some alien prison camp."

"We're not going to die," Bryce asked.

"C'mon," Jamal scoffed, gesturing toward the zombie horde. "Do the blueskins look like they have a good health care plan? We're disposable. Like…like…like diapers."

"Ew!" Cherie said. "Jamal, can you come up with a better metaphor? I don't want to be a dirty diaper."

They laughed, but their hearts weren't in it.

Then, their bracelets flashed "Work." As he made his way back to the tunnel, Bryce turned to find Merry. She smiled at him and gave a brief wave.

Not much later, Bryce and Jason had filled their bag with the blue mineral. Again they were the first to return to the cell. They sagged onto their mats and lay in silence for a few minutes. Bryce stared up at the dark, craggy ceiling of the cell. He wondered if life back on the farm had returned to normal. After all, the cows still needed to be milked. Were his aunt and uncle looking for them? He didn't know how they could possibly know where to start. For all they knew, he and Amanda could be anywhere on earth. No, they couldn't depend on Aunt Sammie and Uncle Kyle to help them, or any other adult for that matter.

Jason finally broke the silence and brought Bryce back to the present. "Dude, you were on fire today. You're like a natural born alien the way you use those tools."

Bryce had to laugh. "Yeah, my parents would have been proud. First place award in mineral digging for evil aliens."

"Would have been?" Jason said quizzically.

"Yeah," Bryce said. "They died in the Great War."

Jason got quiet. "Sorry, bro. I didn't know. I have a cousin who died in the war too," he quickly added.

Bryce sat up and pushed his hair out of his face. "I don't

normally tell a lot of people about my parents. I was living with my aunt and uncle in Alhambra after it happened. I thought I was safe."

Jason nodded. "We all thought we were safe. Before the war, my family lived near LA in a big house. My dad's a dentist. Then the war comes, and my mom got the idea that we need to leave, to hide from the aliens after the harvesting started. So we move to this little farmhouse in the middle of nowhere. But, guess what? The aliens got me anyway."

"I guess that's irony," Bryce said with a wan smile.

"Yeah, Mrs. Garcia would be proud. We finally understand irony."

A little later Jamal and Reese limped in.

"Well, look what the blueskins dragged in," Jason said.

Jamal made an obscene gesture and collapsed on his mat with a groan.

Reese smiled. "Looks like you two are the superstar diggers," he said. "Be careful—they might give you two bags tomorrow."

Jamal groaned from his mat. "Digging is not fun. Not one bit."

"That is ten times worse than cleaning out the barn stalls," Reese added.

"I don't know nothing about that, country boy," Jamal said, cracking a smile. "Not a lot of barn stalls in Oakland." He looked around the room. "I wonder when my sister and Amanda will be coming in."

"They'll be back soon," Bryce said. He wished he felt as confident as he sounded.

Jamal wiped his brow, smearing dirt across his forehead. "Oh, man," he said. "I talked to Cherie during lunch. I know she was polite about it, but she's exhausted. She shouldn't have to do all the work."

"Amanda's not lazy—this isn't like her."

"I'm sure she's not, normally," Jamal said. "But this is obviously not a typical situation. I think that you should work with her from now on, especially since you're the professional at this mining."

Bryce felt stung by Jamal's tone, but if he were in the boy's shoes, he might agree with him.

"I tried to work with her this morning, but the guards threw me down the tunnel with this guy," Bryce said, thumbing his finger at Jason.

"This guy, huh?" Jason said, pretending to be offended. "We'll see how much work 'this guy' does the next time we work together."

A new Special arrived with dinner before the girls got back. Bryce was disappointed that it wasn't Merry.

"Hey," Bryce said to the boy as he turned to leave. "We've got two still working. Can you leave us their food?"

"Why?" the boy sneered. "So you can steal it? If you don't get your work done, you don't get fed."

Jamal jumped to his feet, his hands curled into fists. "That's my sister you're talking about!"

The boy nodded toward the door where the guards leered. Jamal got the message and sat down on his mat again.

"Look," Bryce reasoned. "We're new here. We want to do our jobs and survive, just like you. Can you leave us the food? We won't take it, I promise."

The boy pondered the request for a moment. "I can do it this time since you're new. But next time, tell them that they have to be back in the cell by dinnertime." He dropped the two bags on the floor and left without another word.

"What's wrong with that guy?" Jason asked. "He acts like he's better than us."

"In his mind, he is better than us," Bryce said. "We're just diggers. He's got a job where he'll survive for a while."

Jason slammed the straw into the green bag. "I'm going to eat—all that tunnel work and I'm starving."

"Yeah, me too!" Reese said. He held up the bag and frowned. "But this isn't exactly food. I'd kill for my mom's meatloaf right now."

"Or pizza," Jason added. "Pepperoni and olives. I could eat an extra-large pie right now all by myself."

Jamal shook his head. "Will you guys stop talking about food? You've got me salivating, and all we've got to eat is this alien slime."

Bryce stared at his drink but didn't pick it up. He watched the others suck up the green liquid then slowly drift away. One minute they were sitting up, laughing, talking, smiling, and the next they were prone, lying on their backs, and staring at the ceiling. Finally, their eyes closed, and they slept like the dead.

He didn't want to give in, at least not yet. He knew eventually he would have to drink the blueskins' poison, if only to temporarily stay alive, but for now he wanted to think. He wanted time on his own, time to plan. They couldn't stay here; he already figured out what that led to. Staying meant your brain and body rotted until…until you were no longer of any use to the blueskins. What happened after that he could only suspect.

The air in the cell was hot and stuffy and reeked from the odors of unwashed bodies and sweat. He wished he could carve a hole to the outside to bring in some fresh air.

He lay back on his mat, trying to think of home. Instead of his home in San Diego with his parents, it was thoughts of Aunt Sammie's farm that floated in unbidden. He felt guilty that it was the first place that he thought of, not the home that he shared with his parents before they died. But it had been two years since he left, and during that time, life on the farm with his aunt and uncle became the new normal. His missed his aunt's smile, which reminded him of his mother's. He missed his uncle's corny jokes. He even missed his chores on the farm.

Now his life was turned upside down again by the blueskins.

And yet he didn't hate the aliens. He didn't think of them as something to hate. They were a force of nature, like a hurricane, something to be resisted and overcome, not despised. If he hated them, that made them worthy in a sense. And they were not worthy.

Bryce wasn't sure how long he sat there when the door opened. Cherie trudged through, limping. Her clothes were torn and filthy. Several of her fingernails were broken and bleeding. She looked around, caught Bryce's eye for a moment, and then collapsed on her mat.

Amanda followed, barely able to walk. She caught Bryce's eye, nodded, and dropped like a bag of cement on her mat.

When the door closed behind the guards, Bryce scrambled up from his mat and handed Cherie a drink.

"Thanks," she said softly.

Then he scooted over to Amanda. He gently touched her shoulder. She gave no response.

"You okay?" he asked.

She remained silent with her eyes closed. He turned her over carefully. He could see her chest rise and fall with each breath.

Good, she's alive.

But for how long?

Bryce stared at her. It was amazing what two days at the Imjac camp could do to a person. Dirt covered her face and her lower lip was split. Bryce dragged her by her armpits and laid her gently on her mat. Her eyes remained closed, though Bryce couldn't tell if she was awake or asleep. He put her drink next to her on the mat in case she woke in the night and was hungry.

We've got to get out of this place soon, or it's going to kill us all.

But first, he needed a plan to get through tomorrow.

CHAPTER
SIX

"*Swing low, sweet chariot, coming for to carry me home.*"

Bryce opened his eyes and looked for the source of the noise. Jamal lay on his back, softly serenading the ceiling.

Jamal noticed Bryce's stare and stopped. "Sorry, did I wake you?" he said. "Just singing a church song."

"Don't apologize," Bryce said. "It was good."

"Well, in that case," Jamal said with a devilish grin, "*SWING LOW, SWEET CHARIOT, COMING FOR TO CARRY ME HOME!*"

Cherie sat up with a jolt. "Jamal, are you out of your mind?"

He shrugged. "Maybe. Maybe I have tunnelitis. Stick a guy in a tunnel too long and it's liable to addle his mind."

Jason covered his ears. "Make it stop. That is the worst singing in the history of mankind."

Bryce laughed. "Wait until you hear me sing." He remembered a corny rock song that his dad used to blast in his truck. "*Every rose has its thorn. Just like every night has its dawn. Just like every cowboy sings his sad, sad song…*"

"Oh, no!" Jason said, jumping up from his mat. "I'm going to have old red face throw me off the cliff now!"

They were all laughing now, except for Amanda, who still lay on her mat in the corner with her back to them. She still struggled in the tunnels, gamely going out to work each day but coming back and collapsing on her mat each night. She barely spoke to the others and only drank the green juice because Bryce made her. This was not the bubbly, confident cousin that Bryce knew from home.

"I know a few country tunes," Reese offered, but before he let out a sound, the cell door opened, and Merry entered with breakfast drinks and a fresh bucket of water. Bryce's stomach rumbled, and his mouth watered at the thought of food.

"Morning, Merry," he said as she handed him his bag. "Can you take this back to the kitchen? I ordered eggs and bacon."

He thought he noticed her mouth twitch. Almost a smile this time.

"Eggs and bacon?" Jason said. "Stop mentioning real food. You're killing me!"

"I wish I could take it back," Merry said with a note of sadness. Then she glanced over at the blueskin guards who stood just outside and finished handing out the drinks. Before she left, she looked back at Bryce and smiled.

When the cell door closed, Jason scooted over next to Bryce and dug an elbow into his ribs. "I think you are really sweet on her."

Bryce blushed. "I'm just being nice. Just because we're in a hell hole doesn't mean we can't be nice to people."

Bryce felt a twang of guilt as he said this. There was a less altruistic reason for being friendly with Merry: they needed allies if they wanted to survive in this place. That didn't mean that he wouldn't have been nice to her anyway.

"Whatever," Jason said, patting Bryce on the back. "That doesn't explain why your cheeks are red, bro."

Everyone laughed, again except for Amanda, who hadn't moved.

Bryce scooted over to her. "Hey, sit up. Breakfast is here. Pancakes, just the way you like them, smothered in butter and maple syrup."

"You should not be teasing at a time like this," she said grumpily. She sat up and took her drink without complaint.

That's a good sign.

Bryce also drank his alien concoction, even as he knew it was destroying his mind. He examined his cousin as he pulled on the straw. She looked better than she did yesterday, but a far cry from the healthy, happy Amanda he knew back on the farm. The shadows cast by the orange light gave her the look of a living skeleton. Her hands and face were covered with the black dust from the tunnels.

"We're going to work together today," Bryce said. "But understand, you have to help me help you."

Amanda held his gaze. "I'm ready to do that. I'm ready to work."

Cherie pursed her lips but said nothing. Bryce and Amanda had tried to work together for the last couple of days with no success. For whatever reason, the aliens didn't like mixing up partners.

Then the door opened, and it was time to head to the tunnels.

When they reached the worksite, they marched in a line up the ramp, and the guards assigned them to tunnels. Cherie lined up in the front, furthest away from Amanda. Bryce had Amanda line up last in their group of six with him in the fifth spot, hoping to be put together. When they finally reached the front of the line, Bryce ducked into her tunnel. Amanda paused at the opening, but luckily, the blueskin guard shoved her inside.

Bryce stopped a few steps into the tunnel.

I need to know the problem before I can solve it.

"What's going on? This isn't like you not to work."

"Let's just go," she said tersely. "I'm fine."

Bryce shrugged and started down the tunnel into the darkness. A minute later, he looked back, and Amanda wasn't behind him.

He sighed and moved back up the tunnel toward the entrance.

Halfway back, he found Amanda seated, with tears rolling down her cheeks.

"Okay," he said. "Remember when you said that you would help me help you? This is not helping."

Amanda looked up at him with teary eyes. "It's not the work...I've never told you this before, but I'm claustrophobic. Like really, really claustrophobic. Remember when we go to the doctor's office, and I always take the stairs and not the elevator? It's not because I like the exercise. I can't stand small spaces. Perfectly fine if you live on a farm. Not so great if you suddenly have to work in tunnels."

"Oh," Bryce said. He wondered why it hadn't come up before. But claustrophobia was a lot better than some of the other possible explanations for her behavior. "Why didn't you tell me?"

"It's not something I'm proud of," she replied, kicking a small rock to the side. "Besides, I haven't had to deal with it in a while."

At least I know what her issue is now. Knowing a problem is the first step to solving a problem.

"Good point." He searched his memories for a moment. "I've dealt with something like this myself. Let's go slow and see if we can get you through this. But you've got to promise to stay with me."

She nodded. "I promise."

"Follow me." He led the way down the tunnel, the alien tools tucked under his arm. The air seemed hotter and stuffier in this tunnel than in the one he worked in with

Jason. Twice he stopped as he crawled along to make sure that Amanda stayed behind him.

"I'm still here," she said meekly after he turned the second time.

So far, so good.

The tunnel narrowed, and Bryce had to begin to crawl. His sore arms burned after a few feet, and it felt like the scabs that had formed on his elbows tore open. He moved for a while when it registered to him that he couldn't hear Amanda behind him. He turned back and saw the outline of her shape sitting in the tunnel fifty feet back.

Rats. This is going to be tougher than I thought.

He quickly crawled back to her. She sat against the tunnel wall, her face in her hands.

"I thought you were going to help," he snapped.

She looked up, and Bryce could see tears form in the corners of her eyes. "I...I can't. I can't do it." She buried her face in her hands again. "I told you, I'm claustrophobic, okay. Severely. This tunnel is totally freaking me out...It's just too hard."

"Listen, I think I can help you. My dad helped me get over a fear, but it requires a little imagination. Can you give it a try?"

She looked at him hopefully. "You had a phobia? I thought you had no fear. *Bryce the brave*," she said mockingly. "What were you afraid of?"

Bryce smiled as he brought up the memory. He sat and leaned back against the tunnel wall. "It sounds kind of dumb, but I was afraid of the open water, which was really strange because you know my parents were in the Navy. My dad loved to take his boat out and go fishing, but I would never go with him. He tried to bribe me with candy bars and ice cream, but I always turned him down. Finally, he helped me to get over my fear using visualization."

She looked at him skeptically. "How can I visualize anything while stuck in the middle of a tunnel?"

Bryce nodded. "That's exactly the point. You imagine yourself somewhere else, not in the tunnel. Now close your eyes and take a deep breath. Now imagine your favorite place in the world. Did you guys ever go on vacation to somewhere really cool?"

Amanda shrugged. "We didn't take a lot of vacations on the farm. But once we drove out to the coast during the summer. We went to the beach and had a picnic."

"Okay, great. I can work with that. Now close your eyes. Imagine yourself walking on a beach. The sun is shining, and a gentle breeze is blowing in off the ocean."

Amanda closed her eyes.

Bryce continued. "The sky is clear and blue. Small waves are crashing into the shore, and as you walk along the beach, you make sandy footprints. Good so far?"

Amanda smiled. "Yep, I can picture it."

"Now take some deep breaths and really feel like you're there. Think about the sounds, the smells, the feeling of the wet sand between your toes."

Soon, a serene look crossed her face, and she breathed slowly and steadily.

"Now count to three and open your eyes. How do you feel?"

Amanda smiled. "Better."

"Now you go in front of me. Every time you feel like it's getting to be too much, too overwhelming, I want you to stop, close your eyes, and put yourself on the beach. Can you do that?"

"I can try."

She traded places with him and slowly began crawling toward the end of the tunnel. Twice she stopped for a moment to close her eyes and breathe, and Bryce thought that she might want to go back. But she kept going, and soon they reached the end of the tunnel.

Bryce scooted next to her and took out the searcher.

"Are you ready?"

A look of steely determination crossed her face. "Yep, let's do it."

He held the searcher in front of him and felt it come to life as its probes reached into the earth. He looked back at Amanda, who gave him a thumbs-up.

A few hours later, they emerged from the tunnels for lunch. They had filled the bag more than halfway. Amanda worked steadily; Bryce was surprised by her endurance, which nearly matched his own.

Break was already in full swing. Bryce took a long drink of water from a bucket and plopped down next to Jason.

Jason leaned in. "How'd it go with your cousin today?" he whispered.

Bryce held up the half-full bag. "I think she might be better than you, former partner."

Jason looked offended. "Whatever, bro. If I was with you, that bag would be completely full, and we'd be heading back to the cell."

"Want to bet your green slop dinner that we'll finish before you?" Bryce said, grinning.

"No can do," Jason said. "I'm a growing boy. Can't risk missing out on my delicious alien brainwashing liquid."

Amanda sat next to Cherie and whatever tension they had yesterday seemed to be over. Bryce felt grateful for that —they would all need to cooperate if they were going to survive.

As Bryce sipped his green drink, he watched the zombies. They looked placid, like the animals that they were, waiting for the signal to go back to work. He wondered how long it took before the drinks turned your brain to mush. One week? One month? A year?

All too soon, the screens on the wristbands flashed "Work." Bryce noticed that Amanda looked almost chipper as they went back into the tunnel. He led the way again with Amanda close behind him. This time, she made it to the end of the tunnel without stopping. With Bryce at the helm, they dug through the mountain quickly.

"You're a natural with that thing," Amanda said, marveling at his progress with the digger.

He laughed. "It's strange—I almost feel like it's a part of my body when I use it."

"It didn't work that way for me," she said. "It felt just like the barn shovel. And this thing—" She held up the searcher. "—I don't know what this feels like."

They had nearly finished filling the bag when Amanda's searcher hit something hard.

"Got something big here," she said.

"What?" Bryce asked, crawling over to her.

"Let's find out."

He dug at the wall, exposing a Frisbee-sized vein of yellow rock unlike anything they had seen before. It was a brilliant yellow, like the sun, with concentric circles of orange radiating through it. Bryce used the end of the digger to chip some of the rock off. It was softer than the blue mineral, almost chalky.

"What do you think this is?" he asked, holding up a chunk.

She took it from his hand. "Strange. Some kind of mineral. It's like soapstone." She ran her fingers over the rock and shrugged. "I bet there are probably a bunch of different types of rocks under this volcano."

Bryce put it in his pocket. "Maybe the aliens will want to take a look at it. Might score us some brownie points. Maybe we'll get an extra helping of green goop for dinner."

Amanda laughed. "Or another extremely thin mat to sleep on."

Soon they had filled their bag, and the bracelets glowed with the message to return. As usual, two blueskin guards met them at the entrance to the tunnel and led them to the silos, where the blue material was processed.

A tall boy with broad shoulders was sliding the full bags through an opening in the silo. Bryce handed the bag to the boy, who accepted it without as much as a glance.

Bryce turned away to head back to the cell when he remembered the yellow mineral in his pocket. On a whim, he turned back and showed the rock to the boy.

"Do you know what this is?" Bryce asked. "We found it in the tunnel."

The boy's eyes grew wide. "Yellow!" he screamed. "Yellow! Yellow! Yellow!" He pointed at Bryce and backed away.

The two guards rushed toward them. Bryce held the mineral in the palm of his hand to show that he meant no harm.

"What's going on?" Amanda asked in a panic.

"I don't know," he answered.

Two alien guards aimed their blasters at Bryce.

"What's wrong?" Bryce questioned. "I don't want it. Here, take it!" He gently tossed the rock toward the aliens.

Twin blasts shot from the alien guns. Bryce felt pain race across his body, and he collapsed to the ground, unconscious.

CHAPTER
SEVEN

IT STARTED WITH A BLINK. Then slowly, agonizingly, Bryce opened one eye, then the other. The orange light of the cell made him immediately shut his eyes for a minute more. Then he opened them again, slowly, slowly, until he could stand the light.

Next, he tried to lift his head off the mat, but it felt like it weighed a thousand pounds. So he just lay there for a few minutes, absorbing the sounds around him.

Jason breathed heavily on the mat next to him. Someone else snored loudly from the other side of the room, maybe Jamal or Reese.

Using every ounce of willpower, he rose to a seated position, groaning with the effort.

"You're awake!" Amanda said and sidled up next to him.

Bryce nodded, which hurt a lot. Every muscle in his body raged. "How...did...I...get...here?" he said.

"After the blueskins shot you, I pulled you back," she said. "I was afraid that they were going to throw you off the cliff."

Bryce shook his head, then immediately regretted it. "But why? Why did they zap me in the first place?"

"It must have had to do with the rock we found."

The yellow rock—the mineral he found with Amanda. That was the key. He showed it to the boy at the silo, and he had called out an alarm. But why did they shock him? What scared them about that yellow rock?

"You dragged me all the way here?" Bryce was amazed. It had to be nearly a half-mile between the cells and the mountain.

"I am a farm girl after all," she said, flexing her muscles. "Here, Merry left you this." She handed Bryce one of the green drinks. "Everyone thought you were dead, but I checked your pulse and made sure you were breathing. I knew you were alive."

"Thanks," Bryce said.

"We were talking while you were knocked out," Amanda said. "Nobody could figure out why they reacted like that. Jamal said that maybe they're allergic to it. Reese said that maybe on their planet, the color yellow is tacky. No one really agreed with him."

"I think Jamal is probably right," Bryce said. "But to be honest, it hurts to think. It hurts to breathe. It hurts everywhere."

"Is there anything I can do?"

"No, I think I'll be fine. I just need to rest."

She yawned and covered her mouth. "I'm glad you're okay, but I'm really tired. I'm going back to sleep." She slid over to her mat and lay down.

Bryce sipped his drink and thought about Jamal's theory. An allergy of some kind would make sense. He couldn't think of another reason that the Imjac would react so strongly. But something in the back of his mind told him that he needed to find out.

His eyes flapped open, and it was morning.

"Well, look who's finally awake," Jason said from the mat next to him. "Welcome back to reality, bro. How are ya' feeling?"

Bryce took a quick assessment of himself as he sat up. The flaring muscles had cooled to a burning ache. His head had cleared; his thoughts no longer felt like they were swimming in mud. He would survive the day. Hopefully. But he realized that there was no long-term survival here. No hope. The blueskins lied: they said that if Bryce and the others worked and did what they were supposed to, they would be okay. And they *had* been following orders. He thought he was doing the right thing by bringing the yellow rock to the aliens' attention, and yet, they attacked him. They were unpredictable no matter what they said about things turning out okay if they worked hard.

Then it hit him: the Imjac didn't have to play fair. This wasn't a classroom or a soccer team. There were no rules. The blueskins could kill him and there would be no consequences, other than they would lose a worker that they could easily replace.

He looked around the cell. Everyone was up on their mats, drinking and talking.

He wished he had a plan, but all he had at this point was motivation. His soul ached to get off this island and away from the blueskins. And he knew that he couldn't and wouldn't escape without Amanda and the others.

"Listen, you guys," Bryce said, steadying his voice. He didn't know why he felt a little nervous about his speech, but he did. "I don't want to die here."

"Well, who does?" Cherie said, laughing darkly. "We thought you might have died last night. We're glad you didn't," she quickly added.

"Exactly," Bryce said, seizing on her reply even though it was made in jest. "Which is why we need to escape as soon as we can."

Jamal shrugged. "Yeah, we know."

Bryce was taken aback a bit. The whole big speech he had planned went out the window.

Reese turned toward Bryce. "Okay, but I have a question. How do we get out of here if we don't even know where here is?"

Bryce felt the wind taken out of his sails. Reese brought up the same question that had been troubling him. How do you escape from a place if you don't even know which direction to go?

"I've been thinking about that," Bryce said. "I'm pretty sure that the ship took us west but not too far west. I don't think we were in the air long enough to go all the way across the country or across the Pacific."

"Besides," Jason added. "If they were going to take us over to the East Coast, why not just pick up some kids there? I agree. We must have gone west."

"I don't know about you," Jamal said. "But I was completely blacked out when we took off. I have no idea how many hours we flew. And the Pacific is a darn big ocean. Besides, the alien ships might travel a lot faster than our planes."

"What's your point, brother?" Cherie asked.

"We could be anywhere," he said sanguinely.

The thought of not even knowing where they were in the world made Bryce's head spin. Even if they could escape from the camp, how would they know where to go? If they flew for hours, they were likely thousands of miles from home with no way to get back.

"Alright, we need to figure out where we are. But do we agree that escape is the best plan?" Bryce asked.

"We're in," said Cherie and Jamal together.

Reese nodded. "Count on me."

"You know I'm in, bro," Jason said.

All eyes turned to Amanda, who had remained silent.

Amanda said. "I'm in too. I want to get out of here more than anything in the world."

Bryce smiled. It was nice to know that you had teammates, even if the game was unlike any he had played before, and the stakes were their lives. For the first time since he had been at the Imjac camp, he felt hope.

———

Unlike the day before, they left the cell together. Bryce noticed that they seemed to have a sense of purpose as they marched to the site.

He thought about something his mom always told him: know the territory the battle will be fought on. Good advice for a war, or an escape. His head swiveled back and forth in search of any information as they walked. The sun was behind them, which meant they headed west. As they crested the hill near the worksite, Bryce thought he caught a glimpse of man-made buildings in the distance. He made a mental note of the location in relation to the Imjac camp. He looked around for other clues: animals, plants, trees, but nothing provided an obvious clue, other than they were surrounded by water. An island, for sure. But where?

As was the plan, he would ask the others what they noticed when they got back to the cells later. Maybe someone else noticed something that he didn't.

Bryce worked with Amanda again. That morning they had been moved to a new tunnel; the old one where they had found the yellow mineral had been collapsed by the blueskins. That told Bryce the Imjac indeed feared the mineral.

The digging went quickly that morning, and they filled

their bag just after lunch. Bryce was getting faster at this. Amanda too. But she was not nearly as quick as he was.

They walked the bag to the silo, manned by a long-limbed blonde girl.

"What are you two doing here?" she said, frowning.

"We're done," Bryce explained, extending the bag to her.

Her eyebrows rose. "You're done? Already. Let me see," she said, grabbing the bag from Bryce roughly.

Bryce looked at the suit she wore. Black and sleek, it reminded him of a wetsuit. He noticed that all of the Specials got the same uniforms.

Those uniforms would be good for the tunnels.

"You can't cheat these things, you know," the girl lectured. "A couple of diggers tried to fill a bag with rocks once. Let's just say that it didn't work out well for them." She moved her finger across her throat and feigned dying. Laughing at her own joke, she held the bag up to a scanner, which beeped. "I guess you are done. That must be some kind of record. Congrats, I guess."

They turned to go, then Bryce quickly turned back. "Can I ask you something?"

"Shoot," the girl said, not looking up from her work.

"How do you become a Special?"

"You just answered your own question?"

"Huh?"

"You've got to be special."

That night before the dinner delivery, the door to the cell opened unexpectedly.

The chatter stopped, and they looked at each other nervously. Was this good news or bad news?

No one moved.

"I'll go check it out," Jason said finally.

He went out the door and immediately poked his head back into the cell. "You guys better get out here. Mr. Fancy Pants wants us right away."

The gray, misty evening held a surprise for them. The man in the tattered pants stood in front of the cell with several guards behind him. Bryce at first thought that they were there for him, that there would be some additional punishment for finding the yellow rock.

But then the man spoke. "New members of the Imjac Camp, this evening you will be taken for your weekly bath. Please follow me."

At first Bryce was skeptical: was this some kind of trick? He stared at the interpreter but couldn't get a read on the man. They fell in line, and soon Bryce let his guard down. The others seemed almost giddy at the prospect of cleaning up.

After picking up the other new arrivals, the man in the tattered pants led them on a winding path away from the basin. The path ran parallel to the ocean for a while, but between two small green hills, they turned inland. Soon the ground became sandy and difficult to walk through. Thick green shrubbery bordered the path.

Bryce tried to make a mental map of the island as he walked. He knew that the work camp lay west of their cells, and now they were more or less moving in the opposite direction of that, meaning they moved east. The volcano loomed behind them in the center of the island.

At last, they crested a hill and reached a fork in the path. The interpreter stopped and addressed the group.

"We have reached the bathing area. Boys will head in that direction," he said, pointing toward the path to his right, "and girls will head that way." He pointed in the other direction. "Do not contemplate escape. You will be well guarded, and hundreds of miles of ocean lie between you and the nearest land. You may also wash your clothes at the beach if you choose."

He turned and led the boys down the path. Bryce saw the girls heading down the other path with the blueskin guards in the lead.

An inlet with a small, pebbly beach awaited. Steep cliffs the color of elephant's skin rose on each side. Climbing the cliffs to escape would be impossible—they were too steep, with few hand and foot holds. The ocean water extended into a blue infinity in front of them. Seabirds floated above the surface of the water, searching for prey.

Despite the gray sky and mist, the air was refreshing. Bryce found himself running toward the water, following the other boys. When he reached the shore, he stripped to his underwear and dove in. The water was warm, but it still shocked his system. He took a mammoth breath and submerged for as long as he could, finally shooting through the surface when his lungs were about to burst. He rubbed the saltwater through his hair, massaging the dirt from his scalp. When he was satisfied that he was clean, he went back to the shore for his clothes, which he dunked under the water, rubbing the dirt off. Then he wrung out his pants and shirt and lay them on the beach to dry.

Large holes had broken through the knees of his jeans and elbows of his sweatshirt. The toes of his canvas shoes were torn open. He didn't have to wonder why the zombies' clothes were merely shreds.

By now, the zombies had reached the shore. They took no joy in their trip to the ocean, marching to the beach in a single file line, walking calmly into the surf with their clothes still on. Once they reached the waist-deep water, they dunked themselves twice, promptly walked to the shore, and lined up again.

Bryce wondered how much time the blueskins would give them to bathe. It was nearing dark, so they would have to get back soon. But this was also a perfect time to scout the island. He returned to the water and turned over on his back, floating backwards over the gentle surf. He rose up and down over the small waves, kicking easily so as not to arouse the suspicion of the guards. As he moved away from the shore, none of the blueskins showed any concern.

They must be pretty confident that we can't escape from here.

Soon he was one hundred feet from the shore and had swum out to the edge of the cliff. He wanted to see beyond it, to form a mental map of the island. He kicked harder now, not worrying about the guards. Finally, he reached a point where he could just see around the cliff. Stopping to tread water, he thought that he could make out a dock with small boats tied to it, and buildings beyond that.

There is civilization here. Other people who might help us.

Just then his bracelet began flashing "Return." He dove into the waves and broke into a fast crawl stroke. He had been a strong swimmer when he lived in San Diego, and it felt good to be in the ocean again. He made it to the shore in a few minutes, put on his damp clothes, and lined up with the rest of the kids.

"See anything interesting out there, seal boy?" Jason asked as they walked to the basin.

"Maybe," Bryce said shivering. "We'll have to talk later."

"Man, I thought a shark was going to get you," Reese said, shaking the water from his curly blond head. "Just gobble you up like a little fish." He made a snapping motion with his hands.

Bryce smiled. "You've been watching too many movies," he said.

"Silence," one of the guards hissed, and they stayed quiet until they reached the cell.

———

The next day, Bryce worked the tunnel with Amanda, trying to piece together all that he had seen the evening before. He was sure they were on an island now. He thought about the fact that the man with the tattered clothes said that they were hundreds of miles from the nearest civilization. But where could that be? And what about the town he saw? Did people still live there, and, if so, would they help?

So absorbed in his thought, he missed the fact that Amanda was talking to him.

"Bryce, are you even listening to me?" she asked, obviously annoyed.

"What? No, sorry," he said sheepishly. "Lost in thought. What were you saying?"

"Never mind." She let out a sigh and went back to work.

He and Amanda had become a good team. Since she had conquered her fear of the tunnels, Amanda proved to be adept at handling the searcher, even speedier than Jason had been. If she found where the blue mineral was buried, Bryce could dig it up in minutes. The tunnel was still hot, cramped, and dusty, but at least they were only there for a few hours. When they filled the bag, Bryce suggested that they rest a bit before heading out to the silos.

"Why? We're done. We can head back to the cell," Amanda said.

"I know," Bryce said. "But there's no hurry, right? We're going to be there all night." In truth Bryce had an ulterior motive for waiting. They turned in their bags first yesterday. Doing it two times in a row might draw notice. Attracting the attention of the blueskins didn't seem wise, especially if they were planning an escape. He had already paid the price when he turned in the yellow mineral.

They waited in the heat of the tunnel for a while before heading to the silo to turn in their bag.

They beat the others to the cell anyway.

Later, they lay on their mats, relaxing until the others came in. Bryce couldn't wait to share his discovery of the town. He lay on his back, staring at the ceiling, wondering how he could get a better look. Would he have to wait until his next bath? That might be a week or longer. But there didn't seem to be another opportunity. They were locked in the cell until it was time to work, and then brought directly back to the cell. The Imjac didn't give tours of the island.

Amanda broke the silence. "What do you think?"

Bryce looked over at her. "About what?" he asked, scratching the side of his head.

"What I was telling you about in tunnel. I know where we are."

Bryce bolted up off his mat. "You what?"

"I know where we are. *Exactly* where we are. I just don't know whether it's good news or bad news."

"Where are we?" Bryce asked excitedly.

"We're on an island chain called *Islas del Diablo*. Specifically, *Isla Cuerno.*"

Bryce was dumbfounded. "*Islas del Diablo*?"

"It means the Islands of the Devil. The island that we're on is called Horn Island, probably because the volcano is sticking straight up in the air like a horn."

"How do you know this?"

Amanda smiled, obviously pleased with herself. "I did a report in seventh grade on the islands. Part of my project was making a topographical map of the area. I recognize this place from the shape of the island and the island across the strait." She put a finger up to her lips. "I forgot, you guys bathed at a different beach, so you didn't have the same view that we did."

"But how can you be sure?"

"Remember how the guy with the glasses told us we're hundreds of miles from other lands? Well, there are only a few islands on earth that isolated, and most of them are tropical. This is obviously not Hawaii or Tahiti."

Bryce suddenly wished he had paid more attention to geography in school. He clapped his hands together. "Okay, that's a great first step! We know where we are."

Amanda shrugged. "I don't know if it's really great news," she said glumly. "We're far from home. Hundreds of miles over ocean water. Not exactly swimmable, even for you."

"Aw, geez." Of course, she was right. Even if they could escape from the camp itself, how would they cross hundreds of miles of ocean?

Reese and Jason came into the cell soon after, and later Jamal and Cherie. Cherie was limping as she entered.

"It's nothing," she said. "I just slipped a bit coming down from our tunnel." She winced as she sat on her mat and groaned as she took her shoes off. Even from where he sat, Bryce could see the swelling in her ankle.

After everyone settled, Bryce broke the news. "Okay, guys, Amanda and I have a couple of things to tell you."

"What, bro?" Jason said.

"Spit it out, dude, 'cause I am *tired*," Jamal complained. He said it like two words, ti-red.

"You guys remember when I swam out past the cliff? I saw a town."

The others registered surprise.

"Hold on. There are other people on this island?" Reese asked. "Real people, not just Imjacs and their teenage slaves?"

"Yep," Bryce said. "At least I think there are. I didn't technically see any. But I did see boats and buildings."

Cherie sighed. "So what's the big deal?" she asked. "There's a town nearby. How does that help us?"

"Well, sis," Jamal said. "We might have people to help us get out of here."

"Exactly," Bryce said.

Bryce could sense the mood change in the room. He could see the hope light up in their eyes.

"I have something to tell you too," Amanda offered, tentatively. "I know where we are."

"You know where we are?" Jason said, sitting up on his mat. "Where?"

"The Islas del Diablo."

"The what?" Reese said, putting his hand behind his ear like he didn't hear correctly.

"The Islas del Diablo…it means Devil's Islands. They're off the coast of Mexico."

"Devil's Islands? That's a weird name," Cherie commented.

"They're volcanic, as in lava, ash, smoke," Amanda said. "Hence the name. And the island that we're on has the biggest volcano."

"So that's a volcano?" Reese said.

"Exactly."

Jamal shot off his mat and paced excitedly. "This is good news, right? We know where we are, and there are people nearby."

"There *could* be people nearby," Cherie countered.

Jamal stopped pacing and held up a finger, like a professor making a point. "Okay, there could be people. But there are boats, and we know where we are. We can steal a boat and head home."

Bryce shook his head. "It's not that simple."

"Why not?" Jamal asked.

"Tell him, Amanda."

Amanda gulped. Bryce could tell that she was hesitating because she didn't want to destroy their hope. "Because Devil's Islands are in the middle of the Pacific. We're hundreds of miles away from land, let alone home."

"Hundreds of miles!" Cherie said, slapping both hands against her mat.

Jason just thumped the palm of his hand against his forehead.

"I have a question," Jamal said. "How are you sure that we're in the Devil's Islands or wherever?"

Amanda pushed her hair behind her ears. "I did a report in seventh grade on them. I had to make a map as part of it."

"Okay, so you're sure just because you did a report?" Cherie scoffed.

"Look, I'm not just some dumb farm girl," Amanda said. "I get straight A's and I won the science fair in my middle school all three years. Here's my evidence—besides the report I did—there are only so many island chains in the middle of the ocean. The water is cool, so we're in the Pacific. Plus, we're obviously not in the tropics based on the weather. Have you noticed how it stays light late into the afternoon? That only happens if you are pretty far south in latitude, which the Devil's Islands are. Satisfied?"

"You convinced me, girl," Jason said.

Jamal nodded, and Reese just sat there with his jaw open.

"I'm glad we know where we are," Cherie said. "But how does this help us? We're in the middle of nowhere!"

"True, we're far from home," Bryce answered. "But my dad taught me that if you're trying to go from point A to point B, you had better know where point A is before you get started. Plus, we know which direction to head—east."

As they talked through the night until bedtime, Bryce could tell that the tenor of the room had changed. Escape was possible. A ray of light in a dark tunnel.

But one troubling question tumbled through his mind as he drifted off to sleep: how could they avoid turning into zombies before they made their escape?

CHAPTER
EIGHT

THE NEXT DAY in the tunnels, Bryce brooded over a seemingly unsolvable problem: in order to escape, they needed to scout the island and make contact with the local people—if there even were any. But they were under control of the Imjac from the moment they woke up until they went to bed. Guards followed them to the worksite, led them to the tunnels, and then back to the cell again. To explore and eventually escape, they needed to sneak out from under the blueskins' relentless watch. But how?

That morning they all pledged to use any sliver of freedom to scout the island. Everyone seemed hopeful, even after the sobering news the night before that they were hundreds of miles from home, just like the Imjac interpreter said. It wasn't exaggeration to scare them. It was the truth.

Maybe it was just knowing where you were in the world. Maybe it is enough to know what the journey is, no matter how long.

The tunnel seemed hotter and stuffier today. Amanda worked next to him, humming softly as she maneuvered the probe. After the first couple of days, they worked in silence. They didn't even need to talk to switch roles. One of them would simply stop working, and the other would move in. It felt natural, synchronized.

It's amazing what you can get used to.

After working for a time that morning, Bryce wanted to take a minute away from his thoughts. He hadn't come close to an answer to their problem. He stopped his work, set the digger on his lap, and turned to Amanda.

"What do you miss the most about the farm?" he asked.

She pushed her hair behind her ears. "Oh, lots of stuff. I've been trying not to think about it too much. I think most of all I miss my mom and dad. And the farmhouse. I even miss the cows."

Bryce nodded.

"What about you?" Amanda asked. "What do you miss most?"

Bryce laughed. "I think I miss breakfast the most. Your mom's biscuits are the best."

Amanda furrowed her brow. "You must hate them. The blueskins, I mean. First, they kill your parents, and now they kidnap you."

Bryce picked up a piece of black rock and absentmindedly threw it against the tunnel wall. "Of course I do. But I'm not the only one who lost something during the war. We all have lost one thing or another. It's just my loss was bigger than most."

"I used to feel guilty," Amanda said. "That my parents survived and yours didn't."

"And?"

"I realized that if my parents had died too, you wouldn't have had anywhere to go."

"You're right."

Bryce missed his parents, although with each passing day their memory drifted further and further away. At first he felt guilty about this, that he was letting them down if he had a good day or didn't think about them much. But eventually he realized that they would want him to be happy. They would want him to feel at home with Aunt Sammie and Uncle Kyle.

He went back to pushing the digger into the wall. A flat section of tunnel wall the size of a pizza box collapsed, exposing a large yellow patch of rock like the one that had gotten him in trouble.

"Look what I found," he said, using the prongs of the searcher to pry the slab of rock from the earth. "The same stuff that got me shocked to unconsciousness."

"Oh my God," Amanda said, looking nervously back toward the tunnel's entrance. "Let's bury it before they find out. They might kill you this time."

Bryce considered for a minute. "You're right—we should cover it up. But I'm going to mark the spot where we found it. It might be useful to find out why they're so afraid of it."

Amanda nodded, and they dug out a section of the tunnel wall and buried the yellow mineral. They engraved a small X above where they buried it, small enough that you wouldn't notice it unless you were looking for it. Not that the Imjac were ever in the tunnels anyway.

When Amanda wasn't paying attention, Bryce carved out a marble-sized piece of the rock and squirreled it away in his pocket.

With their bag filled a short while later, they headed out of the tunnel to the worksite. The sun shone brightly through an opening in the clouds, and Bryce shaded his eyes as they emerged from the tunnel. Approaching the silo, Bryce noticed that the man in the tattered clothes and Red Scar watched him from the central controls.

Bryce handed the bag of mineral to a silo worker, who fed the bag into an opening. The interpreter and the large alien continued to stare at him.

"Why are they looking at you?" Amanda whispered as they walked toward the cell accompanied by a guard.

"I don't know...I hope it doesn't have anything to do with the yellow rock." He stuck his hand in his pocket and clutched the small sample he had taken from the tunnels.

On the walk back to the cell, Bryce slowed his pace to allow the guard to get a few steps ahead. He wanted to look around while he could. The sea stretched out to the horizon on his left. As the trail crested a hill, Bryce saw furrowed fields and a small white house in the distance.

Farms mean food. And maybe help.

He wondered what would happen if he took off in a sprint toward the farm. Probably an all-out manhunt. If the blueskins caught him, they would almost certainly pitch him off the cliff. If they didn't, they might hurt his cellmates to make an example of what happens if you run away. He wouldn't escape without Amanda and the others, let alone do something that might cause them harm. He would wait.

He remembered his mother's advice: *if you want something, be prepared to wait for it.*

She was talking about a bike that he was saving for; waiting this time might kill him.

———

Later that afternoon, Jamal and Cherie charged into the cell bursting with excitement. They sat down together on Cherie's mat, Jamal holding his hand behind his back in a strange way.

"We saw something today," Jamal said.

"More like we saw someone," Cherie added.

At that Bryce sat up on his mat like the others.

"Saw who, bro?" Jason asked, his eyebrows floating up his forehead. "Just spit it out already."

"Well, we don't know exactly who," Jamal said.

Reese lay back down on his mat. "I think you two fell on your heads on the way back here."

"Is that so?" Cherie said, a mischievous grin on her face. "Show him, Jamal."

"First, I have to tell them the story. We were walking along back toward the cell. We're taking our time because, no offense, we spend enough time here with you all. The guard is like fifty feet ahead of us, and Cherie and I are just strolling along. Then I hear this rustle in the bush next to us. It sounded like an animal."

"A big animal," Cherie added. "I jumped back."

"I just kept walking. This island is too small to support a large predator. I thought it might be a dog. But this animal, whatever it is, followed us, all the time staying behind the bushes. After a minute or two, I kind of figured out that it was a human. You know, based on the way it was moving. Besides, most animals run from humans."

"Unless they're about to eat them," Reese added.

"Right," Jamal said. "That's true. So we're walking along, and Cherie suddenly turns and says, 'Who's there?'"

"I thought it was someone who escaped or something."

Jamal continued, "All of a sudden, this little head comes poking over the hedge and shoves something in my hands. Then he runs away like a jackrabbit."

Bryce was intrigued. "Who was he?"

"No idea," Jamal said. "One of the local kids, I guess. Dark skin, dark brown hair. Looked Hispanic. He couldn't have been older than ten."

"What did he give you?" Jason asked.

"These," Jamal said, bringing his hand from behind his back. He held a small, colorful package. "Cherie wanted to keep them for ourselves, but I insisted on sharing. One for all, all for one."

"I did not," Cherie said, elbowing her brother playfully in the ribs.

"What are they?" Bryce asked.

"Candy," Jamal said.

Everyone jumped to their feet and gathered around him excitedly. Jamal tore open the packaging.

"Hold on, hold on. Geez, you guys act like you never had candy before," he said. The candy sparkled even in the dim orange light. "Okay, I'm going to hand these out equally."

No one argued. Each ended up with two pieces of soft, chewy candy. They ate their newfound treasure in different ways. Jason shoved both candies into his mouth and chewed loudly. Jamal and Cherie nibbled slowly, whittling their pieces to nothing. Reese let it sit on the edge of his tongue for a minute as though he were in disbelief at having real food. Amanda ate one, then saved the other for later. Bryce took a small bite and chewed slowly. The sweetness hit his tongue like a sledgehammer.

"Wow! I don't know if I'm just hungry, but this might be the best candy I've ever had," Reese said.

"These are the best," Jason added. "And I don't even like soft candy."

Amanda giggled.

It's amazing what seems like a luxury when you have nothing.

"That was delicious," Bryce said after they had finished eating. "Do you think that he'll bring us more?"

Jamal rubbed his chin thoughtfully. "I don't know…I sure hope so, though. I wonder if this has happened to anyone else."

"Good luck asking the zombies," Jason said. "They're not going to be much help."

Suddenly, the door opened, and Merry entered with their dinners—green juice bags—and a fresh container of water. Bryce quickly hid his candy wrappers under his mat, and the others did the same.

Nothing to see here. Although based on their interactions so far, Bryce doubted that Merry would turn them in.

The open cell door let in a welcome breeze, but Bryce could also hear Imjac hovercraft flying around and see lights flashing in the distance. Several blueskin guards sprinted past the entrance, shouting in their strange alien tongue, their suits swooshing as they ran.

Merry's furrowed brows and pursed lips told him that something was wrong. She quickly gave each of them their juice bags and turned to leave without a word.

What was happening outside?

———

There was no breakfast the next morning.

Guards roughly lined up the newbies outside the cells. Instead of being led to the worksite, the guards led them in the opposite direction. Bryce recognized that they were moving toward the area where the ship landed. Toward the cliff. Toward the spot where Red Scar had killed the boy.

Oh no.

They reached the clifftop, and the guards ordered them to stop. Pushed and prodded, they formed a line facing the sea. High clouds dotted the sky, and the ocean stretched endlessly before them. Bryce envied the seabirds that hovered over the water, looking for breakfast.

Three hundred miles in that direction, and we're home.

"Why are we standing here, bro?" Jason said out of the side of his mouth. "Just to enjoy the view?"

Bryce shrugged, but in the back of his mind, he knew. *They caught someone, and this is a show for us. To intimidate us. To make us not want to leave.*

But they were already as scared as they were going to be.

Red Scar and two guards walked out first in that stiff

alien stride. Seeing the blueskins side by side, Bryce was once again struck by how much larger Red Scar was than the others. It looked like a father alien standing with his sons.

The man with the tattered pants ambled out to join them.

Red Scar grunted and hissed at them for a full minute, the small Asian man nodding with every utterance.

When the large alien finished, the man translated. "Your gracious and powerful Imjac hosts have brought you here this morning to show you the consequences for those who seek to break the rules. The procedures are simple: work when you are told; then return to your housing units to rest." He paused to let his words sink in. "Yesterday, someone tried to escape the Imjac camp and was easily captured. You will now see the consequences for one who tries to flee." With that, he nodded at Red Scar, who hissed an order to a nearby guard.

The blueskins dragged the escapee forward. He was bent over, using his feet to drag two rows of earth as he went. Bryce recognized Sam LaPell. The boy looked up as he passed and caught Bryce's eye. He wore a look of terror, with tears streaming down his cheeks.

"No, no, no," Sam shrieked.

But once in the shadow of the enormous alien, he quieted. Red Scar stared at Sam like he wanted to eat him. Then he moved with astonishing speed. Grasping the back of Sam's neck with his huge alien claw, he wrenched the boy off the ground like he was filled with straw. Red Scar turned to the newbies and growled and hissed again.

"This guest of the Imjac decided that the conditions were not good enough for him," the man in the tattered pants interpreted. "Today he will meet his fate. Escape is futile. Remember, serve the Imjac, and you will not be harmed."

Yeah, your brain will just end up like scrambled eggs. And you'll never see your family again.

Red Scar turned toward Sam, but the boy kicked at the big alien and somehow wrenched away from his grasp. The giant blueskin flailed at Sam, who ducked under Red Scar's reach. Sam turned to run, but the guards blocked his escape on every side.

As the guards slowly closed their circle around Sam, he stood frozen. Trapped in a triangle with Red Scar, the guards, and the cliff on each side, Sam chose the cliff. He sprinted to the edge and jumped with all his might. His arms and legs spun circles as he reached the height of his leap, then slowly disappeared from sight.

Cries of anguish erupted from the line. Someone collapsed and was immediately lifted to their feet by their neighbors.

A lump formed in Bryce's throat. He didn't like Sam, but to see a life thrown away stung.

Red Scar stared angrily over the cliff. Then he let out a short hiss and stormed off, obviously disappointed he couldn't deal with Sam himself.

"Back to work," the short Asian man said, clapping his hands.

Bryce saw twice as many guards around the work camp that day. He imagined that the escape attempt had put Red Scar on edge. If so, making it off the island would be even harder. Was it worth it in the end? To plan and plan and plan, only to be caught and killed by the Imjac?

No, it's worth it. Anything to get out of here and make it home.

But would the others feel the same?

Later that afternoon, in the cell, the group sat on their mats, exhausted from another day's worth of tunneling.

Dinner had been delivered, but at Bryce's suggestion they had put off drinking so they could talk.

"I don't know if I can take too much more of this," Jamal said. "My back is killing me."

"My *everything* is killing me," Amanda said. Lately she had become much more a member of the group, especially since she had become an effective worker in the tunnels.

"My ears are killing me," Reese added. "Jason's nonstop rapping is painful. Don't you know any country tunes?"

"It's J-Money to you, country boy," Jason said, laughing. "And my rapping is awesome! *Yo, my name is J-Money and I come from the OA. If you mess with me, you're gonna pay.*"

Reese pointed at Jason. "See! See! It's horrible."

They all laughed. For a moment, life felt normal: a group of friends just hanging out and talking.

"Poor Sam," Cherie said, and sighed.

"Poor Sam? He got what he deserved," Jamal countered.

"Yeah, he was a sneak," Jason said. "I remember he stole some money out of my wallet in the locker room once."

"Wait a second," Reese said, obviously offended. "Besides Amanda, I'm the only true local here, and I've known Sam since kindergarten. He was always a bit of a troublemaker, but he wasn't a bad guy. His family...his family was just really messed up. I feel terrible about what happened today."

"I think Reese is right," Bryce said. "Sam wasn't a friend of mine, but he didn't deserve to die like that. No one does. He died trying to escape, something we all want to do. We still want to try to get off the island, right?"

No one answered. They sat in an uncomfortable silence for a minute.

"I don't know," said Cherie. "The way Sam died is my worst nightmare. If one person can't get away on their own, what chance do six of us have?"

Jamal and Reese nodded in agreement. Bryce saw the hope of escape slipping away.

"Hold on a second," Bryce said. "You're right, Cherie—one person couldn't get out of here. But six of us together are stronger and smarter than one person. And we'll have a plan. We won't just try to sneak off in the night."

"I agree with Bryce, and not just because he's my cousin," Amanda chimed in. "I don't want to die like Sam either. But I sure don't want to slowly starve to death and die in some dark tunnel."

"Yeah," Jason added. "The options are not good—we likely die either way. But I'd rather try to make it home than know for sure that I'll never see my family again."

Jamal and Cherie exchanged a look.

"We're in again," Jamal said.

"Jamal, you didn't even ask me!" Cherie complained.

"I read your mind. We're twins, remember?" Jamal said.

All eyes turned to Reese.

The blond-headed farm boy broke into a big grin. "Well, I'm not going to hold you guys back. Let's get out of here."

Bryce brought the conversation back to the escape plan. "Did you guys notice the extra security around the basin?"

"Yeah," Cherie said. "Our chances of escape went from difficult to impossible."

"Nothing is impossible," Bryce argued. "Besides, they won't keep this security up for long—they'll go back to their old habits. Everybody does."

Jamal shook his head. "You just said 'everybody' like you're dealing with people. The blueskins aren't people, so who knows how they'll react? This may be normal now."

Bryce nodded at the boy's logic. "You might be right. I guess we'll have to wait and see. Should we eat?" He picked up his drink from the mat in front of him.

"Wait!" Jason said, slapping his hand on the earth in

front of him. "I forgot to tell you. I saw the boy again. At least, I think it was the boy. I never saw him the first time."

Bryce's mouth began to water at the thought of more candy. "Where did you see him?"

"Not far from the cell," Jason said. "As we were walking up. Maybe ten or fifteen feet from the path."

"Are you thinking what I'm thinking?" Bryce said.

"More candy?" Jason said, rubbing his stomach.

"No," Bryce said. "Although that would be nice. This kid probably has parents, grownups who might help us get out of here."

Bryce watched the others drink their dinners and drift off to sleep. He held off, until his angry stomach got the better of him. In the end, he had half of his drink and tossed the rest. Sleep came easily, with happy thoughts of people nearby willing to help them escape.

CHAPTER
NINE

THEY DIDN'T SEE the boy again, but not for a lack of trying. Each trip to the site, Bryce walked as slowly as possible, his head swiveling left and right as he walked.

"I need more candy," Jason complained one night. "We need to find that kid."

"Jason, the goal is to get out of here," Bryce said. "Not to have candy. I want to talk to him about the town and to see if there is anyone there that might help us."

"Well, that would be good too," Jason said quickly. "But a little more candy would still be nice."

The truth of the matter was that they hadn't made any progress in coming up with a plan to escape. The blueskins followed predictable patterns, true, but the patterns left little in the way of chance.

Bryce wasn't defeated. *Every puzzle has a solution.*

The next morning held an unpleasant surprise. Red Scar himself loomed at the checkpoint where the guards handed out the bags, the man in the tattered pants next to him. When it was Bryce's turn, Red Scar growled and hissed, and the guard handed Bryce two bags instead of one.

Bryce moved to hand one of the bags back to the guard. "You've made a mistake."

"There has been no mistake," the man in the tattered pants stated. "Fill two bags today."

Amanda started to argue, but Bryce pulled her away.

"Great, Bryce," Amanda said under her breath as they walked to the tunnel. "You *had* to show off. Now we've got to do twice the work."

Bryce felt his face flush. This wasn't fair—Red Scar was punishing him for being efficient. He had never seen another group with two bags. A thought crossed his mind. Maybe this wasn't a punishment; maybe it was a test. But should he try to pass the test or fail?

By the time they reached the tunnels, Bryce had made up his mind. He would take on the Imjac's challenge. Passing might lead to rewards or privileges. Besides, he knew how the Imjac dealt with failure.

When they reached the dig site at the end of the tunnel, Amanda sat down, dejected. "Now we have two bags to fill. What are we going to do?"

"We're going to fill them," Bryce answered. "And fast."

"Somehow I knew you were going to say that."

He attacked the tunnel wall with the searcher, ignoring his aching body. Amanda fed off his energy, jumping in with the digger and gathering the shiny blue stones. Before lunchtime they had filled one bag and partially filled the second.

"We had better slow down, or they'll give us three tomorrow," Amanda joked.

Bryce thought about that for a second. "If they give us three, we'll fill three." He felt his competitive juices flowing.

If they want to test me, I'll pass.

At lunch they told the others that Red Scar had given them an extra bag to fill.

Jamal let out a long, low whistle. "Man, makes me glad I'm not the superstar rock digger."

"That's bull," Jason added.

"Speaking of bulls, my dad always says the prize cow meets the butcher first," Reese said.

"What does that even mean?" Cherie asked.

Reese shrugged. "I don't know. But he said it all the time. I think it has to do with showing off or something. You know, if you're a cow, you definitely don't want to go to the butcher."

"I'm not showing off." Bryce bristled. "I don't want to help them. But maybe this is a good thing. Maybe this can lead to something."

"I hope it doesn't lead to two bags for the rest of us," Jason said.

Bryce didn't respond. He had always been competitive and didn't back down from a challenge. And that's what the second bag from the blueskins was: a challenge, an obstacle that he had to overcome. He jumped up before lunch was even over. "Let's get back to work," he said to Amanda, gesturing with his thumb toward the tunnel.

Amanda rolled her eyes and reluctantly stood up. "Tomorrow, one of you guys is working with Captain Miner here."

The others laughed.

When they marched to the silo with their second bag early that afternoon, Red Scar and the small Asian man watched them from the central controls. Bryce glanced in their direction, and he saw Red Scar and the interpreter talking. About what, he didn't know. He felt satisfied, though. They gave him a second bag to fill, and he and Amanda filled both bags faster than most could fill one.

Jamal and Cherie beat them back to the cell that afternoon. But Bryce and Amanda made it back before Jason and Reese.

Bryce lay down on his mat as tired as he had ever been. He had proved his mettle, but he also wondered if it was worth it. Would he have to fill two bags every day while everyone else just got one? He couldn't work like this forever. Sensitivity to the alien technology or not, he was, after all, still human. And working overtime for the Imjac didn't get them any closer to escape.

————

The next morning the guard again handed Bryce two bags to fill. But as Bryce turned to walk to the tunnels with Amanda, the guard pulled her back and pushed Jamal in his direction.

"You work!" the guard growled.

Amanda feigned a look of relief. When Bryce shot her a dark look, she stuck her tongue at him.

Jamal rolled his eyes and threw his hands up in despair. "Of course! I'm the lucky one who gets to work with Mr. Two Bags!"

Bryce just gritted his teeth and marched to his tunnel with Jamal trailing behind him, complaining all the way.

Halfway down he stopped and turned back to Jamal. "Any idea why they split up Amanda and me?"

Jamal nodded. "I have a real good idea. They are isolating the variable."

"Isolating the variable? What's that mean?"

"They're trying to figure out if it's you or Amanda who works so fast. Or maybe both of you. They split the two of you up to see who the MVD is."

"MVD?"

"Most Valuable Digger. I made that up myself," Jamal said, mockingly patting himself on the back. "We know that the answer is you, but they can't be sure. Which is why you are graced with my presence in the tunnel today instead of your cousin."

"Hmm? Makes sense when you put it that way."

"The question is, what will they do when they find out it's you who can find this blue junk so fast?" Bryce didn't have an answer for that.

And so they began to dig.

Truth be told, Bryce was exhausted from the day before. His muscles burned more than they had any day here, and his hands were raw from digging through the black rocks. Blisters lined his palms and fingers. But if Red Scar thought that he could break him, he had another thing coming.

Jamal proved to be an able partner. He had long, thin arms and dexterous fingers and was able to nimbly maneuver the searcher through the dirt. Jamal sang to himself softly as he worked, words that were drowned out by the whirring of the alien tool.

"We had better slow down, or they'll give us another bag," Bryce half-joked as they switched positions.

"If they give us a third bag, I am walking off this island and swimming home," Jamal said, resting the digger on his lap. "It's amazing, what you can do with these tools. If I didn't know better, I'd think that you were part blueskin."

"I don't know what it is," Bryce said, digging the searcher into the wall of rock. "Once when I was five, I took apart my dad's cell phone. He was not happy. But that didn't stop me from taking apart his laptop."

Jamal laughed. "I guess we all have our gifts. It's handy that yours is working with freakish alien technology."

"Thanks, I guess."

"So why do you think that this"—he held up the alien tool—"works better for you than us?"

"I can't really explain it. When I pick up one of those tools, I feel like the tool becomes a part of my body, something I don't have to concentrate on to control. Almost like another hand or foot."

"Wow, that is weird. Are you sure your parents were human?"

"Yeah, I'm sure."

After that, Jamal kept his thoughts to himself. This made the work quick and steady, but Bryce missed his cousin's company. He imagined Jamal felt the same about his twin. Then again, the way the brother and sister communicated sometimes—maybe they relished a little space between them. Maybe there was such a thing as being too close.

At lunch, they turned their first bag in at the silo and went to sit with the others.

"How did your morning with Wonderdigger go, Jamal?" Amanda teased.

Bryce just smiled. He was used to his cousin's teasing and knew it came from the right place.

"Just fine. I may have found a new digging partner," Jamal said, drawing a dirty look from his sister. "We already finished our first bag and started our second. Better than you slowpokes."

Jason held up his half-filled bag. "We just have half a bag to go. I bet we'll beat you back to the cell by an hour."

"Yep," Reese added. "We sure will. While you two over-achievers are digging away, we'll be relaxing in luxury."

"You call our cell luxury?" Cherie chided.

"Hey, I grew up on a farm. I've slept on hay before. The cell's not half bad."

Bryce downed his drink. "We'll take your bet, Jason. C'mon, Jamal. Let's get going."

"But we just got here," Jamal complained.

. . .

They worked even faster that afternoon. Showing Red Scar that he could fill two bags was one thing. Beating Jason and Reese back to the cell for bragging rights was another. Jamal seemed to pick up on the competition too. No sooner would Bryce locate mineral, than Jamal would scoot over and dig it out. Then Bryce would slide in for more finding. Back and forth, back and forth, until they filled the second bag.

When they finished, they sat back and rested.

"I think we filled this bag faster than the first one," Jamal said. "I hate to say it, but I'm a little proud of myself. And of you too, of course."

"Of course. Think we beat them?" Bryce asked, slinging the bag over his shoulder.

"Only one way to find out," Jamal said and started to crawl toward the entrance.

Suddenly, the tunnel emitted a large groan. The ground shook around them, sending dirt and debris raining down from the ceiling. Bryce crouched, covering the back of his head with both hands just as he had done countless times in San Diego during school earthquake drills. Jamal backed up against the wall and covered his head.

After what felt like a few minutes, the shaking stopped.

"What the hay was that?" Jamal said, brushing the dirt from his hair. "I thought this mountain was dormant."

Bryce could feel his heart pounding in his chest. An earthquake drill was a far cry from an actual quake underneath a 7,000-foot-tall volcano.

"Well, we know this is a volcano," Bryce reasoned, shaking the rocks and dirt from his hair. "It's not surprising there would be some seismic activity."

Jamal held his hands to his head in disbelief. "Some seismic activity! Who are you, some kinda professor? We just had a half a mountain fall on our heads."

Bryce laughed. "It wasn't that bad...I wouldn't want to

be down here if it got worse, though. It could cause a tunnel to collapse."

"Let's get out of here," Jamal said. "For once, I cannot wait to get back to the cell."

They crawled out of the tunnel into a dull, gray world. The earthquake set the worksite on edge. Several tunnels *had* collapsed. Many diggers stood outside their tunnels, their half-filled bags in their hands, refusing to go back to work. Red Scar stormed around the central area, hissing and clicking loudly, the Imjac guards racing to follow his orders.

Bryce saw Cherie and Amanda nearby and flashed them a thumbs-up. They waved back.

"Do you see Jason and Reese?" he asked Jamal.

"Nah," he said. "They probably beat us back."

The guards began to push the diggers back into their tunnels, threatening those who resisted with their blasters. Eventually, digging resumed and calm was restored.

Bryce and Jamal took the laden bag to the silos. Again, the small Asian man and Red Scar observed him as he approached the silo. Bryce ignored their stares and tried to calm himself. Why were they so interested in him? As casually as he could, he handed the bag to a worker and turned to join Jamal on the walk back to the cell.

"Wait," the interpreter called out to Bryce in accented English. "We would like a word with you."

Bryce and Jamal stopped and turned back.

"No, not you," the interpreter said, gesturing toward Jamal. A guard stepped in front of Jamal and shoved him in the direction of the cells.

"I'm going. I'm going," Jamal said. "See you back home, Bryce."

Bryce waved and continued toward the interpreter and Red Scar.

As he drew closer, a stone formed in his stomach, and he felt his forehead become wet with perspiration.

The ten steps Bryce took toward the Imjac leader felt like one hundred.

"What you are doing has not gone unnoticed by the Imjac," the man said, his face a puzzle. Red Scar loomed behind the man, his viper's eyes sizing up Bryce.

Bryce's heart skipped a beat. Did the Imjac suspect that he was trying to escape? His mind raced as he thought of what they might know. Could they have listening devices in the cells? He had definitely said some incriminating things; they all had. Why was he being singled out?

"What am I doing?" Bryce offered finally, trying to hide the waver in his voice.

The man's face broke into a thin smile. "Do not worry. The Imjac just recognize that you are a very efficient worker. The best there is."

Relief washed over Bryce. "Oh," he said. "Thanks, I guess."

The man pushed his glasses up his nose and gestured toward the pocked side of the volcano. "There is a future beyond the tunnels. If you are interested, that is."

Bryce felt like saying he would sooner serve a pig, but he bit his tongue. Besides, a thought tingled in the back of his mind. It's true that the path they were on was a dead end—there didn't appear to be any way to escape. Maybe this opportunity, whatever it was, could be the key to getting off the island.

Before Bryce could say anything, the man in the tattered clothes nodded at Red Scar. "We will speak again tomorrow." And with that, he and Red Scar walked away.

"What was that all about?" Jamal asked as Bryce entered the cell.

"An opportunity," he said. "I think. I'll tell you about it when Amanda and Cherie are back."

Jamal flashed him a thumbs-up and lay back down on his mat.

Jason and Reese beat them back to the cells and were asleep on their mats. Bryce thought he could see a satisfied grin on Reese's face as he dozed.

Bryce sat down on his own mat with a groan. He assessed his clothes as he sat there. Even though they bathed yesterday, his shirt was filthy again. The Specials had newer clothes, black uniforms like the Imjac. But what could they want of him? Sure, he was good at digging, but there was only one of him. Were they actually offering him a position as a Special?

His back ached from being bent over for hours in the tunnels. His elbows were sore from holding the trowel in place as it dug through the rock. More than that, the constant exposure to dim light had begun to affect his mood. He had begun to feel tired all the time—as soon as they got back to the cell, he wanted to sleep. Every day he did a mental assessment, quizzing himself on math problems and trying to remember details from his childhood. *What was the name of Dad's boat? What park did Mom used to take me to after school? What is the name of Aunt Sammie's favorite cow?* He passed all of his mental tests, but he knew it was a matter of when and not if the green drink would take its effect.

Which made the proposition from the Imjac all the more interesting. Bryce shook his head to remind himself that he wasn't leaving the tunnels for his own comfort; it was to help everyone.

He couldn't wait to tell the others.

CHAPTER
TEN

WHEN EVERYONE WAS BACK from the tunnels and dinner had been served, he broke the news. It did not go well.

"So, you're ditching us?" Reese said accusingly after Bryce told them about the offer from Red Scar.

"No, I'm not leaving you guys," Bryce said, defensively.

"That's what it sounds like to me," Cherie added. "I thought we were in this together."

Jamal just glared at Bryce, but the message was clear. He felt as betrayed as the others, maybe more so after working with Bryce today.

Only Amanda and Jason took Bryce's side. "I think you should do it," Amanda said. "You can learn more about this place. You might be able to scout around and find a way to escape."

"Exactly," Bryce said, pouncing on Amanda's comment. "It's not like I'm switching sides—this is reconnaissance. I'll be figuring out the weak spots in the Imjac defenses. I'll be looking for a way to get us out of here. Amanda is my cousin—I'm not leaving here without her. Or any of you."

"I agree," Jason said, nodding profusely. "I trust you, bro."

He looked around the cell. They had been here for less than two weeks, but already the Imjac camp had taken its toll. The baby fat was gone from their faces, their clothes were torn and ragged, their hair filled with tiny particles of black dust that seemed to get everywhere. He understood what his friends were feeling now was desperation. But it didn't make their mistrust hurt any less.

Reese shook his head. "You won't come back for us. Once you switch sides, you'll stay on their side. You'll be one of them. A Special."

"You'll be a traitor," Jamal said. "A Benedict Arnold!"

Bryce slammed his fist into the dirt floor so hard his knuckles started to bleed. "Don't say that! I could never join their side. You don't understand—they killed my parents. My parents hugged me goodbye one morning and never came back. They died fighting the blueskins. I hate them as much as anyone."

The mood changed in the room as Cherie, Jamal, and Reese exchanged guilty looks.

"I'm sorry," Cherie finally offered. "We didn't know… How did they die?"

Bryce gulped. Telling this story felt like wrenching his heart from his chest every time. "My parents were both Navy pilots. When the Mothership landed, they were with the main battle group that defended Earth. They were great pilots, but the alien aircraft had better technology. I still remember the day I found out. I was in fifth grade, and my teacher, Mr. Perryman, got a call on the phone in the middle of class. We all knew the call wasn't good news—half the class was made up of Navy kids, so we knew about the risks of war. When he called my name and sent me to the office, I knew that something happened to one of my parents. I was bracing for it. But I never suspected that both of them would die on the same day." Bryce's voice cracked as he finished.

Amanda, who sat closest to him, put her hand on his.

After a minute, Jason broke the silence. "Listen, the track that we're on isn't getting us anywhere. Wake up, we head to the tunnels. After digging, we head straight back here. There's no chance to find out anything."

"Right," Bryce said. "This will give us a chance."

Reese shook his head. "I'm sorry about your parents, Bryce, but this isn't the right thing to do." He lay on his mat, turning his back toward them.

Bryce could tell that Jamal and Cherie weren't convinced either.

They'll believe it when I get us out of here.

————

As they stepped out of the cell to a still, gray morning, the man in the tattered clothes stood off to the side with a blue-skin guard. He gestured for Bryce.

"Have you made your decision?" he asked.

"Yes," Bryce said. "I'll do it."

"Excellent choice," the man said. "After all, the alternative is certain death." He began walking briskly in the opposite direction of the work camp. "Please follow me."

Bryce started after him, not before looking back at the others. Amanda smiled at him, and Jason gave a slight wave, but Jamal, Reese, and Cherie looked away.

Why can't they understand that I'm doing this for all of us?

He cleared his mind of emotions and followed the interpreter and the guard on the winding path toward the worksite. They walked without conversation, although the man hummed a tune that Bryce didn't recognize. Bryce shivered in the morning cool, but after a few minutes of walking, his body warmed up.

They reached the worksite, and the interpreter led Bryce to the central controls, which were bookended on each side by the towering silos. The hoverboards buzzed around the site, and the mining machines were busy digging new tunnels into the volcano. Specials manned the silos, feeding the bags of blue minerals into the towers' gaping maws.

Without hesitation, the man led Bryce to Red Scar, who watched them approach. Bryce's feet suddenly were made of lead. He felt his knees start to quiver, his stomach flutter as he stood before the immense alien.

Hold steady. Be confident.

Red Scar studied him with his viper eyes. The man in the tattered pants said something to the large alien, who then looked at Bryce with curiosity. There didn't seem to be any malice in his stare, but Bryce still felt on edge. He remembered how easily and mercilessly Red Scar killed the boy when they first arrived, and then there was the incident with Sam LaPell, though, technically, Red Scar didn't throw poor Sam off the cliff.

Apparently satisfied, Red Scar said something to the interpreter, who translated. "You are probably wondering what role the Imjac would like you to fill."

Bryce nodded. He wanted to get on with this as quickly as possible. Being around the aliens sickened him.

"The Imjac are not satisfied with production from the tunnels," the man said. "They need more of the blue mineral. It is very important to their efforts. You will help with that."

Bryce was puzzled. "Me? How?"

"The Imjac keep track of everyone's production based on feedback that the tools provide. You are highly efficient for a human. The best there is by far."

Red Scar growled and hissed. Bryce saw his forked black tongue flicker in and out as he spoke. He wondered how the interpreter could learn such a brutal, inhuman language.

"The leader would like to add that even an Imjac miner would be impressed with your results with the tools."

Amazingly, Bryce thought he saw Red Scar smile, which made him look like a snake right before it swallowed a rat whole.

"Thank you." *This is all an act. Think of the others. Keep pretending.*

"But there is only one of you and many tunnels in which to dig."

Bryce nodded. "What would I do exactly?"

The Asian man nodded. "Excellent. To the point. You will have free range around the worksite. You are to move from tunnel to tunnel as directed by your information band and assist the workers so they keep their production levels up. You will teach them to be more efficient, to be more like you."

"Like a trainer?"

The interpreter smiled. "Yes, exactly like a trainer. A teacher of sorts."

The man pointed at the band around Bryce's wrist. "You will, of course, receive a new band that will have different allowances. You will be permitted to move around the worksite and the island...during the day."

One of the guards stepped forward and removed the bracelet from Bryce's wrist, installing a new band with a larger face. Bryce tried to stay stoic, but inside he was pleased. Now he would be able to move around the site freely. Of course, he knew that he could be traced, but if he was careful, he could gather information that could help them escape.

"But be aware, your movements will still be tracked," the interpreter added, as if the man had been reading Bryce's mind. "You will also receive a uniform so you will stand out from the...others. The guards will know that you are a Special."

Bryce nodded. Bryce looked up and realized that Red Scar was still staring at him again. A shiver of fear ran up his spine. Could the large blueskin know that he was thinking of escape?

A guard shoved a black uniform into Bryce's hands, one like the other Specials had. They all stared at him for a moment, and Bryce realized that they expected him to change right there. Luckily, there were just a few silo workers around, and they seemed busy with their tasks. Only the interpreter looked away as Bryce took his clothes off and put on the uniform.

To the aliens, I am just a piece of meat, a tool for a task.

The uniform fit snugly but moved well with his body, like good athletic wear. He slid his canvas shoes back on his feet but left the rest of his clothes in a heap.

Red Scar hissed and grunted.

"Remember, you are to improve production any way that you can," the man translated. "Visit the tunnels where there are laggards and help them. You can use any tools that you wish, but more mineral must be found."

The man turned toward Red Scar again, and the enormous alien uttered something else. "Of course," the man said, "you must understand that there are consequences if production does not get better."

Red Scar gazed at Bryce, who held his stare.

The words echoed in Bryce's ears as he walked around the worksite. He realized that before he could begin scouting the island, he needed the Imjac to trust him. That meant being a model worker and not doing anything that might invite suspicion. Once he had their trust, he could start scouting the area for a way out. If he started acting strange before then, they might send him back to the tunnels. Or worse. No, he reasoned, first he had to do his job as if he were just happy to be a Special.

For a while, he stood in the shadow of one of the towering blue silos. By now, the diggers were in the tunnels, and only the silo workers and guards roamed around the site. Bryce noticed that there was no one like him, a free agent of sorts. He stood there, wondering when he would start his new job. Nervously bouncing from foot to foot, he glanced at the guards as they made their routes around the site.

Boom! Boom!

Two explosions at the base of the mountain shot rocks and debris into the air. Bryce noticed the explosions were in the area where the tunnels had collapsed after the earthquake. Did more tunnels just collapse? He raced over to see if anyone needed help.

As he approached, he noticed a tall boy in a Special uniform standing outside a tunnel. He held footlong metal cylinders in each of his hands.

"What's going on?" Bryce asked him.

"What does it look like? We're making some new tunnels." The boy had black hair that flopped down over his forehead, almost hiding a mean stare. "Watch out!"

Suddenly, an alien engineer drove a drilling vehicle right past Bryce, missing him by inches. The alien drove the bit into the side of the volcano until the vehicle disappeared from sight. It emerged a minute later, and the Special walked over to the new hole.

"What are you doing?" Bryce asked, feeling a bit foolish but also curious.

"Sealing the tunnel with a mine. Keeps the walls intact so they don't fall down. Tell that to the jerks who died in the earthquake yesterday, though. Didn't work out so well for them." He pressed a button at the top of the mine and tossed it down the shaft. "You should probably back up."

Boom!

Debris and dust erupted from the hole.

"Get out of here before you get hurt," the boy said. "The blueskins get touchy about who has access to these babies." He held up a mine.

Bryce wandered back to the silos.

None of the guards bothered with him, and the silo workers ignored him too, content to do their work. Bryce examined the silos more closely as he stood there; they looked very much like the grain silos near Aunt Sammie and Uncle Kyle's house, tall and cylindrical. But at the top, a tube extended straight up for twenty feet or so, narrowing as it rose until it formed an outlet no larger than a garden hose.

His new wristband began flashing a symbol, an Imjac starburst. What was he supposed to do now? Did they think that he could read Imjac?

Bryce approached one of the silo workers for help. It was the same boy who turned Bryce in to the Imjac for having the yellow mineral, the one who got him blasted. Bryce didn't want to ask him for help, but he didn't know who else to turn to. Going back to the interpreter and Red Scar to ask for help might make him seem like he wasn't capable.

Bryce bit his lip and suppressed his anger at the boy. *He was probably just doing his job.*

He walked over to the boy and pointed to the starburst image on his wristband.

"Do you know what this means?" he asked.

The boy looked annoyed at being interrupted from his work. "It's an Imjac number. Match it up with the number on top of the tunnel." He pointed in the general area of the tunnels and turned back to his work.

So much for help.

Bryce faced the volcano. For the first time since arriving

he remembered that all the tunnels were inscribed with a pattern burned into the earth above them. He felt stupid for forgetting, but he didn't need to know them before—he entered whatever tunnel the Imjac assigned him. Now he had to find the tunnel with the symbol that matched his wristband display. But as he stared into the base of the volcano, he saw hundreds of tunnel openings. It could take all day just to find the first tunnel. Red Scar said that there would be consequences for not producing. He would have to work fast.

He decided to start at the bottom ramp and work his way up. As he studied the Imjac symbols, he began to notice subtle differences between them. In some, the starbursts were larger and had rays that extended from the center outward. In others, two or three large circles sat in the center of the burst, not just one. As he moved up the ramp, he began to quickly eliminate the tunnels. A pattern emerged. The symbols on the first level had a large circle surrounded by smaller circles. The number of smaller circles got correspondingly larger as he moved along the ramp. When he went to the second ramp, he noticed that the symbols on the second level had two large circles.

The symbol on his band had bursts and two large circles. That meant the tunnel he was looking for was on the second level.

He finally found the matching symbol halfway up the second ramp—it was his old tunnel! He scampered up the path toward the tunnel. He reached the entrance and crawled inside frantically. He soon saw a faint light ahead of him. As he moved closer, he could make out two figures outlined in the dim light.

"Amanda!" Bryce called out.

"Bryce!" she said. "Is that you?" He could sense the desperation in her voice.

He finally reached the end of the tunnel and saw the panic in his cousin's face. Tears streamed down her cheeks, and her eyes were red.

"Is it the claustrophobia?" Bryce asked. "Remember to close your eyes and picture the beach."

Amanda shook her head. "It's not the tunnel. It's him. They partnered us together this morning." She pointed toward the boy who sat next to her. Even in the dim light, Bryce could make out his sallow complexion. He stared blankly into the wall, his eyes glazed, his mouth open wide. Drool pooled in the corner of his mouth.

This zombie had reached the end of the road. Bryce moved closer to the boy. "Are you okay?" he asked him.

The boy gave no response. Bryce put his hand on the boy's spindly chest and felt it rise in fits and starts, like an old car chugging up a hill.

He was alive, but who knew for how long.

"Was he like this the whole time?" Bryce asked.

"No," Amanda shook her head. "But he was moving slowly when we first started. I had to literally pull him down the tunnel. Then he wouldn't work—I had to do both jobs." Tears started rolling down her cheeks again. "Is this what's going to happen to us, Bryce? He was probably just like us once, before the blueskins. Are we all going to die in a dark tunnel?"

"No, we're not. We are going to get out of here. But today, right now, we need to get through this."

Bryce examined the boy again. He was looking worse by the minute.

Bryce found Amanda's nearly empty bag. "Let me get you caught up."

"Okay, but what are we going to do about him?"

"I'll help him later. First, let's just move him out of the way. Give me a hand."

Bryce moved directly behind the boy and pulled him

from under his shoulders. Amanda grabbed his feet. He felt amazingly light, like a Halloween skeleton and not a real flesh-and-blood human being.

But he was a human once. He was someone's son, someone's pride and joy. And now he is just an empty shell because of the Imjac.

With the boy down the tunnel and out of the way, Bryce grabbed the digger and went to work intently. Working together, he and Amanda nearly filled the bag in less than an hour.

Bryce stopped and turned to Amanda.

"You should be able to do the rest yourself," he said, wiping sweat from his brow.

Amanda nodded. "What about him?" she asked, pointing to the boy, who hadn't moved since Bryce propped him up against the cave wall. His eyes stared blankly at them, but he was clearly alive.

"I'll bring him out," he said, "and let the Imjac know."

"Thanks," she said. "I don't know what I would do without you."

"You're welcome," he said, giving her shoulder a squeeze.

He moved behind the unconscious boy and wrapped his arms beneath his armpits and around his chest. He began to heave. Without Amanda's help, it was grueling work; before long, his back and legs burned. Finally, he reached the mouth of the tunnel and, with one final yank, sat the boy right outside the entrance, facing the worksite.

He ran down to the main level of the worksite and grabbed a bucket of water and brought it back to the boy. He tried to spoon water into the boy's mouth, but it just ran down the sides of his face. The boy was beyond drinking, beyond help.

Running down toward the silos, he saw the interpreter standing with two Imjac guards.

"That kid needs help," he said, pointing to the tunnel.

"What kid?" the man said, not understanding.

"There is a boy who was working with my cousin," Bryce said. "He wouldn't work. He just stared off into space. I dragged him out of the tunnel."

The man let out a deep sigh. "Another one," he muttered. He turned and said something to one of the guards that stood next to him. The guard marched off toward the ramp where the boy sat.

"Aren't you going to get him help?" Bryce asked, puzzled.

The man shook his head. "There is no help for him now."

Bryce watched in horror as the Imjac guard began dragging the boy away by his feet, the boy's arms flailing behind him like a doll's.

"Wait! Stop!" Bryce said and began to run toward the guard.

The interpreter grabbed him by the arm firmly. "Stop, fool! If you interfere, you will share his fate."

Bryce stood and watched helplessly as the guard took the boy away.

He walked away from the interpreter and sat on the ground, crisscross style. He picked up a handful of black rocks and tossed them to the ground in frustration.

That's the fate of all of us unless we can escape.

He sat for a moment, reminding himself of his focus, gaining the Imjac's trust and scouting the area. He tried to push thoughts of the boy out of his mind. After a minute, he rose and took a deep breath.

Then his wristband flashed with another alien symbol. Back to the tunnels.

Soon it was lunchtime, and the diggers emerged from the darkness, shielding their eyes from the light after hours in the tunnels. Bryce could see his cellmates sitting together, and another worker handing them their lunchtime drinks.

"I guess I'll go have lunch," Bryce said, almost to himself. He didn't feel hungry at all after what he just saw, but he began to walk over to where the others had gathered.

"Bryce, your time as a digger is over," the man said. "You'll no longer eat with them. Please follow me."

Of course, I never saw a Special eating with us.

He felt a pang of sadness as he turned away from his cousin and the others. He could feel them watching him as the man led Bryce across the worksite and onto a path leading away from the ocean.

They walked for a short distance in silence until they reached the walkway of an old house, with a sagging roof, broken windows, and peeling white paint.

"What is this place?" Bryce asked.

The man didn't respond. He walked up the creaky front steps and opened the door.

Bryce followed him inside. The house had been converted into a dining hall: all of the furniture that would normally occupy a house had been replaced with tables and chairs of all types and colors, which looked like they had been scavenged from a dump.

At the tables were the silo workers and a few messengers. Bryce saw Merry sitting across the room, and she smiled and offered a wave. The others sat in small groups talking quietly. Bryce then noticed two blueskin guards stationed in the corner, their yellow eyes scanning the room.

The man led Bryce to a kitchen in the back of the house. A short, stout woman stood over a stove, stirring a large metal pot with a wooden spoon. The interpreter grabbed a bowl and spoon from the counter next to the stove and presented it to her.

"What's for lunch, Maria?" the man asked brightly.

"The same, the same," the woman answered in a heavily accented voice. She dipped a ladle into a giant pot and poured something into the bowl. She then balanced a piece of crusty bread across the top.

The man bowed in thanks. "Gracias, Maria," he said.

Bryce grabbed a bowl and spoon and watched anxiously as the woman ladled his soup into the bowl. The soup looked and smelled exquisite, full of chunks of fish and vegetables. "Thank you," he said and walked back into the dining room.

The woman gazed at Bryce with sad eyes, nodded, and went back to stirring the pot.

Bryce thought about sitting next to Merry, but she had finished her lunch and was heading out the door. She looked back before she left and gave him a smile.

"Over here," the man with the tattered pants called from a nearby table.

Bryce froze. He didn't want to sit next to the interpreter, especially on his first day as a Special. Wasn't he on the side of the Imjac? But then he thought of his ultimate goal, escape. The interpreter probably knew more than any other human about the aliens and the site. He might be able to glean some valuable knowledge.

Bryce pushed aside his doubts and sat down. The smell from the soup made his stomach growl. He dipped his spoon into the bowl and dug in. He gulped down four spoonfuls before he realized the man was staring at him.

"Forgive me," the man said. "You must be hungry. They don't really give diggers enough to eat."

Bryce noted that the man said *they* and not *we*. Was he not on the side of the Imjac?

"No," Bryce admitted. "Not nearly enough. Especially considering how hard the work is. And it's not really food."

The man nodded and picked up his spoon and began to eat.

Bryce noticed that the other Specials were sneaking stares at him. He wondered if the man normally ate alone.

They must be wondering who I am. Or maybe they're wondering why I'm talking to this interpreter. Hopefully, they don't think that I'm on the side of the Imjac.

"What is your name?" the man asked after a few bites. He seemed to be in no rush to eat.

"Bryce."

"Bryce," he said, nodding. "I am Cai Lun. It is a pleasure to meet you."

"It's nice to meet you too," Bryce said, not meaning it. It felt like a betrayal to be sitting with this man, to be eating this food, to be, well, comfortable, while his friends sat on the ground and drank green goop that was slowly rotting their brains.

The man studied Bryce for a moment and went back to his food. By now Bryce's bowl was nearly empty. He wanted to ask for seconds but realized that it might be pushing his luck on his first day. He picked up his bread and was about to tear it in half to soak up the drippings in the bottom of the bowl, but then he stopped himself. Amanda and the others hadn't had real food since the boy gave them candy over a week ago. The guilt of enjoying a real meal set in.

"Do I eat all of my meals here from now on?" Bryce asked.

"Yes," Cai Lun said. "And you won't be sleeping in your cell any longer. I will show you where you will stay with the other Specials."

Bryce nodded, trying not to show panic. He would be cut off from his friends. How could he communicate? How would they plan their escape? He felt even guiltier now.

The band on Bryce's wrist flashed "Work." Lunchtime

was over. He shoved the bread in his pocket and rose to leave.

The man still sat, casually eating. "Bryce?"

"Yeah?"

"Despite what you think, I am not one of them."

CHAPTER
ELEVEN

Bryce soon wondered if becoming a Special was worth it.

He hustled from tunnel to tunnel. No sooner had he left one than his tracker would signal another had fallen behind. Crawling in and out of the cramped tunnels exhausted him. His arms and shoulders burned from the constant moving on his hands and feet. He missed his old position as a digger. Before, he was usually back in his cell right after lunch. But being a Special was an all-day job.

There were positives, however. The alien suit protected his elbows and knees and allowed him to move smoothly through the tunnels. He ate real food now. More importantly, he now had freedom to scout the worksite.

While he raced from tunnel to tunnel, he added to his mental map. He knew the Imjac more or less kept the workers in the same tunnels, and all the tunnels were marked with a symbol. If he found the symbol for each of his friends' tunnels, he could communicate with them. He could bring them messages and plan for the escape. He could smuggle in food so they wouldn't be dependent on the green drinks. It would be almost as good as if they were all together.

Between alerts from his tracker, Bryce ducked into random tunnels, hoping to track them down. He knew where Amanda worked, but not the others. The problem was that there were hundreds of tunnels, and only one of him.

Finally, in the late afternoon, the blueskin symbols flashing on his wristband stopped. He took a deep breath and sat down. The sun hovered over the horizon—it would set in an hour or so. Exhausted, he wanted to crawl back to the cell and lay on his mat.

I'll try two more tunnels and then head back.

He only needed one.

He was halfway down the tunnel when he heard familiar voices.

"We're almost there, bro."

"Man, I can't take another minute of this. Let's finish up."

"Shh. Someone's coming."

Bryce recognized the voices of Jamal and Jason and started to crawl faster.

"Hey, guys," Bryce called out as he reached them. A knot pitted in his stomach. After this morning, he wasn't sure how he would be received.

"What? Who's there?" Jamal called out.

"It's me, Bryce." He crawled forward until he was a few feet from the boys, and they could see him by the dim light of their wristbands. "I've been looking all over for you guys."

Jamal eyed him coolly. "Why, so you could report back to your masters?"

Bryce felt his muscles tense, then took a deep breath. *Jamal is not the enemy. He's just angry and confused, like the rest of us.*

"Easy, bro," Jason said. He turned toward Bryce and

gave him a fist bump. "What have you been doing all day, Mr. Special?"

Bryce filled them in on his day, leaving out the part about the boy being dragged off to the cliff.

"Hold on, you had real food?" Jamal said.

Bryce nodded. Then he remembered the piece of bread in his pocket. "Wait, I've got something for you guys." He dug into his pocket and pulled the bread out. "Here," he said, tearing the bread in half and giving a piece to each of them.

"What is this?" Jason asked, holding it up to his tracker's light. "Is this bread?"

"Yeah, it's a little crushed, sorry. It took me a while to find you guys."

"Real food? Unbelievable," Jamal said and took a tentative nibble.

Jason sniffed at it, then took a giant bite. "It's good," he said with his mouth full.

"I will eat squashed bread anytime without complaint," Jamal said when he was finished. "I am *soooo* tired of that green drink."

"I will eat squashed bread in a tunnel," Jason said, with a wry grin. "I would eat squashed bread through a funnel. I think I like it, Bryce-I-Am."

The boys laughed.

"Hey," Jason said," show Bryce what we found."

Jamal reached into his pocket and held up a piece of yellow rock.

"Is this the mineral that you and Amanda found before?" Jamal asked.

Bryce took it in his hand and examined it by the light of his wristband. "Yes, this is it." A thought formed in his mind. "Can I keep this?"

"You want to keep it?" Jason said. "Didn't that get you blasted by the blue guys before?"

"I'll be careful. Don't worry." Bryce's wristband flashed another alien symbol—someone else was behind. "I have to go. I'll try to bring you food when I can."

"We won't see you at home, bro?" Jason said.

"No, they want me to sleep somewhere else, I guess," he said. "But it's good…I've already seen a bunch more of the island." With that, he turned and started to crawl back to the entrance.

He had made it only a short way when he heard Jamal's voice. "Bryce?"

"Yeah." He turned back.

"I'm sorry for doubting you."

"No problem," Bryce said. "We're in this together. Until the end."

———

Later, Bryce stared down at the worksite from the third tier. He had just helped a couple of zombies fill their bag. They had not deteriorated to the level of the boy who worked with Amanda earlier, but Bryce could sense they were close. When he spoke to them, they didn't respond. It wouldn't be long before the Imjac disposed of them. The thought made Bryce sick to his stomach.

Only the silo workers and guards remained at the worksite that earlier buzzed with activity. The kids manning the silos loaded the bags into the giant Imjac processors, plucking the bags one by one from the stacks beside them. Being a silo worker was a good job during the middle part of the day when all was quiet. At the end of the day, when the enormous stacks of mineral bags stood by each silo, it looked like the worst job at the site. Bag after bag had to be loaded into the silos' gaping maw. Bryce knew that when full, the bags felt like the heavy sacks of oats that he helped Uncle Kyle with on the farm. It made sense that the silo workers were bigger than the diggers, who had to fit in small spaces.

The sun had nearly fallen below the horizon behind him. Bryce looked in the opposite direction. *East*, Bryce thought. *East like the rising sun. That's where we need to go.* First things first—he needed to scout the camp and the surrounding area. But not today. The guards around the camp still eyed him warily. Right now, one stood at the end of the ramp not one hundred feet from him, his blaster on his hip. Bryce knew that if he so much as hinted at running away, he would be dead before he could take ten steps. The guards were quick with their blasters and deadly accurate. Not to mention, unforgiving.

*All the more reason to get away. But first…*His stomach growled.

He walked back toward the silos, hoping to find Cai Lun, but he was nowhere to be seen. He walked up to the nearest guard and pointed in the direction of the building where he had dinner.

"I'm going to eat," he said, pointing toward his mouth and pretending to bite.

"Eat," the guard hissed and started Bryce toward the cafeteria.

With more than half of the Specials still working at the silos, there were plenty of empty tables in the cafeteria. Bryce saw Merry and a few of the messengers sitting together at a table, eating in silence. The only sounds were the scraping of spoons against the metal bowls and the cook's movements in the kitchen. Bryce once again noticed the guards in the corners of the room.

He strode into the kitchen, grabbed a bowl and spoon, and walked over to the cook, Maria. She ladled a bowl of what looked to be the same seafood soup that he had eaten for lunch and balanced another piece of crusty bread across the top of the bowl.

"Thank you," he said, but she had already turned away toward her next task.

Bryce found a seat directly across from Merry.

"What's up?" he said casually.

Merry smiled. "How did you end up a Special? You've only been here a few weeks."

Bryce shrugged modestly.

He felt someone clap him on the back. "This bloke's a world-class digger." It was the gapped-toothed boy, who scooted next to Bryce. "The rumor is he's a magician with the tools...The blueskins gave him two bags, and he got them done faster than most."

"That's not entirely true," Bryce protested.

"Ah, don't be bashful," the boy said, his mouth full of bread. "At least it got you out of the tunnels. Get your brain turned to mush staying there. My name is Mitchell." The boy extended a filthy hand, which Bryce shook.

"Bryce."

"No...more...talk," one of the blueskin guards hissed.

The blueskins sure are a paranoid bunch. They should be.

Since he wouldn't see his friends until tomorrow, Bryce decided to finish his meal. He tore the piece of bread in half and dunked it into the savory broth. He opened his mouth wide before chomping down and closed his eyes to relish the flavor. When he opened them, he saw Merry eyeing him curiously. He smiled at her and shrugged.

When he finished dinner, a guard led him down a well-worn path. It was nearly dark now, and a pale sliver of a moon peeked above the horizon.

Soon the hill sloped up, leading to a small white church, still recognizable despite the fact that the cross had broken off. It reminded Bryce of the San Diego mission he had visited as a child with his parents. As he walked closer, he could see the church was in a state of disrepair. The windows had been boarded up, some roof tiles were broken, and the bright white paint that covered the building had chipped away, though parts of the structure had been shored up with alien metal.

The guard unbolted the door, shoved Bryce inside, then slammed the door behind him. The inside of the structure was small; Bryce counted twenty pews, ten on each side with a wide walkway down the center that led to the altar. Light seeped in from the remaining stained-glass windows that adorned the walls. Bryce assumed the open door at the end of the room was a bathroom.

Good. At least there aren't any guards in here.

Another boy lay on a pew at the far end of the room. He wore the Specials uniform, but his was worn on the elbows and knees. Bryce wondered what his job was. He looked over at Bryce, blinked twice, then looked away.

After identifying a stack of mats in the corner and next to that a pile of blankets, Bryce was unsure which pew to take. Did people own the pews like they would own their beds on the outside? In the end, he took a pew to the right of the entrance, in the corner opposite from the boy. He could always move if it belonged to someone else.

He sat down and took his shoes off, emptying the accumulated dirt on the floor. He looked at his filthy hands and decided that he had better clean up in the bathroom. He walked down the aisle, looking to see if the boy was paying attention to him. But the boy just stared at the ceiling. The bathroom was dark, and there was no soap, but just to have running water was a luxury. He washed the dirt from his hands and ran water through his hair. He dried his hands on a ratty T-shirt that was hung on a nail.

Before returning to his pew, he walked to the boarded-up windows. They had been hastily covered, so there were gaps between the boards. He could see an Imjac standing guard outside the church. He assumed there would be one on the other side of the building as well. He watched the guard for a while. The blueskin stared at the building without wavering. Bryce marveled at the aliens' ability to stay absolutely still, even for hours. He had seen guards maintain the same position all day. It didn't seem natural, even for an alien species.

He returned to his pew and lay down. He felt lonely; he missed Amanda and his friends. He questioned if he had made the right decision to become a Special after all. If he had stayed in the cell, they would have at least been all together.

Bryce's hand probed his pocket and came across the yellow rock he had taken from Jamal and Jason.

Why are the aliens so afraid of this material?

He thought of a way he might experiment with it. He checked on the boy, who was still ignoring Bryce. He transferred the yellow mineral to the opposite pocket, away from the boy's view. He didn't think that the boy would notice or even care, but it was better not to take chances. He began to grind the yellow mineral to powder using his fingernails, scraping it bit by bit. It was a slow process and made the tips of his fingers raw. But after a while, he reduced the mineral to a rough sediment, good enough to try out what he wanted. He stared at the ceiling and eventually closed his eyes.

Bryce woke in the middle of the night. The moon cut slivers through stained glass, providing a dim light. Not wanting to miss a chance to scout for useful information, he sat up on his pew and looked around. He could barely distinguish the bodies in the darkness, but he knew most of the pews were occupied. Heavy breathing and the occasional snore filled the room. It was much colder in the church than the cell, but it was less stuffy too.

He threw his blanket off and walked to the entrance to try the knob. It was locked. He put his shoulder against the door and could tell that more than a deadbolt held it in place.

They really don't want us getting out of here.

He wanted to get a look outside, to see if they posted guards at night. He tiptoed toward the windows, hoping not to wake anyone as he crossed the room. Everyone in the room needed their sleep. Not to mention, some of the Specials could be on the side of the blueskins. If someone caught him acting suspicious, they might pass that along to the Imjac for favorable treatment. He would need to be careful.

Loose-fitting boards formed a large gap between two windows on the other side of the room. He had to pass between two occupied pews to reach them, though. He inched his way along, holding his breath as he passed between two Specials sleeping on the pews. Finally, he reached the window and peered out. He could make out a guard standing outside the entrance and quickly ducked. Had the guard seen him? He held his breath, expecting at any moment for the blueskins to burst through the doors.

When nothing happened after a minute, he stood up again and looked out the window again. He noticed then that the guard had his back to the building, looking out toward the worksite. He hadn't been watching the church at all.

Strange. I wonder what he's staring at.

And then Bryce saw a brilliant flash of light burst off the ground and into the sky, a thousand lights twirling into one massive pulse. It was one of the Imjac's collector ships. A mixture of awe and hate filled his gut as the ship hovered over the worksite for a moment and sped into the sky.

The guard began to turn around, and Bryce ducked to the floor. He moved away from the window and crept back into his bed, crawling under the thin cover. He lay there for a while, wondering what the collector had been doing at the Imjac worksite, but no answer came. Soon he fell asleep.

It seemed that just a minute later, two Imjac guards noisily burst into the room.

"Wake!" one of them hissed. "Wake now!"

Gray light spilled in through the windows. Bryce looked around at the other Specials. There were about twenty kids in all. Some he recognized as silo operators, but others were new to him. Merry was there, of course, and Mitchell as well. A tall boy with broad shoulders sat on a front pew in the center of the room. He looked older than the others, perhaps sixteen, with pale skin and long black hair. Bryce recognized him as the Special who used the explosives to create the tunnels. The boy stood up, stretched lazily, and marched to the bathroom, shoving someone out of his way as he went.

"Mind him, now," Mitchell said, from the pew next to Bryce. "Darius is the one who gave me this." He pointed to the gap where his front tooth should have been.

"I'm not afraid of him," Bryce said, defiantly.

"You should be," Mitchell said. "Darius is in good with the Imjac. Thinks he's one of them."

Bryce nodded. He once again missed his cellmates; even if being a digger was miserable, at least he had good company. He wondered how Amanda was doing. Had the claustrophobia come back?

Bryce sat up and tied his shoes. As he bent over, he scooped up some of the dirt he had emptied from his shoes the day before and put it in his pocket with the yellow mineral. Then he made his way to the bathroom, passing the other pews. He nodded at Merry, who smiled at him when he went by. In the bathroom, he splashed water on his face and pushed his hair out of his eyes, savoring the coolness of the water. Then he followed the others to breakfast.

A brisk wind blew in their faces as they marched along the trail. The sun tried occasionally to poke through the clouds but failed. Still, his suit shielded him from the cold, much better than his clothes did.

Bryce positioned himself in the rear of the line; only the guard trailed behind.

Perfect. If I'm going to try this, now's the time.

He reached into his pocket and gathered as much of the rock mixture in his fingertips as he could. Then with one quick motion, he tossed it into the air behind him, letting the wind carry it backwards toward the guard.

Two steps later he heard a loud thump. He turned and saw the guard writhing on the ground, his black-gloved hands grasping at his face as he screamed in agony. Bryce moved closer. Red pustules began popping up on the blue-skin's face where the yellow dust had struck him.

"Hellllppp," the guard gasped.

By now the others had gathered around the fallen guard, looks of panic on their faces. Bryce instantly realized why they were worried—if they were blamed for this, the punishment would be severe, maybe even deadly. Because he was closest to the guard, Bryce had to appear blameless.

"What happened?" Darius demanded of Bryce, shoving a fat finger into his chest.

Trust no one. "I don't know," he lied. "I was just walking, and he fell." He studied the boy's face, and he appeared to believe him. "I'll run for help," Bryce offered. "I'm fast."

Before anyone could object, he took off on a full sprint to the worksite. He realized the more concern he showed for the guard, the less likely it was that he would be blamed for what happened. And there was no doubt what he had done. He had no idea what to expect from the yellow dust, but he never imagined it would work like that. To completely incapacitate a guard with a small handful of dust—his mind raced with possibilities.

This might be our way to escape. If they don't suspect that I had anything to do with it, that is. If they do, I'm dead. We're all dead.

With the wind at his back as he ran, Bryce made good time to the worksite. He found Cai Lun standing with two guards at his side near the silos. The diggers were just entering the worksite, and Cai Lun monitored their progress. The guards raised their weapons in alarm as Bryce ran up.

Bryce stopped and held up his hands to show he meant no harm. "We need help," he said, pointing toward the direction where the guard lay. "One of the guards fell down. He's hurt—bad."

And I did it.

Cai Lun turned to the guards and translated what Bryce had said. "Lead the way," he said to Bryce, pointing in the direction from which he had come.

The Specials had formed a circle around the fallen guard by the time Bryce, Cai Lun, and the guards reached the area. The guards forced their way in, while Cai Lun stayed back next to Bryce. One of the guards bent over his fallen comrade and poked at him with his weapon. The blueskin lay motionless on the ground.

"Is he dead?" Bryce asked.

Cai Lun shrugged. "I don't know." He turned to the group. "What happened?" he asked, looking from face to face.

Bryce's heart raced. What if someone saw him throw the dust? Would they turn him in? Luckily, they all looked toward the ground and stayed silent. For once, the fear that the Imjac inspired had worked against the aliens. Safe for now, he exhaled.

When no one spoke, Bryce broke in, "I was closest to him. He was walking right behind us one minute, and then I heard him fall. He asked me to go for help, so I came for you."

One of the guards held a sensor over the blueskin on the ground. He turned to Cai Lun and grunted and hissed.

"Apparently, he's dead," Cai Lun said without emotion.

"What? How?" Bryce said, his throat tightening. True, he held no love for the blueskins, but to kill another was a step he hadn't even contemplated.

Cai Lun shrugged again. Bryce was amazed that the older man could stay so emotionless in the face of something like this. He thought he'd looked unmoved over the zombie Amanda had been assigned with, but this was a new level of stoic. The guards showed even less emotion. They simply grabbed their comrade by his arms and dragged his body away.

"They don't even seem like they care," Bryce said.

Cai Lun nodded. "You don't become masters of the universe by being softhearted. He will be replaced." He turned back toward the group. "Go to the mess hall and have your breakfast. I will send a guard to watch you." Then he turned and marched back the way he had come.

No one talked as they walked toward the hill, even though there were no guards around to keep them silent. Bryce thought about breaking the silence but realized that he was new to this group. If they wanted to walk around like a bunch of monks, let them.

The group bunched up as they reached the entrance to the dilapidated house. Bryce held back, with Merry at his side. Just before he walked in, she grabbed his arm and pulled him to her.

"I saw what you did," she whispered into his ear, then stepped in front of him into the dining hall.

CHAPTER
TWELVE

BRYCE WAS STILL SHAKING as he brought his breakfast—fish soup again—to the table. He again sat near Merry and her friends, hoping that they wouldn't notice the rattle of his spoon against the bowl. He tried to catch Merry's eye, but she looked away. Was she avoiding him on purpose? With the guards positioned nearby, he wouldn't be able to talk to her about what she saw anyway. In the end, he gave up trying and just ate.

What exactly did Merry see? Did she know about the yellow powder? After her friendly gestures, it seemed unlikely that she was on the side of the blueskins, but he couldn't be sure. Maybe her friendly ways were just to get him to trust her. If she planned on telling the Imjac that he had killed the guard, his plan of escape would be over.

He would be over.

Darius sat with the silo workers. Like Bryce, he seemed to have a unique position with the Imjac. They spoke in hushed voices, occasionally looking at Bryce. He avoided their stares. Did they suspect him in the guard's death? Then, he remembered that he was new, had appeared out of nowhere. Maybe their talk was just normal curiosity.

Bryce saved his bread for the others but savored the soup. He wondered if he would get tired of having the same meal for breakfast, lunch, and dinner. At home, before the war, he complained often about the food his mom served. *Meatloaf again!* If he got home, he would never take food for granted again.

He couldn't wait to meet up with Amanda and the others and tell them what happened. He wasn't sure how the yellow mineral fit into the escape plan, but he knew it was an important part. He spooned up the last of his soup, put his dish on the tray, and headed to the worksite under the watchful gaze of a blueskin.

Luckily, he wasn't immediately called to a tunnel, so he decided to check on Amanda first. He knew it might draw suspicion to visit tunnels unnecessarily if the Imjac were watching him. The Imjac seemed as suspicious as humans, if not more so. Yesterday, he felt the guards constantly monitoring him, eyeing him as he moved from tunnel to tunnel. He would need to make his visits to his friends seem like a part of his job.

He strolled up to the front of Amanda's tunnel and casually waited, glancing at his wristband from time to time. Guards were posted at the end of every walkway, and two guards on hoverboards circled the worksite. He waited until the nearest guard turned his head and ducked inside the tunnel.

He found Amanda working the digger at the end of the tunnel. Cherie sat next to her with the searcher resting on her lap.

Bryce was surprised that they would work together again but said nothing.

"I thought I'd give my brother a break today," Cherie explained as if reading his mind. "Even twins need a little time away from each other." She paused for a moment, then smiled. "Actually, the guards just pushed Amanda and me in the tunnel together. But I am happy to be away from Jamal for a day."

Bryce nodded as if he understood. As an only child, there were times he would have traded an arm for a brother or sister. Maybe that's why he and Amanda grew so close. Two only children finally getting a sibling.

"Who is he working with?" Bryce asked.

"Some new kid…There was a shipment last night."

"A shipment?" That explained the Imjac ship that he saw taking off. It was a collector, taking off to harvest new workers. More diggers that soon would be turned into zombies. He felt the bile build up in his stomach.

"Besides," Cherie said, "Amanda needed an upgrade after working with that zombie yesterday."

"Some upgrade!" Amanda said, giggling.

Cherie stuck out her tongue at her.

"I brought something for you guys," he said, digging into his pocket. "It's a bit crushed, sorry." He tore the bread in half and handed a piece to each of them.

"Bread!" Cherie said. She held it under her nose and sniffed it as if it were a flower. "Jamal said you brought them bread yesterday. I was so jealous!"

"Real food!" Amanda cried, snatching it from his hand.

While the girls ate, Bryce told them about what happened with the mineral and the Imjac guard.

"Do you think you killed him?" Amanda asked, her eyebrows furrowed in concern and her eyes wide. Bryce could tell that she was shocked. So was he, really. He had never even punched someone in the face before. His parents told him to stay out of fights. When he had to defend himself, he just wrestled his opponents to the ground until they gave in.

"Yes, he died," he said. "That powder—it's like magic. The guard fell down in a heartbeat."

"There's still some here in the tunnel," Amanda said. "Right where we buried it."

"Good," Bryce said. "But we should leave it there until we have a plan. No use getting caught with it before we know what we're doing."

"I want some of that powder," Cherie said, making a fist with her right hand. "I can't wait to take out a few blueskins."

Bryce shook his head. "We can't rush anything. If they find out we know about the yellow mineral, they'll kill us for sure. And that would be a serious flaw in our escape plan."

Thankfully, Cherie nodded in agreement. "Yeah, I'll take escape over death any day."

Bryce's wristband blinked with an Imjac symbol. "I've got to go. Leave the mineral here for now and be careful who you talk to about it. You never know who's listening."

He said goodbye and crawled out of the tunnel. Thick gray clouds now filled the sky. The wind blew mist into his face.

Great, another day in paradise.

He spent the rest of the morning crawling in and out of tunnels. Something was happening with the zombies—they were fading all at once. A knot formed in his stomach as he thought about what that meant. It wouldn't be long until the blueskins dumped them off the cliff.

The same question nagged at him: How long did the diggers last before they turned to zombies? Weeks? Months? A year? He would have to ask Cai Lun about that.

When his wristband finally signaled for the lunch break, he was exhausted.

As luck would have it, Cai Lun was hunched over a bowl of soup in the food hall as Bryce limped in for lunch. Bryce grabbed a bowl of soup—some sort of meat and vegetable this time——and a piece of bread. He looked around the lunchroom, but Merry wasn't there. Cai Lun motioned him to sit at his otherwise empty table.

The two sat eating for a minute before Cai Lun broke the silence. "It seems you have had a busy morning." He gestured at the crusted dirt on Bryce's elbows.

"Yeah," Bryce admitted. "Busier than the last two, that's for sure." He thought about broaching the subject of the zombies. Could he trust Cai Lun? He stared at the older man's placid demeanor.

The older man searched his face. "Is something wrong?" he asked softly.

Bryce nodded and leaned in so the others in the room couldn't hear him. "Some of the zom—er, kids who've been here awhile...they're kind of cracking up. It's like their batteries have expired. Like the boy I told you about yesterday."

Cai Lun shook his head and sighed. "It happens. It is that way with the green juice."

Bryce gulped as he thought about his friends. "Is it going to happen to everyone?"

"All of the diggers, yes," Cai Lun said. "But not to everyone." He gestured around the room to the other kids eating in the dining hall. "Some will live...longer."

Bryce felt the vein pop out of his forehead. "And *that's* okay with you?" he hissed, loud enough and with enough venom that one of the guards in the corner glanced his way and took a step toward the table.

All chatter in the dining room stopped.

Cai Lun held up a hand, and the guard stopped and moved back to the corner. "Calm down, Bryce, and think," Cai Lun said, leaning in toward Bryce so the others wouldn't hear. "We are in no position to change things. We have no armies and weapons. You are a boy, and I am a small man, a scholar. We cannot challenge the Imjac."

Bryce felt himself cool down. "What should we do?"

"Survive." Cai Lun rose from his seat. He handed his piece of bread to Bryce. "Perhaps you can find a taker for this," he said with a grim smile.

Bryce took the bread and nodded a thanks. How could Cai Lun know that he was bringing bread to his friends? No matter. He would try to steer clear of the older man. Anyone who ignored what the Imjac did to kids was no friend of his.

Still, Bryce had to admit there was logic in what Cai Lun said. He couldn't fight the Imjac; the best armies on Earth had tried and failed. And he was just a teenager, with no army or weapons. Maybe his best bet was to survive after all.

At least until he could escape.

———

Know your enemy.

That's the lesson Bryce's dad, a fighter pilot, taught him at a young age. "When you're up in the air, just you and the other guy, both of you have guns and missiles. Both of you know how to fly. How are you going to win?"

Bryce was stumped. "Shoot first?"

His dad laughed, a high-pitched giggle that didn't match his personality. "Well, maybe. But the most important thing you can do is study the guy. See how he reacts. When you move one way, what does he do? When you know him, you really know him, that's when you win."

And even though he didn't really have enemies when he was young, he had opponents. Opponents with traits and habits that could be exploited after careful study. Once at a YMCA basketball game, Bryce learned that the opposing point guard couldn't dribble with his left hand. Bryce spent the whole game shifted to the boy's right side, not allowing him to dribble past or to pass the ball and shut down the team's offense. Bryce's team won by thirty points. At a junior chess tournament, Bryce saw that his opponent, a girl with red pigtails and freckles, twisted her hair around her finger when she had made a mistake and left one of her pieces in danger. Bryce put her out of her misery in minutes.

But the Imjac camp was no basketball game or chess tournament. The enemies were real, and the stakes were life and death.

The rest of the afternoon Bryce spent his time observing the Imjac. He noticed for the first time the guards had different symbols on the breasts of their suits. As he passed each guard, he stared at the symbols carefully, noting their shape. After studying the marks, he decided that the marks were unique; he wondered if they represented the concept of a name, just like the symbols over the tunnels represented numbers. After all, alien or not, individuals need to be identified.

Bryce again noted that the Imjac guards were able to stay unnaturally still for much longer than a human could. They could stand with their legs locked for hours without moving. He wondered if it had anything to do with their mechanical gait. Their movements were robotic and stiff, although the guards could move swiftly when needed. And on the hoverboards, the Imjac could cover territory in a flash.

At first the guards watched him carefully as he moved from tunnel to tunnel. When he left a tunnel, the nearest guard would mark it in his wristband. But now, a week later, they barely gave him a second glance. Maybe, like humans, they got bored too. And being an Imjac guard must have been mind-numbingly dull.

Twice Bryce walked to the edge of the worksite at the top row of the tunnels and peered over the edge. On the west side of the mountain, he could make out the threatening bulk of the Imjac Mothership. Later, he wandered to the other side, toward the east, and spotted the town that he had seen before.

It was small, no more than a dozen buildings, but definitely human. He stared for a minute, trying to make out signs of life. For a fraction of a second, he thought that he made out a person, but in the end, he couldn't be sure. It might have just been a shadow from a passing cloud. He thought about the boy who'd given the twins candy. The boy had to live somewhere, and the town was a likely place.

At the very least, the town might be somewhere they could hide out from the Imjac after they escaped. He looked back toward the church; it lay a good half mile from the worksite in the opposite direction from the town. The town seemed to be the same distance away from the worksite as the church, meaning that escape was roughly a mile away. He thought back to all of the miles that he ran in P.E. classes —they might finally come in handy. All he needed to do was use the yellow powder to overpower the guards outside the church and sprint like crazy. In six minutes flat he could be free.

I can do it. I can escape.

Then he thought of Amanda and the others. Yes, he would be free, but they would be facing certain death, but not before slowly losing their minds to the green juice. They would rot away in the holes in the mountain until their brains turned to oatmeal, eventually to be tossed off the side of the cliff. He gulped. He couldn't do that—let his cousin and his friends turn into fish food. No, they would all escape together or not at all.

Placing his hands in his pockets, he felt the two pieces of now-squished bread. Time to make some deliveries.

———

That night he dreamed he was walking up the long driveway to the farmhouse. He could see Uncle Kyle and Aunt Sammie sitting on the porch waving to him. But for each step that he took forward, the house moved further and further away. He sprinted, running faster and faster, but the house zoomed away, until it was a small dot on the horizon. Suddenly, he felt something land on his chest. His eyes shot open. He sat up with a start and gasped in shock when a soft hand was placed over his mouth.

"Shh," Merry said, standing over him. Even in the dim light, her eyes sparkled like the sea. She took her hands off his chest and motioned for him to follow. He saw her move through the shadows as she tiptoed to the other side of the church, then down to the end of the hall.

Bryce sat up and carefully looked around to see if anyone stirred, but the rest of the Specials were sleeping. He stood up and glided past the pews to where Merry stood waiting for him. As he came closer, she grabbed his wrist and led him down a hallway behind the altar.

She stopped, and he nearly bumped into her.

"We need to talk," she whispered.

Bryce stifled a yawn. "Apparently. But in the middle of the night?"

"In case you haven't noticed, we don't have a lot of opportunities for conversation. This isn't exactly summer camp."

"You're right," Bryce said. Whatever she wanted to talk about must have been important to risk being noticed by the others. "What do you want to talk about?" he asked, but in his mind, he knew.

Merry's eyes narrowed. "What did you do to that guard? What made him drop to the ground like that?"

Bryce paused for a moment. Could he trust her?

She sensed his reluctance to talk. "You can tell me. Although I definitely wouldn't trust everyone in there." She nodded in the direction of the pews. "Think about it. If I was with the Imjac, I would have turned you in when I saw it."

Bryce wasn't convinced. "What did you see?"

"I saw you throw something in the air, and the blueskin hit the ground like a stone. Now are you going to tell me, or should I go back to bed?"

Bryce sighed. "I found this mineral in the tunnels, this yellow stuff. Here." He pulled a small rock from his pocket and put it in her hand. "I thought it might be valuable to the Imjac, like the blue mineral. Except when I showed it to one of the silo workers, the Imjac zapped me."

Merry nodded. "I remember that."

Bryce continued. "I wanted to know why they reacted that way. What were they afraid of? So I performed an experiment. I ground up a little of that powder and tossed in the air at the guard, and you saw the result. I had no idea it was going to do that."

"It killed him," she said. Bryce thought he could detect admiration in her voice, mixed with a little fear. "Can you get more of it?"

"Yes, I think there's more, lots more. But I don't think we should dig it up now. We need a plan. If we start using it now, they'll get suspicious. My goal...is to get out of here."

Merry's eyes lit up. "Mine too," she said. "I want it more than anything. When you come up with a plan, count me in. There are *others* too. Others we can trust." Someone shifted on their pew, and she looked around nervously. "We'd better get back. I'll go now. You wait for a few minutes."

Bryce stood in the dark obediently for a few minutes before he went back to bed. As he crept into the body of the church, everyone else seemed to be asleep.

But there was one who wasn't.

CHAPTER
THIRTEEN

THE GUARDS STOMPED in just before dawn.

"Wake! Wake! Work!" They hissed, prodding those slow to get up with the ends of their blasters.

These guys are charming.

Bryce yawned and sat up. It had been two days since his talk with Merry, and he hadn't slept well since. He tossed and turned each night, despite the fact that he was working harder now than he had ever worked before. This morning he felt like he was balancing a ten-pound weight on his head. And he had another punishing day in the tunnels in front of him.

Bryce waited in line to washup in the bathroom. He learned the unwritten rules quickly: the girls had access to the bathroom first, then the higher-ranking boys, starting with Darius. As the newest Special, Bryce cleaned up last, which meant that he had only a minute or so to splash water on his face and rinse his mouth out.

Bryce was still figuring his place among the Specials. There were cliques: the silo workers, the deliverers, and the tunnel builders. But there was no one else like Bryce. He was the Special's Special, leaving him no one to commiserate with or complain to. The other Specials seemed friendly enough, offering a hello or a nod, but he missed Amanda and his friends from the cell.

He wondered about his conversation with Merry that night. He was still unsure about the girl's motivation and whether he could trust her, so he didn't reveal too much. But she was as close to a friend as he had among the Specials. In any event, she hadn't pulled him aside again to talk to him since that night. Actually, she didn't speak to him much in front of the other Specials at all.

Smart. If someone did see us talking that night, it would look even more suspicious if we seemed friendly.

When he walked out of the front door of the church, Cai Lun stood a few feet away with two Imjac guards looming behind him.

A lump formed in Bryce's throat. Had they discovered what happened to the guard yesterday already? Had they come to pick him up and toss him off a cliff?

Bryce averted his gaze and got in line with the other Specials.

"Bryce," Cai Lun said, waving him over. "I'd like you to come with me."

The eyes of the other Specials turned to him. Every muscle in his body froze. Bryce stopped and stared into the older man's face, trying to read whether he was in trouble or not. Cai Lun betrayed no emotion but signaled that Bryce should walk beside him.

They took a path in the opposite direction from the dining hall. The morning was cloudy but not cold. A breeze brought with it the briny smell of the ocean.

Cai Lun led Bryce past the work camp and up an incline. They crossed a paved road, cracked and crumbling from disrepair. Big, colorful flowers grew from stalky plants next to the path. They moved toward the coast, toward the cliff where the ship had landed, where the boy had been tossed into the ocean by Red Scar. A knot formed in Bryce's stomach. Was Cai Lun leading him to his execution? Bryce glanced nervously at the two guards that followed them. He wished that he had brought the yellow powder with him. If he could take care of the two guards, he felt certain that he could run faster than Cai Lun. He could make it to the town and look for help. But without the powder, he was helpless.

As they walked, Cai Lun stared straight ahead and said nothing.

The trail led to a steep embankment. Cai Lun turned to the guards and said something to them in the Imjac language. They stopped and Cai Lun walked on.

"Follow me," Cai Lun said and began scampering up the hill.

The older man moved with surprising strength and agility. Bryce struggled to keep up.

"They let you walk around unsupervised," Bryce said, looking at the guards that they left behind.

"The Imjac are much like humans in many ways," he said. "They become as trusting and complacent as we would. They would not let me walk around unaccompanied all day—no, I am much too valuable to them for that. But for short journeys, they see no worry. They see us as weak humans that cannot harm them. I guess the war proved them right."

"I say it's more like arrogance than complacence," Bryce countered.

"You may be right. But no matter—it serves our purpose today."

Bryce wondered what that purpose was. The trail finally reached the flat top of a butte, a circle of forty feet in diameter. Cai Lun strolled to the center and stopped. Bryce joined him, his mind working nonstop. Why were they here?

"Look," Cai Lun said, pointing into the distance.

Directly in front of them, an immense Imjac Mothership rested in the center of the plateau. Made of the same impervious blue metal that won the war, it glistened even under the clouds. An entrance ramp had been extended from the body of the ship, making the ship look like a large blue fish with its mouth open, ready to snap up unsuspecting prey.

A ship like this killed my parents.

Bryce scanned the horizon. He realized that, other than the top of the volcano, this was the highest point on the island. He spun around. He could see the worksite coming to life from here, the cells where the diggers lived, and the mountain looming behind them.

"You can see everything," he said.

"Yes, that is why I brought you here." Cai Lun pushed his glasses up the bridge of his nose.

The comment puzzled Bryce. "You brought me here so I could see the Imjac ship?"

"No," Cai Lun scolded. "You are here because I want you to know what you are up against. You are not like the others...You struggle to be free, whereas the others accept their fate. But you must see the Imjac for what they are before you can accomplish anything. So, what do you see?"

A bevy of Imjac guards and workers hovered around the entrance to the ship. Two collector ships, like the one that caught Bryce, lay next to the Mothership, like small children next to their enormous mother.

"I see the blueskins working next to their ship."

"What else?"

Bryce shielded his eyes from the sun. "I see two ships like the one that caught me."

"Yes, those are collectors. What else do you see?"

"Behind the ship I see some strange-looking tubes attached to metal bases. They have hoses sticking out of the back of them."

Cai Lun nodded. "Good. And what do you think those are for?"

Bryce thought for a minute, but nothing came to mind. His frustration boiled over. "Can't you just tell me? I don't know why we're up here."

Cai Lun turned to him. "Forgive me. In my former life, I taught students not much older than yourself. I found that it is better to allow someone to see things for themselves than be told about them. I have other reasons to show you rather than to tell you. Are you satisfied with my answer?"

Bryce nodded. "I guess."

"Good. Look again carefully. What do you think the tubes are used for?"

The sun suddenly burst through the cloud cover, causing Bryce to squint. "They hold something…water maybe. Maybe they're giant fish tanks." He laughed, as it sounded silly, but stopped when he saw Cai Lun nodding at him. "Wait, I'm right?"

"In a sense." The interpreter pointed toward his temple. "Now think, what kind of fish needs a tank that big?"

Bryce turned toward the ocean. "Maybe the Imjac catch fish in the ocean and keep them in the tanks. Then they eat them."

Cai Lun shook his head. "No, but that is an interesting thought. I will give you a clue: things are not always what they appear."

Bryce rubbed his chin. Suddenly, it came to him. "The Imjac…those tanks are for the Imjac…That's why they always smell so sea-like…but I don't understand. They walk like us—they don't seem fishy."

Cai Lun pushed his glasses up his nose. "That is all I can tell you. You must put the rest together yourself."

Bryce grabbed him by the arm. "Wait! Why are you helping me?"

Cai Lun stopped and faced him. "As I told you, I am not on their side. Come, the Imjac will get suspicious if we take too long."

They marched down the hill toward the waiting guards.

Bryce knew that he had to see those tanks again—and next time, much closer.

————

As he made the rounds that morning, his thoughts came back to the tanks behind the Mothership. Why did the Imjac need them? He started with Amanda and Cherie's tunnel. Only, to Bryce's surprise, he found Reese working with Amanda.

Amanda smiled as Bryce crawled up.

"Hey, Amanda. Where's Cherie?"

"I don't know. They broke us up today—I've got this country boy as a partner." She patted Reese on the shoulder.

"Hi, Reese," Bryce said. He hadn't talked to Reese since his promotion to the Specials. At the time, he was as angry as the others at Bryce. He hoped he'd cooled off by now.

Reese smiled then fist-bumped Bryce. "Rumor has it that you, my friend, walk around with bread in your pockets."

"Most of the time, rumors are unfounded," Bryce said, stifling a grin.

Reese's face fell. "Yeah, I guess sometimes they aren't true," he said, trying to hide his disappointment.

"But luckily for you," Bryce said, "I still have my bread from breakfast." He took the mashed slice out of his pocket and broke it into two pieces.

Reese smiled widely. "You had me there. I thought for sure you didn't have anything."

"Yep, my cousin, the joker," Amanda said. "Hey, Bryce, can I chat with you for a sec?" She nodded in the direction of the entrance, away from Reese.

"Don't mind me," Reese said. "I'm going to savor my bread." He took a big bite and closed his eyes.

Once they were safely away from Reese's earshot, Bryce stopped and leaned back against the wall of the tunnel.

"Any idea where Cherie and the boys are?" Bryce asked.

"No clue," she said between mouthfuls of bread. "You're going to have to check the tunnels. They were up ahead of us, but definitely on this level."

The wristband flashed an alien symbol. Someone needed help. "I'd better go," Bryce said.

She grabbed him by the wrist before he could move. "Wait," she said. "There's something I need to tell you. I think...I think the green juice is starting to mess with my brain."

"What do you mean?" He sat upright.

Amanda pushed a few strands of hair behind her ears. "Lately, I've been feeling a bit off."

"Like that time you dropped the milk bucket on your head?"

"No, I'm serious. I'm not thinking clearly."

"How can you tell?" he asked.

"I can just feel it. I can sense it. My memories have started to fade," she said. "When I think about home, it's hard for me to picture. It's hard for me to imagine mom's face. I go through half the morning like I'm on autopilot. Like a...zombie." A solitary tear rolled down her cheek.

"Are you sure it's the juice and not just being...here?"

"Yes, I'm sure. I thought for a while I was imagining it, but now I know it's real. I can see it in the others too. We've all been getting on each other's nerves, forgetting basic things."

A sense of dread roiled Bryce. Now he had to work even more quickly, or his friends would be lost. *Amanda* would be lost.

"I'd better go."

Amanda nodded. Then she did something very un-Amanda-like—she hugged him.

———

"No, bro, not like that. Hold it with two hands. You gotta stop dropping it—the blue guys are gonna kill us if you break it."

"Hey, Jason," Bryce said as he arrived at the tunnel's end.

Jason was working with a newbie, a boy with brown skin and a flat-topped hairdo. The boy's eyes grew big as Bryce came out of the darkness.

"Bryce, my main man," Jason said, extending a high-five. "Glad you're here, bro. This dude is having a hard time with the digger—I've tried everything."

Bryce smiled at the boy, trying to set him at ease. "What's your name?"

"DeShaun," the boy answered. He seemed to be younger than they were by a few years.

The Imjac are getting desperate for workers to take someone this young.

Bryce smiled. "Okay, DeShaun, you're going to figure this out." He patted the boy on the back and sidled up next to him on the rock wall.

Bryce taught DeShaun how to hold the digger and how to know if the machine had found the blue rocks. Soon the boy held the machine steadily as it cut into the earth.

Jason watched DeShaun dig into the tunnel with admiration.

"Bryce, you're a miracle worker. Jamal and I, we had a system. We got it done! Then we get stuck with these newbies, and now we're back to square one."

Bryce furtively handed Jason the other half of his bread from lunch. "Hey, is your head feeling okay?"

Jason looked offended. "What're you trying to say?"

Bryce laughed. "Nothing like that. It's just that Amanda said her memories have faded. She thinks it's the green juice."

Jason rubbed his chin. "Hmm. Could be stress. I know I forget things when I get stressed out. But I think I'm at the top of my game."

Bryce looked at Jason's basketball sweatshirt. "Okay. Let's just check. Who won the NBA championship last year?"

Jason opened his mouth as if to speak, then stopped. "You know, I forgot that one. Who was it?"

"The Lakers."

"Man, I should have known that. I'm a big Lakers fan. Alright, test me again."

"Okay. What's the name of your English teacher?"

Jason rubbed his chin again as if deep in thought. "Man, I must be having a bad day." Then his eyebrows raised in alarm. "Oh, man. I'm starting to become a zombie!"

At the mention of the word "zombie," DeShaun's head pivoted in their direction and his mouth fell open.

Bryce smiled at the new boy, whose eyes were now as big as Frisbees. "He's just kidding. No zombies. No undead people searching for brains, I promise."

"Yeah, just kidding, bro. No zombies here."

DeShaun shrugged as if they were crazy and went back to operating the digger.

Bryce motioned for Jason to move further down the tunnel, out of earshot of DeShaun.

"So, what do you think this means, dude?" Jason asked with concern.

Bryce paused for a moment. "I don't know for sure, but if I had to guess, it means we need to make a plan to escape sooner than we thought. I'm working on it."

"We'll work on it too," Jason said, and gave Bryce a fist bump goodbye.

Bryce didn't realize how many new kids had arrived until he walked out of the worksite for lunch. The newbies all sat together with their green drinks, like he and the others had when they arrived, looks of disbelief and despair painted across their faces. Their clean, unspoiled clothes made them easy spot. The total number of workers didn't seem to have changed, though. The meaning of this hit Bryce like a gut punch: many of the zombies were no longer here.

After lunch, while visiting a new tunnel, he found Jamal, who looked genuinely excited to see him.

"Just the guy I've been waiting for," he said as he caught sight of Bryce emerging from the darkness.

"Oh, yeah," Bryce said, smiling. "Like you're expecting a lot of visitors. I bet you're looking for a handout."

The newbie that Jamal had been paired with, an Asian girl with long straight hair, looked at Bryce with indifference and went back to work.

"She's from Japan," Jamal said. "Not very interested in conversation. It's been a quiet day."

Bryce handed Jamal the leftover bread. "So why are you excited to see me? Hungry?"

"Well, food always helps," Jamal responded, gnawing at the edge of the bread, "but no, that's not why I wanted to talk to you. I've thought of a way to weaponize the yellow powder."

"Weaponize it? What does that mean?"

Jamal shook his head disappointedly. "You are the son of Navy pilots, right? Weaponize means exactly what it sounds like. Turn the yellow stuff into a weapon."

"And how do you propose we do that?" Bryce asked.

"With this." Jamal held something small and white in his palm.

"What is it?" Bryce asked, holding the silky object up to the meager light of his wristband.

"It's a flower," Jamal said, smiling brightly. "The flower of death, I call it."

Bryce took it from Jamal's hand. It was a cone-shaped flower bud half the size of his palm. "Looks like an ordinary flower to me." He sniffed it. "It doesn't even smell that great."

"Well," Jamal said, a sly look on his face. "It's been sitting in my pocket all day. But here, let me show you something." He took the flower back from Bryce and scooped up a little dirt from the tunnel floor. He poured the dirt into the center of the flower, then twisted the top of the flower's petals. "Here, check it out now." He handed it back to Bryce.

The dirt had been sealed tightly inside the petals. Bryce shook it gently, and the dirt held fast. "Cool! We could store the powder."

Jamal kept smiling. "No, not just store it. I told you, we can weaponize it. Toss it against the wall."

Bryce tossed the flower bomb against the wall. As the flower hit the wall, it blew apart, sending a cloud of dust everywhere.

The new girl stopped working, shot them a dirty look, and uttered what must have been a curse in Japanese. At least, it sounded like a curse to Bryce.

Bryce coughed and waved the cloud of dirt out of his face. "Wow! That really worked. Could we find more of those flowers?"

Jamal nodded. "They're all over the island. I can pick them on the way to and from the cell."

"Nice!" He thought about mentioning Amanda and Jason's memory loss but didn't. Jamal had momentum, and Bryce didn't want to interrupt that. "Can you start collecting these?"

"I've already got a few more in my pocket."

Bryce was smiling as he crawled out of the tunnel toward the light. Smiling because they were in this together. Smiling because a glimmer of hope rested in his heart. Smiling because there was a chance now, a small one, that he could make it home.

When he emerged from the end of the tunnel, his smile vanished. Cai Lun stood at the entrance next to two alien guards. Red Scar stood behind them all, his eyes filled with menace.

Bryce picked himself up and dusted off his suit nonchalantly, but his knees were shaking. "Hi. Do you guys need me to check a tunnel?" he asked coolly.

Red Scar hissed something in the alien tongue.

"Why are you in this tunnel?" Cai Lun asked, his tone as threatening as Red Scar's stare.

Bryce shrugged. "With all the new people, I'm checking on everyone. Seems like everywhere I go, people need a hand."

Cai Lun translated for Red Scar, who stood silent for a moment. Bryce couldn't tell if his logic had reached the alien.

Finally, he said something to Cai Lun.

"You were not signaled to go into this tunnel. From now on, you are only to enter the tunnels marked on your bracelet. Do you understand?"

"Yes," Bryce answered.

Red Scar then said something else. Cai Lun didn't translate; he just looked back at the large alien with alarm.

The last thing Bryce remembered was the two alien guards pointing their weapons at him.

CHAPTER
FOURTEEN

HE WOKE to darkness in the church, something cool resting on his forehead.

"You're awake." Merry knelt next to his pew, holding a cool, wet rag on his forehead, her eyebrows knotted with concern.

Bryce tried to sit up, but it felt like his brain was being boiled.

"Just rest for now," Merry said, gently pushing him back on the pew. "There's no reason to get up. What happened?"

Bryce laughed but stopped when it became painful. "I was hoping you could tell me. The last thing I remember I was talking to Cai Lun."

"Cai Lun?"

"The interpreter."

She looked puzzled. "Did *he* zap you?"

It suddenly came back to Bryce. "He didn't—Red Scar's guards did."

"Red Scar?"

"That's what I call the leader, the big blueskin. His guards zapped me at his request."

"Oh, he's scary. Why did he blast you?"

"He didn't like that I was visiting my friends in their tunnels. Maybe he was suspicious, too. How did I end up back here?"

"When I came back tonight, you were lying here. I tried to wake you for dinner, and that's when I realized that you weren't sleeping."

At the mention of dinner, Bryce's stomach growled. "Dinner? I guess I missed it."

Merry pressed something into his hand. "I brought you a piece of bread."

Bryce finally forced himself to sit up. His head felt too heavy for his neck, as if the weight of it might pull him back down. He made himself chew the bread, even though his jaws ached with every bite.

"Thank you," he said as he finished.

"You're welcome," Merry said, brushing a loose strand of hair behind her ears. "You had better rest—tomorrow could be a tough day for you. At least you're still one of us. They could have sent you back in the tunnels. Or worse."

Or worse. We both know what that means.

He certainly didn't feel much better the next day. Bryce emerged from his first tunnel to a dull gray sky. Even the meager light of the morning made him squint. He limped around the camp, making his rounds, keeping his distance from where Cai Lun and Red Scar stood near the silos. Every muscle in his body felt like it was on fire, worse than after the first time he was blasted. Maybe because this time they used two blasters instead of one. Or maybe it was the cumulative effect of being hit. Whatever it was, he didn't want to be shot by a blueskin blaster ever again.

But he'd gotten off easy.

If Red Scar suspected him of anything other than

visiting his friends, he would have been tossed off the cliff. Getting blasted was a warning: follow the rules or else.

But there was something else too. The fact that he was still alive showed that they needed him. If he was replaceable, he would be lying at the bottom of the cliff right now. He could use that to his advantage.

But that was for another time. Today, he just needed to survive.

Right before lunch, Bryce emerged from a tunnel to see that Cai Lun stood outside, accompanied by a guard.

Bryce dusted his knees and began to stalk off, ignoring the interpreter.

"So, you will not speak to me today?" Cai Lun questioned.

Bryce stopped and turned to face the interpreter. In truth, he was confused. Cai Lun had showed him kindness before, and then yesterday, everything changed.

"Bryce, I did not suggest to the Imjac to have you punished. Quite the contrary," Cai Lun said, pushing his glasses up his nose. "But I am in no position to tell the Imjac what to do. It is the other way around. They keep me here because it is convenient to them. If there were others who could speak their language, I would be as disposable as a digger."

Bryce crossed his arms across his chest.

"I did not come here to argue. Stop acting like a petulant child," Cai Lun scolded him. "I have come here to tell you that your movements are tracked, and, after yesterday, they will be following you carefully. If you want to maintain your current position, your actions will need to be flawless."

Bryce nodded. "Okay."

"I must go," Cai Lun said. "I can afford less than you to appear to be on the human side."

Bryce was left wondering what the older man meant by that comment.

He patted his side pocket that held his bread from this morning. He likely wouldn't see Amanda or his friends, but on the chance that he would, he saved it. Without the bread that he shared with them, they would have to drink the green juice, which was already having its effects. A bigger problem came to mind: how could they plan an escape without communicating?

He felt a gnawing in his stomach, and it wasn't from hunger.

The next night, Merry woke Bryce in the middle of the night. She placed a finger to her lips and signaled for him to follow her. She led him through the pews to a hallway in the back of the church. At the end of the hallway was a door that Bryce had never noticed before.

"Where are we going?" he whispered.

"Shh." She shoved the door open, revealing a small room with a single dingy window that allowed only the faintest light inside. Tall shelves covered three of the walls, filled with cans of various sizes. A broom, a mop, and bucket sat in a corner, leaving a very small open area in the center of the room. Bryce thought that it must have been a maintenance room for the church at one time.

Bryce could see by the dim glow of their wristbands that two other people sat on the floor of the room. He recognized Mitchell, who was sitting next to another deliverer named James.

Merry took a seat with the others and motioned for Bryce to sit down.

Bryce's mind raced. Was this some sort of trap? Should he head back to his bed?

"Oh, have a seat, bud," Mitchell said, gesturing toward the floor. "We're all friends here."

News to me.

Bryce sat down cross-legged and looked at the others.

"What is this all about?" Bryce asked.

"This," James said, sitting up straight, "is a meeting of the Escapers. Unlike those other sheep who plan on sticking around, we want to get out of here. Which is why you're here."

"Escapers?" Bryce said.

"Yeah," Mitchell said. "Escapers. You know, like people who escape things."

"That's funny," Bryce said.

"Why's that?" asked James.

"Because I was an escaper before, where I lived. Well, I wasn't really, but that's what they called me. And it wasn't a compliment. Anyway, I think it's a good name for us." He looked at Merry. "I guess I'm here because of you."

"Merry told us you have some magical powers over the blueskins," James said, his curly blonde hair evident even in the dim light. "And we need all the help we can get."

"So, what have you got? How did you take down that blueskin?" Mitchell asked eagerly.

"I told them what I saw," Merry said guiltily. "I'm sorry. I hope that you don't mind. We're all from the same area. They can be trusted."

"So all your friends can be trusted?" Bryce countered.

Mitchell gave Bryce a cross look. "Hey, we're on your side," he said. "I assume you want out of this camp too, or you wouldn't have done what you did. Are you going to tell us, or what?"

Bryce pondered for a moment. He remembered advice that his mother told him: a secret is only a secret until you tell someone. But his mother was gone. His father also. Because of the blueskins. He decided to take a chance.

"Okay, but you can't tell anyone about this. The blueskins would kill me if they found out. Probably kill all of us."

The others nodded solemnly.

When he was done relaying how he used the powder on the blueskin guard, Mitchell asked, "Can you get more of it?"

Bryce nodded. "There's more in the mountain, tons of it. In my old tunnel. Only…" He thought about Amanda and the others. How would they fit into this escape now that he could no longer see them? Would the Escapers agree to help them? He couldn't leave without them.

"Only what?" Merry asked.

"I can't get into my old tunnel like before. They're watching me now. They're suspicious—the yellow rock would have to come from someone else… My friends, the ones I came here with, they can help."

"But how can you get their help if you can't speak to them?" James asked.

Bryce shrugged. He didn't have an answer for that yet, but he did have a few questions of his own. "How long have you guys been planning to escape?"

Mitchell pulled the sleeves of his sweater up his arms. "Months now. We meet every few nights."

"What is your plan?" Bryce asked, excitedly. Surely a group that had been meeting for months would be a step ahead.

There was an uncomfortable silence as they avoided his stare. Mitchell squirmed in his seat, and Merry tapped her fingers on the floor.

"So, you don't have a plan," Bryce said finally.

"We never had a way to get past the guards before,"

Merry explained. "That was our first roadblock. But with the powder…"

"We might be able to take out a few guards," Bryce said. "But never take on all of them. We'll need a real plan…We need to know where we're headed, what obstacles stand in our way, and how we're going to get past them."

"What do you think we should do?" Mitchell asked.

"I think we should get back to bed before someone notices us missing," Merry said.

"Wait, wait," Bryce said. "Before you go…I'm sure you've started scouting the area too. The next time we meet, we'll make a map."

They left, one by one to avoid detection, until Bryce was alone. When he was sure the person in front of him had time to make it back, he stood and walked out the door into the dark church. He took one step out of the hallway and ran right into a large, shadowy form. Darius.

"What are you doing up?" Darius hissed, grabbing Bryce roughly by the arm.

A thought of punching the larger boy right in the nose whizzed through Bryce's head like a comet. But then he thought better of it; he would be no match for Darius, who was much taller and outweighed him. And with no one to break it up, Bryce would have to depend on the limits of Darius's cruelty to know when the fighting would stop. And he hadn't seen any limits so far.

"Nothing. Took a wrong turn out of the bathroom. That's all."

Apparently this answer seemed reasonable enough to Darius. "Well, get back to bed," he snapped, and gave Bryce a hard shove, causing him to smash his shoulder into the wall.

Bryce walked back to his bed rubbing his bruised shoulder, knowing that Darius was watching his every step. He knew then that if they were going to escape, the older boy would stand in their way.

———

Two days later, Bryce rushed from tunnel to tunnel helping newbies learn the tools.

By lunch he was exhausted. On his way to the dining hall, he saw Amanda and the others sitting together on the far side of the yard. He waved at them but didn't dare go over to say hello—he knew Red Scar was already suspicious. Amanda waved back, but the others pretended that he didn't exist. It had been days since he had visited them and brought food.

They think that I've abandoned them. I've got to find a way to talk to them.

But how could he communicate with them if he couldn't visit their tunnels? There didn't seem to be an easy answer to this. He rolled the problem over and over in his mind as he walked to lunch.

He stopped as something caught his eye. Darius stalked around the site, pushing and shoving the diggers, herding them along. Once, he rammed a boy so hard that he fell down.

Bryce caught Merry's arm as she was passing by with lunch drinks. "What is Darius doing?"

Merry looked disgusted. "That's his new job, I guess. When he's not blasting tunnels, he runs around shoving people around. I guess the blueskins think it will help the newbies dig faster."

Bryce glanced again at Darius, who seemed to be enjoying himself as the big bully. He roamed the second rampart, roughly shoving diggers down the ramp, laughing to himself as they fell.

Someday it would be nice to get that guy.

Bryce took an open seat across from Mitchell in the dining room. Cai Lun wasn't there, which relieved Bryce.

"So, tell me, how's your day been?" Mitchell said in a quiet voice, cheerfully talking with his mouth full.

Bryce shrugged. "Fine, I guess. It's been busy today with all the new kids."

Mitchell shook his head. "Yeah, that's a rough one. I hate to see the sad looks on their faces after their first time down in the dark. I know it shook me bad." He paused for a deep slurp of his soup. "So let me ask you something. How exactly does it work with your job? How do the Imjac know when a team's fallen behind?"

Bryce shrugged. "Must be a sensor in the bag. Can't think of another way."

Mitchell laughed.

"What's so funny?"

"Sorry. Just thought of something. If I were still in the tunnels, I would just work as slow as a snail every day. Then you'd have to come help me and do all the work."

Suddenly Bryce knew how he could see Amanda and the others. "Thanks," he said.

Mitchell looked puzzled. "For what?"

"You just solved my problem."

"I'm good at that," Mitchell said without a trace of modesty.

That night when Merry came back to the church after her shift, Bryce pulled her aside and gave her a message to pass along to his friends the next morning.

"Okay, I'll tell them," she said. "But do you think they'll listen?"

"Why wouldn't they?" he answered defensively, but in his heart, he was less sure. If they truly thought he abandoned them, they might have given up.

He lay in bed that night wondering if they would follow his instructions. Amanda would, and maybe Jason, but if it was just those two, the Imjac would become suspicious. If they were going to escape, they would all need to follow the plan.

They'll do it. They'll realize that it's their only hope.

And halfway through the next morning's shift, he had his answer. His wristband alerted him that another tunnel needed attention, his old tunnel.

He raced up the embankment to the tunnel and ducked inside. His stomach fluttered with nerves as he made the crawl into the mountain. When he reached the end, he saw Amanda was waiting for him along with Reese. She smiled as she saw him and pulled him close.

"I knew that you didn't ditch us," she said.

"No way," he said, backing out of her embrace. "I'm with you guys to the end." Bryce dug into his pocket and came out with the bread from breakfast. Amanda tore the bread in half, giving one part to Reese, who munched on it greedily. "How are the others?" Bryce asked.

Amanda shrugged. "Jason, Reese, and I are on your side, but Jamal and Cherie are mad. Or at least confused."

Bryce clenched his fists. "It wasn't my fault." He told her the story of Red Scar surprising him outside of the tunnel. "He threatened to kill me if I went into a tunnel without reason."

Amanda nodded. "I figured something held you back," she said. "I'll tell the others."

"Yeah, you wouldn't leave us behind," Reese added. "Like my daddy always says, the bell cow always comes for dinner."

Bryce scratched the side of his head. "Does that make me the bell cow?"

"I'm not sure," Reese admitted. "But he says it all the time, so there must be some truth in it."

Amanda interrupted. "So this is how we can see you and keep planning?"

Bryce nodded. "You'll have to take turns being lazy," he laughed. "Make sure that it's not the same person who is behind two days in a row. Try not to show a pattern. They're watching me right now. Do you still know where the yellow stuff is?"

She nodded.

"Good," Bryce said. "We'll need that soon. Also, ask Jamal to keep gathering those flowers. You can pass them to Merry, and she'll bring them to me. I feel a plan coming together."

His wristband flashed again. "I'd better go. Tell the others I'm sorry, but we'll be out of here soon."

"You think so?"

"Have a little faith."

CHAPTER
FIFTEEN

THEY HUDDLED in the cold in front of the dining room after breakfast. Almost all the Specials were there, except for Merry and Mitchell, who were out delivering breakfast to the diggers.

"Why are we standing here?" Bryce asked James impatiently. He was eager to start his day, to see Amanda and the others. A plan was germinating in his mind, and he wanted to put it into action.

"It's bath day," James said blandly.

Bryce looked himself over—he could use a bath. Dust and small rocks coated his knees and elbows and, although he didn't really notice, he was sure that he smelled overripe.

Two guards led the Specials from the church down the road, and at the fork, the boys split off from the girls.

At the beach, Bryce stripped his filthy uniform from his body and rushed into the blue water. He sat down in the shallows and splashed in the cold, refreshing water. He rubbed the salt water over his skin and through his hair, dunking his head to rinse off. Once clean, he soaked his uniform, scrubbed it, and lay it on the sand to dry.

Time for more scouting.

He wanted to see the town, to see if people still lived there. He ran until he was in waist-deep water and dove headlong into the surf. He swam at a good pace, finally reaching the dark gray cliff. He edged out past the cliff and stopped to tread water. From this angle, he could see the town. It was a tiny hamlet, one short street with a few buildings on each side of it. He stared for a moment, hoping to see any sign of life. Finally, he saw something move. Was it a person? A stray dog? He couldn't be sure from this distance.

He looked back toward the beach and saw most of the other Specials getting dressed. He was tired from the swim out and had hoped that he could float back in. But he couldn't be late—the blueskins were already watching him. He righted his body and began a steady crawl toward the beach.

He was halfway to shore when something large bumped him. Panic gripped him. Sharks often bumped their prey before taking a bite. He stopped and treaded water, looking around. No dorsal fin poked through the surface.

Good, not a shark.

Then suddenly, Darius popped out of the water in front of him. He glared at Bryce through beady black eyes.

"What are you doing out here, newbie?" the large boy said, gasping from the effort of the swim. His black hair stuck to his forehead as if glued in place. "Trying to escape?"

"Just swimming," Bryce said.

"What, working in the tunnels isn't enough exercise for you? I'll talk to the blueskins about that," Darius hissed. "Maybe they can give you more to do. Or maybe they'll send you back to being a digger. And you can turn into a zombie, like your friends will soon."

Bryce felt his muscles tense at the thought of his friends.

"You're just as bad as they are. You're one of them. You are a blueskin."

Darius raised his eyebrows. "Why not? They're winners, aren't they? I want to be a winner. And you are a loser."

He reached out and grabbed for Bryce, who dove below the larger boy's grasp. He swam down between Darius's legs and propelled himself underwater. He kicked and swept his arms in front of him with all of his strength. When his lungs felt like bursting, he shot to the surface. He looked back and saw Darius thirty feet behind him.

Reaching the shore and scrambling up the beach, he slipped into his clothes and took his place in the line of boys. As Bryce pulled on his suit, Darius trudged out of the water with a look of fury. Bryce knew that he'd be safe in front of the guards, but later, in the church, he would be on his own.

———

Today, Jason was the laggard. He was working with the quiet Japanese girl, who looked panicked as she saw Bryce crawl in from the darkness.

"Will you tell her to calm down, bro?" Jason said as he munched on the piece of bread that Bryce brought for him. "I mean, this is your job—to help us catch up." He offered her half of the bread, but she shook her head vehemently and pointed toward the tunnel wall.

"It's okay," Bryce said. "I'll help you. Eat." He offered her the bread again and this time she took it with a bow of thanks.

While they ate, Bryce slid over to the wall and grabbed Jason's digger. He felt it form a connection to him immediately, almost linking itself to his mind. Then its claws ripped through the earth, and soon he held a piece of the bright blue mineral the size of a softball.

He held it up, and Jason's jaw fell open. "That has got to be some kind of record," he muttered.

The girl smiled, nodded vigorously, and held open the bag. Bryce obliged and handed the digger back to Jason.

"You can handle it, right?"

"Yep," Jason said, swallowing the last of the bread. "Oh, I almost forgot. Here." He reached into his pocket and furtively put something in Bryce's hand. "From Amanda."

Bryce looked into his hand and saw a few marble-sized pieces of the yellow mineral.

"That's all she could sneak out yesterday," Jason whispered, looking over his shoulder at the girl, who didn't seem interested in their conversation. "It has to be in small batches, or she might get caught."

Bryce nodded. "Okay, good. Tell her to keep it coming. We're going to need a lot more than this if we're going to do what we're planning." Just then his wristband began flashing. "I gotta run. See you later." He extended a fist for a bump, and Jason obliged.

———

That night someone woke Bryce again. Only this time it wasn't Merry's gentle touch on his chest, but two heavy hands that gripped his shoulders roughly.

Bryce's eyes shot open to see Darius's moon face a few inches from his own.

"You thought you could get away with making me look like a fool, eh, scrub," he hissed, looking from side to side to make sure that Bryce's neighbors didn't wake. "I think you're up to something."

Bryce had been in the middle of a peaceful dream. Now he was fighting for his life. He grabbed Darius's wrists and tried to break his hold, but the larger boy's grip held steady.

"Let me go," Bryce gasped. "I don't know what you're talking about."

"I think you do," Darius said. "I think you know exactly what I'm talking about. You're sneaking around here in the middle of the night. Then you swim out halfway across the ocean. Very strange behavior. I know you're planning something; I just don't know what. But when I find out, the Imjac will know next. And they'll do with you what they do with every other piece of waste around here—chuck it off a cliff."

With that, he relaxed his grip and stood. "Sleep tight, scrub. I'll be watching you."

Bryce exhaled deeply as the large boy stalked off toward his pew. If Darius had found the small yellow rocks that Bryce had hidden under his blanket, the blueskins would have killed him for sure.

He'd have to find a place to hide the mineral. But that was for tomorrow. Tonight he had only a few hours left to sleep.

———

The Escapers met the next night. Merry told Bryce ahead of time, so he didn't fall asleep. He lay in his pew until he heard the others, one at a time, get up and tiptoe to the room. He pinched his sides to keep from falling asleep—his eyelids felt like they weighed ten pounds.

Bryce sat up and he looked at Darius's pew. The large boy lay on his back and his eyes were closed, but there was no way of knowing whether he was actually asleep. Bryce slowly rose to his feet. Darius didn't move. He took a few tentative steps. He could see Darius's barrel chest rising and falling steadily. Satisfied that he was sleeping, Bryce made his way down the hallway to the back room.

They sat in a circle on the floor. Someone found an old,

ragged poster tacked to the wall that they turned facedown to serve as their map. Merry produced a pencil from somewhere.

"Okay," she said, handing the pencil to Bryce. "Let's make our map."

Bryce drew a rectangle on the left side of the map. "This is the church. And here is the path that leads to the mountain." He drew a dotted line toward the center of the map. Then he drew a large square that took up the center of the map. "And this is the worksite."

"Where's the mountain?" James asked. "You've got to have the mountain."

"Good point," Bryce said and drew a large circle next to the square.

Merry rubbed her chin. "Why is it a circle? Shouldn't it be a triangle or something?"

"It's a bird's-eye view," Mitchell countered. "We're looking at it from above."

"Oh." Merry seemed satisfied.

Bryce started drawing again. "Now the path to the diggers' cells goes in this direction." He drew a dotted line from the square toward the top of the map.

"No, it's more like this." Mitchell grabbed the pencil from Bryce's hand and changed the directions of the lines.

Bryce rubbed his chin. "I think you're right, Mitchell."

Pleased, Mitchell handed the pencil back to Bryce.

"Now, the Mothership is on a flat-topped hill behind the cells. Would you say it's about here?"

No one answered.

Finally, Merry shrugged. "We've never been there. You have?"

"Yep...well, nearby, anyway," Bryce said. "I may be a little wrong about the placement, but until we know better, let's just draw it in here." He made a large rectangle representing the hill and drew a smaller rectangle to represent the ship. He also sketched some small circles next to the Mothership.

"What are those?" James asked.

"I don't know. Strange tubes I saw next to the Mothership," Bryce answered. "I'm not sure what they're used for. They're tall—maybe over ten feet."

Merry scratched the side of her head. "What could those be?"

"I think I know," James said. He had been studying the map carefully, running his fingers over the small circles. "I think it's where the blueskins sleep."

Bryce snapped his fingers. "I'll bet you're right. How did you know?"

"I was walking back from the cells one day, and I took a route near the water," James said. "I looked over the cliff and I swear I saw a few blueskins swimming in the ocean. And there's something else. I don't think that they're shaped like us."

"What do you mean?" Bryce asked.

James paused, and his eyes drifted up as he tried to remember. "It was a clear day, and they were swimming near the surface. I didn't see feet or arms like you would see on a person. But there's definitely some sort of limbs, like paddles."

"But what about their suits? They have arms and legs just like we do," Merry said.

"That could all be for show," Bryce said. "Maybe they want us to think that they're shaped like us."

"Or maybe they need the suits to survive in our environment," Mitchell added.

That made sense to Bryce. "And maybe without their suits, they're vulnerable."

James crossed his arms. "Maybe they're kind of like fish or squid—they need water to survive."

"That would explain their smell," Merry said, wrinkling

her nose. "Kind of fishy. Kind of stinky."

"Maybe we can use that to our advantage," Bryce said.

Mitchell said, "But how does that help us? They're never going to let us near them when they sleep."

"That's the million-dollar question," James said.

"I want to see them sleep," Bryce said. "I know where the tubes are—I need to see if they're vulnerable while they're in them."

Mitchell shook his head. "Too chancy. What if they find you? They'll know that you got out of here. They'll double the guard, and we'll never get out."

"I agree," James said. "Too dangerous."

It occurred to Bryce that the younger boy looked up to Mitchell. As long as Mitchell was against something, James would be also.

"What do you think, Merry?" Bryce asked.

Merry crossed her arms over her chest. "I don't know. It is taking an awfully big risk."

"But think of it. We could find out a way to cripple their guards, maybe even their leader. We could free everyone."

"You're thinking too big, mate," Mitchell countered. "Any escape has to be small scale, or it won't work. We can't have the whole island running around."

James nodded in agreement.

"What if I just went to look around?" Bryce offered. He needed this plan to work faster than the group realized-- Amanda and the others didn't have much time before the green juice kicked in. They'd been here for much longer and didn't feel the same sense of urgency.

"That's a question for next time," Merry said. "We had better get back to bed." She picked up the map and pinned it back on the wall, poster side out.

Then one by one they crept back to bed. Bryce left last, and as he approached his pew, he stopped and stared at Darius's shadowy form. Darius was oddly quiet after dinner, keeping to himself. Was it just a show to put Bryce at ease so he would make a mistake? The large boy had turned on his side now, facing Bryce, and in the dark Bryce couldn't tell if his eyes were open. Bryce lay down, eventually falling into an unsettled sleep.

———

When Bryce got back to the church the next afternoon, he found himself alone. The other Specials were either making deliveries, working the silos, or in the case of Darius, probably shoving people around.

Now would be the time to find a hiding place for the yellow mineral.

So far, he had stored it on the floor, under his pew. But as his friends had passed more and more of the mineral to him, the pile of rock had become conspicuous. One quick glance under the pew by Darius or a guard would mean certain death. He thought about using the back room where they had their meetings, but it might be tough to access it when he needed it. And as suspicious as Darius had become, he would need to hide the mineral on an everyday basis. Getting to the little room regularly without the others knowing would be difficult if not impossible.

Bryce walked a loop around the church before he noticed a creaky floorboard not far from his pew. He bent down and worked the board back and forth a bit. After a minute of what Aunt Sammie would call "elbow grease," the end of the board came loose. He dug his fingers under and pried it up, carefully avoiding the nails, and reached down into the gap in the boards. Thoughts of snakes and spiders crossed his mind.

Stop being a chicken.

Luckily, the ground was just a few inches below the floor. He grabbed the mineral from under his mattress and then carefully placed it and flower petals down the hole. Before he sealed it up, he made sure he could find the loose board in the dark by counting how many steps away from his bed it was.

He put the board back in place and pressed down on it with his foot to level it with the floor around it. It creaked a little more than it did before, but he didn't think anyone would notice. Many of the boards in the rickety building creaked.

Satisfied that the mineral was safe, he lay back on his pew. Light streamed in through the stained-glass windows, casting a colorful glow. Bryce savored the solitude, something he hadn't had much of since he got here. As an only child, he spent most of his younger years alone with his thoughts. He found that he did his best thinking while he was by himself.

His mind wandered to happier times. He thought of walks along Flat Rock Beach in San Diego with his parents and his dog, Admiral. Admiral would splash in the surf and fetch a tennis ball from the shallow water. His mom would explain how the towering cliffs formed from thousands of years of pounding waves. His dad would sing to himself as he walked, tossing the ball for Admiral without a care in the world.

Those were the days. Before the Great War. Before the Imjac.

Days that would never return. But he could have happiness again—he could make it back to Alhambra. There were good times on the farm with Amanda, Aunt Sammie, and Uncle Kyle. Playing board games after a hard day of farm work. Fishing for bass at the pond. Good meals cooked every day, except for oatmeal, of course.

But to get there, he would have to escape this dreadful island.

———

All the next day, butterflies danced in Bryce's stomach. That night he would scout the Mothership and the mysterious tubes. He knew that they could be key to their escape, and he didn't understand why Mitchell and James couldn't see that. He would go alone, so if he was caught, no one else would be harmed. The other Escapers could still engineer and escape without him.

He returned to the church after dinner to find Darius nosing around his bunk. The large boy unashamedly picked up Bryce's mat and blanket from the pew and rifled through them. Finding nothing, he dropped them on the floor, stomping on them roughly. Bryce stood to the side with Merry and watched all of this play out.

"He's very suspicious of you," Merry whispered to Bryce.

"With good reason," Bryce whispered back.

When Darius turned and noticed Bryce eyeing him, he stalked off without a word.

Bryce walked over to the pew and furtively pressed his foot into the loose floorboard, which squeaked softly. He picked up his mat and blanket and laid them out again on the pew. No harm, no foul.

Of course, if Darius had searched the pockets of Bryce's uniform, he would have found a pocket full of loaded flower bombs, or flowers stuffed with the deadly yellow powder, thanks to Cherie. Bryce would put them below the loose board that night when everyone was asleep. He couldn't be sure how many flower bombs, they would need, but definitely more than they had.

Merry, Mitchell, and a few others were talking quietly in one corner of the church. Normally, Bryce would have joined them, but he had his scouting mission to the tubes on his mind. He had to get closer to them, to see how they could fit into the escape. He thought James was probably right, that they were used by the blueskins to sleep, or recharge. How could they use that to their advantage? They needed the odds to be in their favor as much as possible if they wanted to escape. A scouting trip would also let them know where the guards were posted at night.

Later, he lay on his pew until the Specials, one by one, drifted off to sleep. When he felt sure that everyone had nodded off, he tossed his blanket to the side, crept to the secret room in the back of the church and softly opened the door. The small, dingy window was all that separated him from the outside—the question was, would it open?

It was an old-fashioned window, with ropes on rollers that moved the window up and a latch at the top. He unlocked the latch and pulled up on the handle. It moved up a fraction of an inch. He pulled harder on it, and this time, it moved a few inches with a loud clunk. Did anyone hear that? He froze and listened for footsteps. After a minute of silence, he went back to the window. Now able to get both hands between the window and the sill, he yanked with all his might. The window slid all the way open.

"Where do you think you're going?" called a voice in the darkness.

Even in the dark, Bryce could make out Merry's turquoise eyes.

"We need to see what those tubes are. I'm going to check it out," he said defiantly.

Merry broke into a smile. "I think you should," she said to Bryce's surprise. "And I'm going with you."

Bryce started to argue but soon realized it might be good to have another set of eyes out there.

"What will Mitchell and James think?"

Merry raised two palms and shrugged. "We'll deal with them when we get back." She pointed to his lower arm. "What about your wristband? They can track us."

Bryce smacked his forehead to his heel. "You're right. What was I thinking?" He felt immediately deflated—if he left the church, the Imjac would know it.

"Don't worry." She walked over to the shelves and came back with a flathead screwdriver. "Mitchell taught me a little trick. Sometimes it's nice to take these off and get away for a while. Let me see your arm."

She gently grasped his arm and slid the blade of the screwdriver in between his skin and the band. She twisted back and forth a few times, releasing the teeth of the wrist-band from Bryce's skin.

"Okay, try to slide your hand out."

Bryce did, and the wristband fell to the floor.

Merry expertly took off her own wristband and placed it next to Bryce's.

"Okay, let's go," she said.

And so, one at a time, they spilled out the window. Waist-high bushes and overgrown grasses provided immediate cover. Merry left the window slightly open behind them.

Dark clouds blanketed the sky, drowning out the moonlight. A cool, misty wind blew in from the coast. In the shadows of the church, Bryce knew that he would be nearly invisible in the black Specials suit.

Bryce poked his head up over the brush and couldn't see a blueskin guard on this side of the church.

"We're clear," he said, standing up. "We need to head in that direction," he said, pointing toward the hill where the Mothership lay.

Merry positioned herself for a run.

Bryce grabbed her wrist gently before she could move. "Slowly and carefully, or we'll be caught. First, we need to check if there's a guard on that side of the church. If so, they could see us as we get close. Stay here, and I'll go look."

He moved slowly, staying close to the ground until he

reached the corner of the building. He poked his head around and saw a guard standing at the far corner, near the entrance of the church. He turned and waved Merry over.

She ran to him.

"Next time, move slower. It's easier to notice something moving fast than it is something moving slow."

"If you're a human," she countered.

"Good point. But let's not take our chances. See that guard—can you tell if he's facing in our direction? I can't tell."

She scrutinized the alien. "He's facing away from us," she said finally.

"Are you sure?"

"Ninety-nine percent. Remember those alien designs that they have on their chests? That would be easy to make out, even in the dark. And I can't see one."

Bryce nodded. "Good point. I'm glad I brought you along."

"You're glad you *brought* me," she growled, but he knew that she was teasing.

They turned the corner and crab-walked to the other edge of the wall.

Luckily, the guard stood rock-still.

Bryce gave one last look at the blueskin, who hadn't shifted. But if he turned now, they would be in plain view, and the guard was out of range of a flower bomb.

In one quick movement, he turned the corner, with Merry right after him. They pressed their backs against the building.

Bryce felt his heartbeats return to normal as he breathed deeply.

"*That*," Merry whispered, "was very stressful. Where do we head from here?"

Bryce studied the path to the Mothership. A small gully covered with tall bushes lay between them and the tubes.

There would be plenty of cover if they stayed low. Unfortunately, there would be no cover on the hill that led to the ship. They would be completely exposed. They would have to hope that no one came along, or they would be caught for sure.

"Let's head that way," Bryce said, sounding more confident than he felt. "You go first, and I'll follow."

Merry gulped. "What if the guard sees us?"

Bryce reached in his pocket and showed her the flower bomb. "But I don't want to use it unless we have to."

"Is that filled with powder?"

Bryce nodded.

"Good."

Merry began a bent-over scramble to the gully. Bryce watched the guard as she moved, but the blueskin's attention never wavered. Now it was Bryce's turn. He moved methodically, looking back at the guard every few steps. He was halfway to the bushes when a huge flash of light blazed right above him, followed by a roar that sounded like a tornado. Bryce dropped to the ground as an alien fighter ship dashed by. He waited a minute and then slowly raised his head off the ground to see Merry flash him a thumbs-up from the cover of the bushes. He rose to his feet, looked back at the guard, who was still facing away from them, and loped over to Merry.

"You can come out," he said. "It's just a fighter refueling."

Merry stared at the ship. "I've never seen one before. They're…amazing."

Bryce scoffed. "Yeah, they're amazing, until they destroy your town. Or blow up your city."

Merry pursed her lips. "I guess when you put it that way. Where do we go from here?"

Bryce pointed in the direction of the hill. "We should

still stay low," Bryce said. "Who knows what kind of patrols they have at night."

The blueskins must have felt especially confident because there were no patrols at all. They made it through the ravine quickly and reached the edge of the hill. There was a dirt road between the gully, and ankle-high grass covered the hill that led to the bluff. There would be no cover for the last part of the trip.

"I think I should go up there alone," Bryce said.

"No, I'll go with you."

"Stay here. I'll need a lookout in case a patrol comes. And two of us will be easier to spot than one." What Bryce didn't say was that if he was caught, this trip wouldn't be for nothing. Merry could go back and help the others escape.

Merry seemed convinced. "I'll hoot like an owl if I see anyone."

"An owl? Are they native to the island?"

"Like the Imjac would know the difference. Besides, it's the only bird call I know."

"Good point."

Bryce looked around and crossed the road quickly. There was no point in moving slowly now—he was out in the open and could easily be seen by any guard passing by. The hill was modestly steep and rose about thirty feet from the road.

He was halfway up the hill when he heard Merry hoot from her hiding spot in the bushes. Then he saw them— two blueskin guards slowly moving along the road. He thought about scampering up the rest of the hill, but he might head right into more trouble. Looking to around, he saw no cover nearby. In the end, he ducked his head down and made himself as flat as possible on the hill. The grass tickled his ears and his heart thudded in his chest. The crunching of the guards' boots became louder and louder as they neared Bryce. Merry gave a final hoot, and Bryce could tell the guards were very, very close.

He held his breath, waiting for any sudden movement or a call of alarm. Luckily, the guards continued walking, and the sound of their steps became weak enough that Bryce knew it was safe to lift his head.

He exhaled deeply and continued his crawl up the hill. Reaching the crest of the hill, he lay down again and looked around. He was at the edge of the bluff—the Mothership sat a hundred feet away from him. The tubes stood next to the ship. They were about ten feet tall with the circumference of a basketball hoop. Definitely wide enough to fit a person or an alien inside. A couple of small vehicles were parked next to the Mothership.

I can use those for cover as I get closer.

There were no guards around, but Bryce wondered about electronic security. The blueskins could have sensors around their ship to alert them to intruders.

Too late to worry about that now—it's all or nothing now.

He broke from the cover of the grass and edged up to the side of the vehicles. He was now fifty feet away from the Mothership and seventy from the tubes. Even in the dim light, he could make out blob-like shapes floating in the tubes. The blobs slowly bounced around the liquid inside, reminding Bryce of a lava lamp. Curious, Bryce crawled closer and closer. He was out in the open now.

He put his head down and inched ahead. When he got to within fifteen feet of the tubes, he looked up. James was right. The blueskins were swimming in the tubes, wriggling like squid in the water with their eyes closed. The shape of their bodies wasn't human-like at all. From the shoulders down, their bodies extended into a series of tentacle-like appendages. It was then that Bryce noticed the alien suits lined up behind the tubes, like headless tin soldiers. The Imjac humanoid shapes were just a facade, a way to help them navigate on land. At the bottom of the tubes, Bryce noticed small hoses linked to a larger hose running from the bluff to the sea.

Suddenly, one of the blueskin's eyes opened, a yellow sun in the darkness. Then another and another and another, until all of their eyes were open. Bryce put his head down and flattened into the turf. His heart pounded, and his ears listened for any clue that he had been seen. After a minute, he slowly lifted his head. The aliens had closed their eyes again.

Had they seen him? There was no way to know for sure, but he knew he should leave. He turned and made the agonizing crawl down the hill. When he reached the crest, Merry hooted again. He saw the hovercraft moving along the road in the opposite direction. He waited until the board was safely past, then he went down the hill and met up with her.

"What did you see?" she asked, impatiently.

"I'll tell you on the way back," he said. "We'd better hurry, before we're missed."

CHAPTER
SIXTEEN

Bryce had learned something from his scouting mission to the Mothership, but he wasn't sure what to make of it. The blueskins slept in tubes, but how could they use that to their advantage? Why did all the aliens' eyes open all at once? He hoped the others might be able to help because he was out of ideas.

The Escapers met the next night.

"What do we do now?" Merry asked, as she plopped the map that they had drawn on the floor.

Bryce scratched his head absentmindedly. "Well, we have a general layout. Now we need to figure out our plan."

"That's easy," James said. "Run to the town. People will help us."

"Hah!" Mitchell scoffed. He was still upset about not being told about the scouting mission that Bryce and Merry went on the other night. "I'm not so sure. How do we know that some of the people aren't on their side?"

"Who could be on their side?" Merry protested.

"Darius, for one," Bryce countered. "But I think we're going to have to take a chance with the town. If we try to hide out in the woods, we'll either starve to death or they'll find us. We need help to get off the island."

Mitchell rubbed his hands together, obviously delighted at the prospect of escape. "Let's get going. It'll be great to see my mom. I've been here the longest, you know. Out of everyone. Except for Darius, of course."

"We need to know how to make it to the town at night," Bryce said, "that is, if we're planning on leaving at night."

"They'd catch us for sure if we left during the day," Merry said.

"You're right," James added. "We all have jobs, and they would know right away if we didn't show up. If we were able to slip out at night, we could be gone for hours before they noticed."

Bryce nodded at James's logic. He was glad the small boy was a part of the group. "Okay, so if we're leaving at night, we'll need to know where the guards are on the way to town, so we don't walk right into them. The yellow mineral is really no match for their blasters—it's best if we surprise them with it."

Merry scratched the side of her head. "Okay, so we need to scout again."

"Yep." Bryce hesitated for a second, unsure how to breach the next bit of information. "And there's something else. I need to get my friends out too."

There was an uncomfortable moment of silence.

"But how?" Mitchell asked. "The cell doors are sealed. What are we going to do, dig them out?"

The question hung in the air for a moment.

Merry finally punctured the silence. "Well, I could try my wristband on the door sensors. It works when we do deliveries—who's to say it wouldn't work at night?"

"That's right," James added. "They probably don't shut off access at night. Why would they? They know that we're locked up."

"Good point." Bryce wanted to encourage this line of thinking. Leaving the others behind, especially Amanda, was unimaginable.

"I still think it's too chancy," Mitchell countered. "I bet the scum suckers do cut off our access after deliveries—they've definitely got the technology to do it. Why risk our lives on something that probably won't work?"

"Well, we're going to," Bryce said. "Or you'll do it without me. And without the flower bombs that my friends have been making."

Bryce looked Mitchell in the eye.

"Okay," Mitchell said. "We'll get your friends."

"Tell us about the tubes you saw," James said, changing the subject.

"Well, you were right," Bryce said. "The Imjac are about as human as squid."

"I knew it!" James said, clapping his hands.

"And how does that help us?" Mitchell asked.

Merry pointed to the tubes on the map. "The tubes aren't that far from the road out of town. We could sneak up there and…"

"Disable them somehow," Bryce said. "The more we take out, the fewer there are to chase us."

To Bryce's surprise, Mitchell began to nod. "Yeah, that makes a lot of sense. The fewer of those buggers after us, the better."

That seemed to settle matters. Mitchell sat back on his haunches and bit his lower lip. "I guess we better get to bed then. When do we go on our scouting mission?"

"Tomorrow night," Bryce decided.

———

Bryce tossed and turned on his pew as he thought about the quandary. How would they be able to free his friends from the cell? It's possible that Merry's wristband would work, but if not, what could they do? The cells were dug into the hillsides, beneath tons of dirt and rock. It would take a month to dig them out, not a few hours. And the night of the escape, they wouldn't even have a few hours.

Bryce spent most of the next morning yawning and stumbling around from tunnel to tunnel. Finally, the symbol for Amanda's tunnel lit up on his wristband—it had been two days since he had seen his cousin. He wanted to update her on their plans, and to make sure the group would be ready to go. He wore a smile as he worked his way back to the end of her tunnel.

As he came closer, he saw her profile lit by the dim light of the wristband. Reese worked next to her, the digger in his hand grinding into the tunnel wall. Amanda seemed to be lost in thought, staring at the wall. In the dim light, they both looked thin and drawn, like starving people he had seen on TV.

"Amanda," he called out.

She didn't turn.

Strange. Maybe she couldn't hear me over Reese's work.

"Amanda," he called out louder.

This time she turned and blinked twice in his direction. Her eyes were glazed over, her mouth open, her features expressionless. Then, she shook her head and smiled.

"Bryce!" she said.

"Looked like you were lost in thought for a minute," Bryce said.

She looked at him quizzically. "If you say so. What's up?"

"We're getting close to escaping," Bryce said. "The plan's really coming together."

Amanda stared into his eyes. "Huh?"

And then he knew. The green juice had started its insidious work; Amanda was on her way to becoming a zombie.

"Escaping, Amanda," Bryce said, trying to hide his frustration. "Getting off this island. Going home." He dug a piece of bread from his pocket and handed half of it to her.

"What's this? Bread? Where'd you get this?" She smiled at him in wonder.

"You know. Or at least you should know," he said. "You need to stop drinking the green juice. I'll bring you bread. Listen, tell the others to be ready."

She just nodded. Bryce wasn't sure that what he said registered with her.

Reese turned off the digger, having extracted a small piece of the blue mineral. Bryce handed him a piece of bread and took the searcher from Amanda. He felt the familiar hum of the searcher and watched it do its work. In a couple of moments, he felt the pull of a strong vein of the blue mineral.

"Dig here," he said to Reese. "There should be lots here."

Amanda faced the wall again, staring vacantly.

"Has she been like that all day?" Bryce asked Reese.

"The last two days," Reese said, glancing away. "Something has definitely, uh, changed recently. We've been keeping an eye on her."

"Thanks." Bryce's insides felt heavy. Had he lost his cousin already?

"I heard what you said about the escape," Reese said, gnawing on the bread. "We'll be ready. Here." He handed Bryce a few flower bombs.

Bryce said goodbye to Amanda, who nodded vacantly, and crawled to the light of day. All the while, a pit formed in his stomach. He had no time left. His cousin was changing or had changed. The escape would have to come soon, or it might be too late for Amanda.

As he reached the edge of the tunnel and ducked out of the entrance, his wristband flashed again. He recognized the symbol for this tunnel also—Jamal and Jason had been working there lately.

He quickly found the tunnel entrance. The written alien language had seemed as foreign as Chinese two weeks ago, but now he was able to recognize the symbols quickly and accurately.

Jamal and Jason sat in the darkness of the tunnel with their tools resting on their laps.

"Well, look who it is. The chosen one," Jamal said.

Bryce stopped and studied Jamal's face. Was he still holding a grudge? But Jamal quickly broke into a smile and shook hands with Bryce.

"We thought you'd never get here," Jason said, rubbing his stomach. "Where's the bread? I only drank half of my green juice this morning."

Bryce grimaced. "I'm sorry. I just gave it to Amanda and Reese. I thought it was her turn."

"Amanda's turn was two days ago," Jason started to complain, then composed himself. "It's alright. She didn't do it on purpose. Don't take this the wrong way—I know she's your cousin, but not everything is right with that girl lately, if you know what I mean." He twirled his finger next to his temple.

"Well, that same thing is going to happen to all of us pretty soon," Jamal said. "That is, if we don't get out of here soon. Speaking of which, how's the big plan going, Bryce?"

Bryce sat back and leaned against the tunnel. He told them of the plan to scout the area leading to town and how the aliens slept in the large glass tubes. Bryce also told them about that night's scouting mission.

"If we don't look around, we'll have no way of knowing where the blueskins are positioned at night," Bryce said. "We'd be walking blind."

Jamal nodded. "Scouting is a good move." He rubbed his chin thoughtfully. "I wonder if we could use their sleeping to our advantage. I mean, if you were to drop a little of that yellow powder in the tubes, you could knock a whole bunch of those blueskins out in a minute."

"You could, bro," Jason said enthusiastically. "They don't have too many guards. How many tubes were there?"

Bryce shrugged. "I don't know, maybe twenty?"

"There can't be more than fifty blueskins on this island," Jamal said. "Heck, we do all the work. If you were able to take down twenty, that's forty percent of our problem gone."

"That's a big if. While I was up there, one of them opened an eye, and then the rest of them did. Freaked me out. It would be too dangerous to go from tube to tube to put the powder in. Besides, the tubes are like ten feet tall, with smooth sides. We would need Spider-Man to get the powder in."

"Let me think about it," Jamal said. "I'll come up with something."

"I'll think too, bro," Jason said.

Bryce and Jamal laughed.

Jason's brow furrowed. "What's so funny? I can think."

They all broke into giggles.

As Bryce crawled out of the tunnel, he realized that they hadn't talked about the biggest obstacle in their escape: how to open their cell door the night of their escape.

———

That night, as he lay in his pew waiting until midnight, Bryce went through a mental checklist. He had four flower bombs in his right pocket in case they needed to disable any blueskin guards. Hopefully it wouldn't come to that— he didn't want to set the Imjac on edge before the escape. In his mind, he walked the route to the cells over and over.

If tonight went well, he would press to leave the next

night. But there were a lot of ifs. If they could make it to town. If they could avoid the guards along the way. If the cell opened.

A lot of ifs and no guarantees.

He glanced at Darius, who slept on his pew. His immense chest rose and fell in heavy breaths. Merry had made sure that he would sleep well all week; she'd been spiking his soup with a little green juice when he wasn't looking.

They had agreed to wait for a half-hour after the last person had gone to sleep before meeting in the room. It was difficult to lie here in the darkness with the sounds of sleep surrounding him and not nod off himself. Every time he felt his eyelids getting heavy, Bryce shook his head vigorously until his eyes wrenched open again. The thought of Amanda and the others depending on him helped to keep him awake.

Finally, he saw Merry slip from her bed and glide toward the back room. Mitchell got up soon after and was followed by James. Bryce waited a good, solid minute, looking around the church for any raised heads. Satisfied that everyone else was asleep, he rose, slipped into his shoes, and went to the back room.

They sat waiting for him in the darkness. Wordlessly, Mitchell popped open the window. A cool gust blew in, refreshing the stale air of the room.

James gulped. "Are we sure that this is a good idea?"

Merry patted him on the back. "We'll be fine—we just need to practice the route for tomorrow."

"And if we run into any trouble, I have a few of these with me," Bryce held up one of the flower bombs. "Here are a couple for you, Merry." He dropped a couple of bombs in her palm.

Mitchell nodded in approval. "Good idea," he said.

"Let's get those bands off." Using the flathead screwdriver, he removed Bryce's wristband and then Merry's.

Bryce slipped out the window first, and Merry followed. Mitchell left the window open just a crack.

They crouched down in the tall grass that grew against the wall. Dark clouds obscured the moon again. *So much the better. We'll be harder to see.*

Bryce turned back and waved at Mitchell and James through the window.

"I guess this is it," Merry said.

"Yep," he said. "Let's do this."

CHAPTER
SEVENTEEN

BRYCE HELD a finger to his lips as he looked around. A half moon, partially hidden by low clouds, provided little light. A stiff breeze bit through the gaps in his uniform. He shivered and then put his mind to ignoring the cold. It would only serve as a distraction, and he couldn't afford to be distracted tonight.

They escaped the area around the church easily this time. The guard stood as still as a statue as they crept by, leading Bryce to wonder out loud if he was awake.

"I think I would fall asleep too if I had that job," Merry said.

Bryce pointed in the direction of the road. "We're moving that way, toward the coast. I want to scout our escape route, to see how fast we can make it to town. Remember, stay down and move from cover to cover. I'll go first."

Merry nodded.

They soon reached the trail that led to the beach.

"We need to stay off the path," Bryce said after Merry joined him behind the hedge. "It'll be too easy to see us.

Let's stay to the left, where there's a little bit of cover. I'll go first, then you follow."

Knee high bushes grew to the left of the path. During the day, they bloomed with bright blue flowers. But in the dim light, everything had turned to shades of gray. When he had covered a good distance, he stopped and turned toward Merry, signaling for her to meet him.

Feeling safe, they jogged along, taking in a hundred yards at a time, constantly scanning the skies for blueskin activities. But other than the two guards around the church, the path was clear.

They reached a fork in the road. One road led to where Amanda and the others were kept. The other, Bryce hoped, led to the town.

"On the night we leave, we'll head toward the cells," he said, pointing. "The others can stay here. Then we can all head to town together."

"I guess there won't be much cover for us," Merry said, pointing to the path to town.

Bryce could see what she meant. No plant life on either side of the path, no rocks or embankments, just ankle-high grass. Bryce estimated that for a half mile, they would be completely exposed.

He hesitated. It would be a risk, and a big one. But this had to be done.

"We'll be fine," he said, more confidently than he felt.

He set out with Merry trailing close behind him. They made it just a few hundred feet when she stopped.

"Look!" she said, pointing to the sky.

A single light hung in front of them fifty feet off the ground. It moved back and forth along the path, coming toward them.

"It's one of their hoverboards," Bryce said. He looked behind them. They might make it to cover if they took off in a fast sprint. But running might be noticed, even in the dim light.

"What should we do?" Merry asked, her voice in a panic.

"Drop to the ground on the side of the path and hold completely still. Maybe he won't notice us."

"That's your plan?"

"Do you have a better idea?"

Merry shook her head.

They lay down on the side of the road ten feet apart, flattening themselves as much as they could. Bryce held a flower bomb in his throwing arm and another in his left.

Two chances to hit. No, four. Merry had two also.

The light from the hoverboard wound down the path, slowly moving from side to side, illuminating everything on the road and the area around it. When it moved to within eighty feet, Bryce knew that the blueskin would see them.

"Merry, he'll see us. We've got to take him out."

She sat up and cocked her arm back with a flower bomb ready. Bryce did the same. Forty feet. Then thirty. Twenty. Ten. Then the hoverboard was nearly on top of them. The light passed over Merry first, moved on, then came back to her.

The light shone on Merry like a spotlight in a theater, causing her to shield her eyes from the brightness. The hoverboard began to descend with Merry in its focus. She tried to scramble away, but the light followed her. Bryce could make out the alien's shape against the dimly lit sky and took aim. When the hoverboard dropped to fifteen feet, he released.

Thwack! A direct hit. A cloud of dust erupted around the alien. It reached up with both hands toward its face, and the hoverboard lurched sideways wildly, heading directly for Merry, who sat there, frozen under the harsh light. If she didn't move, she would be crushed by the weight of the alien and the board.

Bryce raced over and grabbed her arm, pulling her with everything he had, just as the craft crashed, missing her by inches. Bryce landed awkwardly on top of Merry.

"Are you okay?" he asked, rolling off her.

"Yeah, I'm fine."

Bryce stood and helped Merry to her feet.

"Do you think that they heard that?" Merry said of the crash.

"Let's not stick around long enough to find out."

Merry touched his arm. "Thanks. You saved me."

"You would have done the same for me."

She pointed at the alien, who lay on the side of the road. "Is he alive?"

Bryce walked over and looked at the blueskin. His skin had red pustules from the powder, and his large yellow eyes stared up to the sky unblinking. Bryce gave him a gentle prod with his foot, but he didn't move.

"I think he's dead."

Merry nodded. Bryce could tell that the blueskin's death bothered her, but he didn't know what to say. It bothered him too, but he knew that it was necessary. Besides, the blueskins wouldn't think twice about killing them.

"Are we just going to leave him here?" Merry asked.

Bryce looked at the alien lying on the path. The hoverboard had fallen to the side of the road, but the alien's body would be obvious.

"You're right. We should move him."

They each grabbed one of the alien's arms and began pulling him off the path.

"Uh, he's heavy!" Merry complained.

"Really heavy."

It took a minute to move the alien off the road far enough where it wouldn't be noticed. With its suit of metal, it felt more like moving a machine than a being that lived and breathed. When they were done, Bryce looked up and down the path for any guards. There were none.

They continued jogging down the path and soon reached a wooded area. The path continued through the trees.

"This way," he said.

Tall, leafy trees grew along the path, providing cover. They moved along slowly nonetheless, stopping every so often to see if the guards had picked up their trail. Lights from hovercrafts circled back around the cells, but they saw no blueskins.

At last, they reached the edge of the town. They crouched behind a large hedge and assessed the town, which consisted of one paved road, with buildings on each side. They were all built of the same style, white paint with clay tile roofs. They reminded Bryce of the mission project that he had done in fourth grade in San Diego. The street seemed deserted, empty except for a few abandoned cars.

"Do you see anyone?" Merry asked.

"No, you?"

She shook her head. "Should we move closer?"

"Maybe," Bryce answered. "But let's stay behind cover." He pointed toward the nearest building, which had a short wall surrounding a garden. "Follow me."

He took one last look to make sure no guards patrolled the street, then loped toward the wall. He dove over the edge and landed on his backside. Merry came right behind him. From their new vantage point, they had a better view. The shop windows were empty or boarded up. The town looked abandoned. Not even a stray cat in sight.

"Looks like this town isn't going to be much help," Merry said, obviously disappointed.

Bryce was about to agree with her when something caught his eye. "Wait, do you see that?"

"What?"

"Look at the third house down. Second floor."

Merry squinted. "What do you see?"

"I see light," Bryce said. "It's so dim, it might be candle-light." Just then he saw a shadow cross the window. "And there's someone there…The town isn't deserted."

Merry smiled. "There's hope."

"Yes, maybe," Bryce said, "but not if we get caught. Let's get back before someone notices we're missing."

Bryce took one last look down the empty street. Even if someone did still live in the town, there was no guarantee they would risk their necks for them. Chances are that their lives had been ruined by the blueskins. The town had clearly suffered. Why take on the risk of angering the aliens for a few strangers? But for now, Bryce put these thoughts out of his head. Even a sliver of a chance of freedom sounded better than staying at the camp.

The moon broke through the low cloud cover, casting a silver light on the ground. Normally Bryce would have welcomed the additional light, but tonight it would make them easier to see. He motioned for Merry to follow and scaled the wall. He looked to the sky but saw no alien ships or hoverboards. He sprinted for the heavy brush.

When they reached the main road, Bryce stopped.

"We should head back a different way," he said. "They probably found the hoverboard by now and might be looking for us."

Merry nodded. "Good thinking. Let's go up that hill— we'll be able to see them before they see us."

They clambered up the slope, paused at the peak, and looked down. The dead blueskin and hoverboard rested where they had left them, and obviously hadn't been found. Bryce turned his eye inland and saw the enormous Mothership. It was a safe distance away; he could barely make out the strange tubes lined up outside.

He pointed the tubes out to Merry.

"It's funny," she said. "They're all lined up like dominoes. It's like you would just need a giant hand to knock them all down."

"That's a great idea, actually!"

"What is?"

"I'll tell you later. We should go."

They finally reached the church, skirting around the bored blueskin guarding the entrance. Then they rattled open the window and clambered inside.

Mitchell and James were still waiting for them.

"You finally made it," Mitchell said. "We thought you guys would never get back."

"Yeah, Mitchell was really worried," James said. After Mitchell gave him a cross look, he added, "I was a bit nervous too. What took so long?"

Bryce filled them in on the dead hoverboard pilot and the trip to town.

"Sounds like good news," Mitchell said when he finished. "We can reach town, and there are people living there."

"And bad news, too" James said.

"How so?" Bryce asked.

"Yeah," said Mitchell. "What's the bad news?"

"It's good that you found people in the town," James said. "But after you killed the alien, the blueskins are going be patrolling like crazy. We'll be lucky to make it one hundred feet without being caught."

Bryce knew that he was right. And his heart sank.

CHAPTER
EIGHTEEN

Despite his physical exhaustion, Bryce could barely sleep that night. They seemed so close now. They knew the route to take to the town. The flower bombs worked as lethal weapons and could disable a blueskin or two that stood in their way. But so much was unknown. Would the blueskins increase their patrols? Would anyone in the town help them? To do so would be risking their own lives. And most important of all, how would they free Amanda and the others? Merry seemed confident that her wristband would work, but until they tried it, they couldn't be sure.

He thought he had a solution to take care of some of the blueskin guards. It wouldn't make it easy to escape, but it would help. The only problem was that it was risky.

He thought of something his father liked to say: no risk, no reward. The reward would be their freedom, but they would be risking their lives.

It had only been two months, but he had almost forgotten what it meant to be free. To be able to make a decision on his own, to go where he wanted when he wanted. On the farm, he had to go to school and do his chores. After that, his time was his own. Now each moment was under the watchful eye of the aliens. He started to imagine coming home, walking up the driveway to Aunt Sammie and Uncle Kyle's house. They would rush down the driveway, to meet Amanda and him, with smiles and tears everywhere.

Amanda…

The next morning, he sat alone during breakfast, choosing the corner of a table that faced the wall, away from Merry and the others. Freedom seemed so close now; he couldn't let it slip away because someone saw them together and grew suspicious. The others picked up on his cues and ignored him too.

Good. They're smart. They can sense it too. We're close. Really, really close.

When he reached the worksite that morning, he noticed an immediate change in blueskin activity. They had doubled the guards. Instead of one guard at each level of tunnels, he saw two, one at each end of the ramp. The ground level around the silos teemed with additional aliens. Several hoverboards buzzed through the air. Now, half a dozen guards surrounded Red Scar and Cai Lun as they stood in the center of the worksite, surveying the action.

Mitchell sidled up to Bryce on his way to manning his silo. "Looks like they found the hoverboard," he said, chagrined.

"Yeah," Bryce said. "They sure did."

"We had better wait a day," he said.

"Why's that?"

"They'll be on edge today," Mitchell said. "Best to give them time to relax again."

Bryce thought about Amanda. Every day that they waited was a day she got worse. But an extra day also gave him the opportunity to cause more trouble. "You're right, we go tomorrow. Tonight, we handle the guards."

Mitchell gave him a look of alarm.

Not only were there more guards everywhere, but Bryce noticed a rough edge to the blueskins' behavior. Diggers who walked too slow were pushed to the ground. More than once a blaster was raised in threat. The guards that watched Bryce nonchalantly before now tracked his every move. Today was a day to tread carefully.

As he walked through the center of the worksite, Bryce caught Cai Lun's eye. He hoped that he could talk to the older man and see what he could tell him about the situation. Cai Lun saw Bryce and nodded his head ever so slightly.

Message sent.

Cai Lun did not disappoint. The interpreter stood waiting for Bryce as he pulled himself out of his first tunnel.

"Hi," Bryce said. "How have you been?"

"There is no time for small talk," Cai Lun said. "Walk with me. Things are very, very dangerous."

"Even for you?" Bryce said bewildered.

"For everyone who is *not* a blueskin."

Cai Lun began to walk briskly up the rampart toward the next level of tunnels. "Check your wristband. Pretend you have just received a signal."

Bryce did as he was told. "What's going on?"

"Another guard has been killed. The first one, the blueskins were willing to overlook, to see it as an unfortunate accident," he said, pushing his glasses up the bridge of his nose. "This time, the Imjac are taking no chances. They are bringing in additional guards. It will be perilous for anyone not following the rules."

It had been almost a week since they had spoken. If possible, Cai Lun looked even thinner and more tired.

Heavy lines sprouted from the corner of his eyes. His eyes were red and glazed.

"I understand," Bryce said. "Whoever did this will surely be careful. When will the guards arrive?"

"I do not know," Cai Lun said, stopping and turning to face Bryce. "But be cautious."

Before Bryce could respond, Cai Lun spun on his heels and walked away.

Bryce sat next to Merry at lunch. He knew that he was taking a risk; three guards were posted inside the dining room instead of the normal two. But this conversation couldn't wait.

"We need to leave tomorrow," he said softly between slurps of soup.

She looked at him with alarm, glancing around to see if anyone had heard. "I don't know—they're on the alert," she whispered. "Why can't we wait?"

"Because more guards are coming," he said. "If we wait, it'll be too late." He didn't mention Amanda. He felt a pang of guilt; after all, he was asking them to take more of a risk for her sake.

"We'll talk later," she said, and got up from the table, walking away from her half-eaten bowl of soup.

Bryce wondered if he was being too pushy. From Merry's point of view, what difference did waiting another week mean? But to Amanda, another week might make the difference between survival and becoming a zombie.

When Bryce met with Jamal and Jason at their tunnel later, he told them about his scouting mission.

"You killed another of their guards," Jason said in disbelief. "They are going to be really pissed."

"No," Jamal said. "The blueskins don't get angry. I've seen it. Getting angry implies that you have emotion…They have no feelings. Those guys would kill their own just as soon as one of us. But it will make them more careful. And harsh. The last thing they would want to do is lose control."

"You're right," Bryce admitted. "This is about control. There are more of us than them. If we all decided to take off in different directions across the island, there is no way they could catch all of us. Or even most of us. They manage us by keeping us afraid."

"What if we did it?" Jason asked.

"Did what?" Jamal said.

"Take off across the island. Like you said, some of us would get away."

Bryce shook his head. "Too chancy. Besides, would you want to be one of the kids who got caught?"

Jason looked downcast. "No," he admitted. "I wouldn't."

Bryce wanted to pick up his friends' spirits. "Listen, we've got a plan," he said. "Let's stick to it."

"We'll be ready," Jamal said.

One thought haunted Bryce as he crawled out of the tunnel: he still hadn't figured out how to get them out of the cell.

———

That night, the Escapers met again in the back room to discuss final plans.

"But what about all of the extra guards?" James asked.

"I know. But Bryce heard that there are even more blue-skins coming," Merry countered. "It will be even tougher to leave when they get here."

"It's tomorrow, or we may never leave," Bryce said. "I would rather take that chance than die here. And even as Specials, we will die here, sooner or later."

They all nodded in agreement and began to review the

plan. Tomorrow night they would have to leave much earlier for the back room. Merry and Bryce would head to the cells to release the Alhambra kids, while James and Mitchell would scout the escape route. Then the boys would double back to meet up with the others, and they would head to town together. They had plenty of flower bombs, but Bryce knew the bombs were best if used on a sneak attack. They would be too easy for the blueskins to dodge in a face-to-face battle, and the blueskins' weapons were far superior.

When they finished going over the plan, Bryce looked at Merry.

"Are you ready?"

"Yep."

James looked at them quizzically. "Ready for what?"

"We're going to take out some of their guards tonight."

James's eyes bulged. "You're going to what?"

"Don't worry," Merry said soothingly. "We'll be safe."

James stood up. "There's nothing safe about this!" he said a little too loudly. "We're so close to leaving."

"You're right, James," Mitchell said. "It's not safe. But neither is trying to escape the blueskins when they're at full strength. This is a way for us to disable some of their troops, to give us a fighting chance tomorrow."

"Don't you think this is crazy?"

"No, for once I think this is a risk worth taking," Mitchell replied, crossing his arms over his chest.

James scanned the others' faces and realized that he had lost. "Okay, but we're going with you."

Mitchell's eyebrows rose. "We are?"

Merry pursed her lips. "I don't know if that's such a good idea. If there are more of us, we're more likely to be seen."

"True," James said. "But it also means two more people to help."

Merry looked at Bryce. "What do you think?"

"I think we should all go," Bryce said. "It will be good practice for tomorrow night. And with what I'm planning, we may need all the help we can get."

Leaving their wristbands in a pile on the floor, they pried open the window and crawled out feet first. Mitchell was last to leave and closed the window behind them.

"Here, before I forget," Bryce said and gave each of them a few flower bombs.

James gulped. "We're really going to do this, huh?"

"We are," Bryce said. "It might mean the difference between escaping and getting caught. Follow Merry and me and move slow and low to the ground. We'll be fine."

I hope.

For all the guards that were visible during the day, security around the church had remained light. They easily snuck around the guards surrounding the church and made it to the bluff faster than before.

They stopped at the base of the hill. In the distance, near the cells, they could see the lights of the hoverboards circling the area.

"They must think that diggers are behind the attacks on the guards," Merry noted. "And putting extra guards there."

"Makes sense, right?" Bryce said. "Who else but a digger would have access to the yellow stuff?"

"But how could they get out to attack the guards?" James asked.

"I bet the blueskins are killing themselves trying to find that out," Bryce countered.

Bryce pulled a bomb from his pocket and nodded at the others, who did the same. They scaled the hill, slowly, stopping every ten feet or so to make sure that they hadn't been noticed. Finally, they reached the crest of the hill.

"First," Bryce said, "we should look for guards. Then we'll head for the tubes."

"Okay," Merry said. "But what will we do when we get to the tubes?"

"Use your idea from last night. About dominoes."

Mitchell and James gave Bryce a quizzical look.

They were interrupted by movement in front of them.

Merry poked her head up first and immediately dove back down.

"There's a guard… there…looking right at us."

Bryce put a flower bomb in his right hand. "On the count of three, Merry and I hit him. If we miss, James, you and Mitchell go. One, two, three!"

They rose to their knees in synchronicity. The guard stood no more than fifteen feet away, his blaster at his side. When he saw them, he raised his blaster, but it was too late. Two bombs hit him, and he fell, grasping futilely at his face.

Bryce and Merry dove back down for cover.

"Did you see any others?" Bryce asked.

"No, did you?" Merry said.

"No. Okay, slowly, let's get up and look."

They all rose to their knees. The guard lay a few feet from them—he must have staggered toward them after he'd been hit.

"If this works, escape will be a lot easier," Bryce said. "Not easy, but easier."

"That's why we're here, right?" Mitchell said, patting him on the back.

The tubes stood fifty feet away, occupied but unguarded.

"I think we're good," he said, and crept toward the tubes. The others followed behind.

Even in the dim moonlight Bryce could see the water in the tubes, filled almost to the top, and in most of them, a dark bulbous shape oscillated inside. Three tubes at the end, near two parked mining vehicles, were empty.

"What are we going to do exactly?" Merry asked.

"Knock down the dominoes, like you said," Bryce answered.

She smiled. "I didn't think you would take that literally."

He turned toward Mitchell and James. "Why don't you keep an eye out, and we'll push the first tube over? If it works like I think it will, it'll run into the others and knock them down. Then we run."

They crept to the empty tube at the end. Bryce placed his hands halfway up the tube. What had looked to Bryce like glass was definitely not; the tube seemed to be made of a firm translucent fabric. He and Merry began to push, digging their heels into the ground and putting all of their weight behind it. Bryce's legs and back raged with the effort. The tube didn't budge, but the water sloshed around a bit.

He wiped the sweat from his brow and turned back toward Mitchell. "You might need to give a hand here. It's heavier than it looks."

Mitchell joined them and pushing and shoving together, they got the bottom of the tube to lift from the ground an inch, then two.

"C'mon, you guys! Push harder!" Bryce said. Bryce felt the last energy from his muscles waning.

"We are," Merry hissed.

But the tube wouldn't go up further. They were stuck.

"James," Mitchell said, "come give us a hand."

Bryce was about to ask how the small boy could help when he heard *thwap, thwap, thwap*. He looked over his shoulder. James sprinted toward them, arms extended, a gritty look on his face.

The small boy slammed into the tube full speed. Then

the tube rose three inches, then four, then five and finally tipped over.

Just as Merry had predicted, the first tube slammed into the second tube, which hit the third, and so forth. After the second tube tipped, they quickly scooted down the hill. When they reached the bottom, they looked up to see all of the tubes had toppled over, spilling their contents, both the water and the aliens.

Giddily, they returned to the church the way they came. Bryce felt the adrenaline pulsing through his veins. The mission went as well as it could have. The blueskins would be feeling threatened now—not even their sleeping quarters were safe. People under stress made mistakes. He hoped aliens would do the same.

Bryce had to remind himself that the Imjac were not people.

When they reached the church, they clambered through the window and fell to the floor, panting from the run back.

"That," Bryce said. "Was awesome."

"It really was," Mitchell said. "James, you were the hero. You saved us. Without you, we never would have knocked that tube over."

James just sat there, a big, satisfied grin spread across his face.

Merry said. "How much do you think it will help, though? Don't get me wrong, it was great revenge and all."

"I guess we'll find out tomorrow," Bryce said.

Mitchell rubbed his hands together excitedly. "Tomorrow! I can't wait. It will be so sweet to get out of here. See my mom, my dad, my brother. Well, my mom and my dad at least. My brother is about as charming as a blueskin."

Bryce patted Mitchell on the back. "You'll see them before you know it."

With happy thoughts of escape swirling in their minds, they crept back to their pews to wait for the next day.

CHAPTER
NINETEEN

BEFORE DAWN THE NEXT MORNING, the church doors burst open. Red Scar and a troop of guards stormed in. The giant alien carried a heavy blaster in his right hand, a murderous look on his face. As Bryce opened his eyes and realized what was happening, his heart sank. They must have discovered he was behind the attack. The escape was over. He would die on this island, along with Amanda and the others.

A blueskin guard threw him to the ground from his pew.

"Easy, easy," Bryce said in a placating tone.

"No talk," the alien hissed.

He stood up and looked around the room. Bryce quickly realized it wasn't just him that was subject to the rude awakening. All of the Specials had been dumped from their beds. The same blueskin who woke him now grabbed him by the arm and marched him to the front of the church.

Soon, all the Specials stood beside him in a line and watched as the aliens searched their bedding, tossing the blankets and mats to the floor. Bryce knew they were looking for the yellow material. He cast a quick glance toward Merry, James, and Mitchell and could tell that they were as worried as he was. What did the Imjac know?

Just then, Cai Lun appeared in the doorway, followed by a guard. He walked to Red Scar's side.

When the search proved fruitless, Red Scar approached the Specials. Bryce took an involuntary step back then caught himself.

Red Scar sputtered and hissed, and Cai Lun translated.

"Last night there was an attack on your Imjac caretakers. If you know who was involved, speak up now and you will be spared."

A moment of dreadful silence followed.

Darius took a step forward. "I know who is behind this." He pointed at Bryce. "It's him. The attacks started when he joined us."

Red Scar looked at Bryce like he could eat him as Cai Lun translated Darius's words.

"What do you have to say for yourself, Bryce?"

Bryce's mind raced. Whatever he said, he had to make it believable. "I had nothing to do with it. You already searched my bedding. Why don't you search me?"

Darius glared at Bryce, but Bryce just looked away.

The interpreter translated. Red Scar hissed and clicked. "You will *all* be searched," the interpreter said.

Bryce glanced at the line of Specials and noticed Mitchell's head drop.

Did Mitchell still have the flower bombs from the last night on him?

The guards went down the line, emptying the pockets of each Special. As they approached Mitchell, he jumped back, reached into his pocket, and threw a flower bomb at the guards. Two guards went down in the explosion of yellow powder. The other guards scattered in fear, while the other Specials stood stock still, shocked by the unfolding scene.

Mitchell leapt over two pews and headed to the door when a loud boom echoed through the church.

A blue bolt struck Mitchell in the back, and he dropped to the ground.

Red Scar stood in the middle of the church, his heavy blaster smoking at the tip.

Bryce felt his eyes well with tears. Merry started from the line to go for Mitchell, but Bryce reached out and grabbed her by the arm.

"No, don't. It's too late for him."

"Let me go," she cried. But eventually she stopped pulling against him and turned toward him, sobbing into his shoulder.

The guards who had retreated came back, pulled aside their dead comrades, and continued searching the remaining Specials. Bryce felt a wave of fear when they got to James, but the boy stood stoically, only the rivers of tears rolling down his cheeks betrayed any emotion.

When they were done, the guards grabbed Mitchell's lifeless body and dragged him from the church.

Red Scar clicked and hissed again. "This is a warning to those who cross the Imjac," Cai Lun said, but Bryce could see the interpreter's heart wasn't in it.

Stunned by the events in the church, Bryce trudged to breakfast with the others. Bryce felt wracked by guilt—he could have taken the bombs from Mitchell and hid them himself. Why hadn't Mitchell hidden the flower bombs? If Bryce hadn't dared the Imjac to search him, Mitchell would still be alive.

No, he couldn't have known that they would search everyone. He couldn't have known that Mitchell still had the bombs on him. But still, Mitchell, his friend, was dead.

The boy who so looked forward to going home would never go home again.

I will go home. We will go home.

He purposely sat alone at breakfast, focusing his thoughts on tonight's escape. His stomach twisted and turned, but he forced himself to swallow a few mouthfuls of bread. The energy would be useful later. The other Specials were subdued, except for Darius, who sat with his group, laughing and talking loudly as if nothing had happened. Without a passing glance toward Merry or James, Bryce left for the worksite.

Low gray clouds blanketed the sky. He hoped that they would stick around; clouds might give them cover from the hoverboards tonight. They would need every break they could get now that they were down a person.

The Imjac guards were fewer in number today but even more testy. He wondered if the toppling of their sleep chambers injured some of them. It certainly seemed so. When he reached the control center near the silo, he counted the guards on duty. Sure enough, there were ten fewer than yesterday. The mission last night was a success. But it came at the ultimate price for Mitchell.

He needed to talk to Amanda and the others. He nervously paced the ramparts, waiting for his wristband to flash from one of their tunnels. They needed to be ready tonight. But by the late morning, he had only been called to a few tunnels. All were panicked newbies who had been partnered with zombies. He tried his best to calm the new kids, to teach them, trying to remember the overwhelming fear that struck him that first day in the tunnels. When he pulled himself out of his third tunnel, he kicked the dirt in front of him in frustration. When would he see his friends?

He turned, and a guard's pale-yellow eyes bore into him. He walked away as nonchalantly as he could, but the more he thought about it, the more self-conscious he became.

They're not watching you. They know nothing.

Nothing that he had learned of the blueskins led him to believe that they had any guile. If they thought he was guilty of something, the aliens would punish him immediately.

Bryce's wristband finally flashed "Return." The diggers spilled out of the tunnels and made their way toward the open area where they would be served their green juice. Bryce spotted Jamal, Jason, and Reese in their usual seats, but where were Amanda and Cherie? He scanned the crowds, but they were nowhere to be seen. Had Amanda finally become a zombie? He scanned the tunnel openings, hoping to see his cousin. Finally, a few minutes later, Cherie led Amanda by the hand to lunch, like a mother guiding a toddler. It pained him to think that his cousin was on the brink of losing her mind. Aunt Sammie and Uncle Kyle would be devastated.

He considered walking over to them. Could he risk it? It might draw attention, and he might be the next one being led to the cliff. But every second would count tonight, and they needed to be ready.

Instead of heading directly to the dining hall, he circled around the worksite. As he passed his friends, he pretended to stumble. He bent down to ostensibly tie his shoe, and without looking at them he said, "Tonight. Be ready," and walked off without looking back.

Confident that he got his message across, he walked to lunch, going through tonight's plan in his mind one more time. This time, it wouldn't include Mitchell.

After dinner, Bryce lay on his pew in the church, staring at the ceiling. A few of the others, mostly silo workers, chatting quietly on their pews. Bryce ignored them, focusing on the plan, going over it again and again in his mind. What-ifs popped up in his mind like gophers from a hole. What if the guards arrived early? What if they couldn't free Amanda and the others? What if the townspeople didn't help them and instead turned them in to the blueskins?

He looked at the light that seeped through the boarded-up windows. The sun had just set, the excruciating wait had begun.

At last, Merry and James trudged in, looking exhausted. Bryce wondered if they felt like they had been balancing on the edge of a knife all day like he had. He shot them a quick glance, and then looked away. Darius strode through the door after them, looking as ornery as usual. He pushed a couple of the smaller kids out of the way and plopped down on his pew. He shot a challenging look at Bryce, who just turned his head.

Let sleeping dogs lie. At least for tonight.

Bryce turned on his back and closed his eyes. A little sleep would be welcome—he might be refreshed for tonight. He rested for a few minutes, never allowing himself to fully fall asleep.

Suddenly, he felt a presence nearby. His eyes blinked open. Darius loomed over him, his face just inches from Bryce's.

"What's wrong with you tonight, loser?" Darius sneered. "You don't look so good. Are you upset because your little jerk friend did something stupid?"

"I'm fine," Bryce said through gritted teeth. "Leave him out of this."

"You don't get to tell me what to do, twerp!" Darius said, swatting at the side of Bryce's head. "I know you were involved too. You, Merry and that other little jerk."

"If you know what's good for you, leave now," Bryce hissed.

Darius sneered. "If I know what's good for me," he said in a singsong voice. "Yeah, right. Just remember, I'm watching you." He turned and walked away, but not before slamming his hip into Bryce's pew, nearly throwing Bryce from the bed.

Merry came over after Darius had left. "I wasn't able to spike his soup tonight. So be careful. I know that he watches us. We should be sure that he's asleep before we leave."

Bryce nodded. One more factor to think about tonight.

The church eventually grew dark, then quiet. Soon the sounds of heavy breathing, accompanied by the occasional snore, filled the room. It was time.

At last Bryce saw Merry steal out of her bed and tiptoe to the back. Five minutes later, James left, taking slow, steady strides. Now it was Bryce's turn. He put his feet on the ground and waited. Then he slid off the pew and crouched down, wiggled the board near his pew loose, and filled his pockets with the rest of the flower bombs. Then he stood and took a long stare at the room, looking for any signs that someone might be awake.

He took his first step.

Easy now.

He cleared his bunk. The small room lay thirty feet ahead. Then freedom. He stopped every three steps and listened. It remained quiet. Finally, the doorknob was in his grasp.

Suddenly, he felt a weight like a brick slam into his shoulder.

"Where are you going, loser?" Darius said, spinning him around with one of his meaty hands.

"This isn't the door to the bathroom?" Bryce said in pretend surprise.

Darius grunted and pushed him aside. He opened the door and stepped in. James and Merry stood by the open window, looking back expectantly. Bryce registered the look of surprise on their faces as they saw Darius standing there instead of Bryce.

"What are you doing here?" James said.

Do something.

Bryce slammed his shoulder into Darius's back, forcing the larger boy into the room and shut the door behind him.

Darius spun and faced Bryce. "What are you three up to? A little kissy face in the closet?" Then he turned back to James and Merry. "Why is the window open?"

Merry looked at him.

Do something.

Bryce did the only thing that he could think of: he slugged Darius as hard as he could in the side of his head. A jolt of pain radiated through Bryce's fist and up his arm. Darius spun around, unfazed, a murderous look on his face.

"I'll kill you," he hissed and grabbed Bryce by the throat. He lifted Bryce off his feet like he was made of straw and slammed him into the door. The air left Bryce's lungs. He scratched, clawed, and kicked fecklessly at Darius's legs, but the larger boys' grip only hardened around his neck.

Bryce saw stars. Then the room began to darken.

Wham!

The grip on Bryce's neck suddenly loosened, and he fell to the ground. He landed on his back, with Darius falling with a thump to his right.

Bryce opened his eyes and lifted himself to a sitting position. Darius lay on the floor facedown, his eyes closed. Merry stood over Darius, holding an old can of paint by the handle. She looked shocked at what she had done.

She shivered. "Is he dead?"

Bryce leaned over to Darius and listened. Faint puffs escaped the large boy's lips.

"He's alive. But we need to leave now. Someone might have heard."

James held his ear to the door for a moment. "I think we're clear. What are we going to do about him?" He pointed to Darius.

Bryce rose to his feet. "Leave him. By the time he wakes up, we'll be out of here. Hopefully," he added.

Neither Merry nor James moved.

"Are we doing the right thing?" Merry said.

James said nothing, but the look on his face and his shaking knees echoed Merry's question.

"This is our chance. To escape. To leave this island and the blueskins," Bryce said. "If we don't leave tonight, we'll die on this island. Imagine going home and seeing your parents. Imagine sleeping in your own bed instead of a church pew. Imagine eating a homecooked meal."

"Well, my mom isn't much of a cook to be honest," James said.

"That's not the point," Bryce said. "We can do this—we have a plan. Now let's go!"

Bryce saw Merry steel herself, and James's knees stopped shaking.

Clearly, Bryce was in charge. They would listen to him, follow him. He just hoped he *was* doing the right thing.

Merry removed their wristbands. Bryce and James dropped theirs to the floor. Merry pocketed hers along with the screwdriver.

And so, one by one, they climbed out the window into the night.

CHAPTER
TWENTY

LAST TO LEAVE, Bryce dropped softly to the ground outside the window. He didn't bother closing the window behind him—it was all or nothing now. A mild breeze blew in from the ocean, and the clouds that blanketed the sky earlier were gone. A bright orange moon and twinkling stars lit up the night and would give them no cover. Even in their black uniforms, they would be easy to spot in the open. He thought about something his father used to say: if I didn't have bad luck, I'd have no luck at all.

Bryce dropped to a crouch, and Merry and James followed his lead. He put his hands to his lips to indicate silence. The next few moments were critical. He crept slowly toward the edge of the building, looking backwards occasionally to make sure that the guards weren't walking the perimeter. When he reached the edge of the church, he poked his head around the corner and saw a guard standing twenty feet away. They had snuck by him before, but this time, more than ever, they couldn't afford to be noticed. They would have to deal with the guard.

Bryce reached into his pocket and pulled out a flower bomb. Merry and James did the same. The guard stood with his back to them, staring in the direction of the Mothership.

"I'll throw first," he whispered. "If I miss, you guys throw right after me."

Merry and James nodded.

He closed the distance to the guard by a few steps. Shorter shots were always better. Lining up his left shoulder, Bryce heaved the bomb. It struck the back of the guard's helmet with a *thwack!* Bryce dropped to the ground as the guard spun around, his weapon pointed threateningly.

Even in the moonlight, Bryce could make out the dust clouding the guard's head. The blueskin teetered for a second, dropped his weapon, then collapsed to the ground.

"Should we leave him there?" James asked.

Merry shook her head. "He's out in the open. Someone might notice. We should move him."

"I agree," Bryce said. "But let's be quick about it."

Hunched over, they scampered to the guard. Bryce gave him a quick nudge with his foot, but, like the others, he was dead. They dragged his body over to the church wall where he would be covered by the tall grass.

"Alright, let's get going," Bryce said.

"Wait," James said, picking up the guard's weapon. "This might be useful." He handed it to Bryce. "You are pretty good with alien tech, right?"

The gun was heavy, made of the same metal that was used to create their impenetrable ships. But the weight was in the handle, leaving the blaster tip light and easy to aim. Bryce held it up as if to practice a shot.

"You're not going to shoot that, are you?" Merry asked.

"Not yet," he said. "Not unless I have to. C'mon, let's go."

They stole away from the church, stopping, starting, then stopping again. A hoverboard patrolled in the distance, near the worksite, but the skies over them were otherwise clear.

They moved quickly and quietly, able to reach the main road in a few minutes. Bryce's senses were on overdrive: the smell of the sea in the air filled his nostrils; his beating heart drummed in his ears; his fingers tingled with anticipation.

In a few minutes they reached a fork in the road. One direction led to the cells where Amanda and the others waited to be freed. The other road led to the town.

"That doesn't look good," Merry said.

Three blueskins blocked the crossroad, all carrying the same heavy blasters that had cut Mitchell down that morning.

"What are we going to do?" James asked.

"First, we are going to get off the path," Bryce said, pulling the smaller boy off the road and into the brush. They crouched behind cover to assess the situation.

The guards were fanned out across the road; no single shot would take all of them down. Unlike the guards posted at the church, these guards were on alert, changing position and scanning the area.

"We could go over the hill," Merry suggested.

"True," Bryce said. "But we would still have to pass them on the way to town with the others."

"We could hit them with these," James said, holding up a bomb. "I've been itching to take out a blueskin."

Bryce shook his head. "We're too far away. We'd have to get closer, and we have no chance against those blasters. But I have an idea. You two stay here."

Crouching, Bryce backtracked down the road two hundred yards, until he was clearly out of sight but hopefully not out of hearing range. He examined the alien blaster. Like the other Imjac tech, he could feel it with his mind. He knew it would work for him. But would it have the effect that he wanted?

He pointed the blaster toward the sky and fired four shots. Then he scampered off the road and ducked back behind the foliage. He slowly backtracked in the brush toward the others.

Halfway back, he could see the three blueskins racing toward the area where he fired the shots.

Bryce found Merry and James where he left them.

"That was brilliant!" James said. "How did you know that would work?"

Bryce shrugged. "I didn't, honestly. But I'm glad it did. James, you stay here behind cover. Be still. Those guards will probably come back. Don't fight them—on your own, you won't stand a chance."

"Yes, sir," James said, giving a mock solute.

Bryce turned to Merry. "Let's go get my friends."

She nodded. "I hope my wristband works."

"Me too."

The twisty path led them to the worksite. During the day, it was a hive of movement and noise, but now it was as silent as a graveyard. The mountain loomed above; with the moon behind it, it cast the worksite in shadow. A chill ran down Bryce's spine.

They continued down the path toward the cells. As they passed each blue metal cell door that would stay closed tonight, a pang of guilt gnawed at Bryce's insides. Even if they escaped, many kids would be left behind to have their brains rotted away by the green drink and die. All to feed the greed of the Imjac.

I'll come back for you. All of you.

Merry saw the guard first. She grabbed Bryce by the arm and pulled him to the side. Then he spotted the blueskin leaning against the hillside, a gray shadow staring into the sky.

I wonder if he's thinking about home like we are.

Bryce erased that thought from his mind. Sympathy for the blueskins wouldn't be helpful tonight. They had no feelings for him or the others. Escape was the aim, at all costs.

He took out a flower bomb and crept as close as he could, with Merry on his heels. Within twenty feet, he stopped. Any closer and there was a chance the guard might see them or hear them. Bryce looked at the blaster—it would shoot from this range, but it was loud and might draw unwanted attention. He turned to Merry and held up a bomb. She did the same.

Bryce threw first. His shot missed, hitting the hillside above the guard's head. The blueskin quickly turned and faced them, his blaster ready, just as Merry's bomb hit him square in the chest. He clawed at his face, cries of agony escaping his mouth. Then he collapsed, facedown.

"That was loud," Merry said, looking around.

"Let's hope it wasn't too loud," Bryce whispered.

They approached the blueskin's body. His writhing had stopped.

"I don't think we have time to move this one," Bryce said. "Let's keep going."

They soon reached Amanda's cell without encountering any more guards.

"Okay, here goes," Merry said and took a deep breath. She waved her wristband over the sensor, but the door didn't budge. She passed the band again over the sensor more deliberately. Again, and again, and again, the wristband passed over the sensor with no result. "It's not working," she said with alarm.

Bryce's heart raced; his thoughts grew frantic. He knew in the back of his mind that this was a possibility. He kicked himself now for not coming up with a back-up plan.

"Is that the only way you ever get in?" Bryce asked.

Merry nodded.

His mind flew through possibilities. They had to escape tonight. Darius was unconscious but would wake. Two more guards were dead. They had crossed the point of no return. He kicked at the door, but it stood firm. Then he heard pounding from the inside. Amanda and the others were awake inside now. That was good. But only if he could figure out a way to free them.

"Bryce, is that you?" It was Reese's voice.

"Let us out!" Cherie shouted through the door. "We're ready."

"Keep it down," Bryce said. "We're trying."

His friends started pounding on the door.

"Bryce!"

"Bryce, we need to get out!"

Bryce searched his mind for an answer. He could see hoverboards in the distance, making their rounds, getting closer and closer. It would only be a matter of minutes before they were discovered. He needed to get them out now.

"I'm going to shoot it with the blaster!" Bryce said.

"Shoot what?" Merry said.

"The sensor. Do you have any other ideas?"

Merry shook her head.

The pounding and shouting continued unabated from inside.

He stepped back. "Move out of the way—this might ricochet." He took aim and started to squeeze the trigger.

"Wait!" Merry said, pulling up the tip of the blaster. "I've got an idea. Shooting the sensor is too risky—if you fry it, your friends might never make it out."

Bryce let the blaster drop to his side. "What do we do?"

"The guard. The guard we killed has a wristband too. I bet it works on the doors."

They ran back and found the guard lying where they

left him. Merry knelt down and removed the alien's wristband.

They hurried back to the cell.

Merry passed the guard's wristband over the sensor. "I hope this works," she said.

Then the door to the cell slid open.

The Alhambra kids rushed out: first Jason, whose basketball sweatshirt was nearly in shreds. Then Jamal, whose trim frame had become almost spindly. Reese lumbered out next with his shock of blond hair that now resembled a mop. They gathered around him, patting him on the back. But where were Amanda and Cherie?

Reese gave him a bear hug and lifted him off the ground. "You did it, man. I didn't think you could," he said, teary eyed.

Finally, Cherie, looking as thin as Jamal, led Amanda out from the cell. Amanda looked straight ahead, her normally sparkling brown eyes dull and sleepy. Bryce grabbed Amanda's hand and gazed into her eyes. "Amanda, I'm here. We're going home."

She gave him the slightest nod.

Bryce breathed a sigh of relief. *Something was awake inside.*

Merry quickly removed their wristbands. "With these off, the blueskins can't track us," she explained.

"Let's get moving," Bryce said. "They probably know the cell door opened."

Two shadows rounded the bend, blueskin guards with their blasters ready.

"Go," Bryce said. "I'll hold them off."

"No, we stick together," Jamal said, pulling out two flower bombs.

"Right, bro," Jason said, equally armed. "We're ready."

Merry held up her own flower bomb.

Reese and Cherie each grabbed one of Amanda's arms and pulled her aside.

Waiting until the guards were in range, they took throwers' stances. The guards continued to move in quickly, not suspecting an attack. Bryce looked back. Amanda was safely out of range.

A blue blast shot through the blackness and landed inches from Bryce's feet.

"Now!" Jamal said, and they threw their bombs. Bryce's shot was off the mark. Jamal missed too. But Jason's shot hit one of the guards directly in the chest, and the alien fell to the ground in a heap. The other guard shot at them, a blast that zipped over Jason's head.

"Bro, that was too close," he said, smoothing his singed hair. Then he aimed another flower bomb, hitting second guard, who quickly fell.

"Dude, I'm on fire," he said, patting himself on the chest.

"You can congratulate yourself later," Bryce said. "Let's go!"

They broke into a run, catching up with the others quickly. Bryce and Cherie supported Amanda, and they moved as a group toward the fork in the road. Amanda slowed the progress. She was reluctant to run, and even when they pulled her, moving at a snail's pace.

"C'mon, Amanda!" Bryce said. "Can you move any faster?"

She stared back at him blankly.

No time for this.

A familiar whirring sound filled the air. Two hovercraft homed in on them. By now, the blueskin guards must have been on full alert. They couldn't stop now—who knew how many troops were chasing them?

"Keep running!" Bryce yelled.

The others didn't need to be told twice. Led by Merry, they sprinted down the path.

With one hand holding Amanda's arm and the other cradling the blaster, Bryce trailed the group.

Bryce turned and fired the blaster with his free hand, sending a blue bolt through the night sky. He missed, but the hoverboards veered from their path. The boards began to fly in a side-to-side motion, like skiers moving downhill, making them harder to hit.

Every few steps, Bryce turned and fired at them, which kept them back.

Then the hoverboard pilots started shooting back. A blast landed in front of them, kicking dust and rocks in the air. Another landed to their right and then left.

Amanda screamed and stopped running.

"Bryce, shoot them again!" Cherie screamed.

Bryce spun and fired several shots, and the hoverboards pulled back, but Bryce knew they would return.

For the next part of the trip, they would be walking in the open, easy targets, while pulling Amanda like a stubborn mule. If they didn't move faster, they would be dead. The blueskins would be coming in force.

"Stop for a minute."

"Why?" Cherie asked, nearly out of breath.

"I want to try something," Bryce said. "It'll make us faster."

Another blast from the hoverboards landed nearby.

"Anything to make us faster," Jason said.

"Amanda, Amanda," Bryce said.

She gaped at him.

"Want a piggyback ride?"

"I don't think she gets it," Cherie said and started pulling on Amanda's sleeve again. "I think we should go."

"Amanda, piggyback ride," Bryce repeated.

Amanda smiled and a spark of recognition lit up her eyes. She climbed aboard Bryce's back.

"You take this," he said, handing the blaster to Cherie.

They started toward the fork again, moving faster this time. Bryce was alarmed at how light Amanda felt on his back. True, they all had lost weight in this ordeal, but she felt like a skeleton.

Then the whirring resumed. The hoverboards found them again.

Cherie turned and tried to shoot the blaster, but it clicked and didn't fire.

"How do you shoot this thing?" she asked.

"Just squeeze the handle," Bryce answered.

"I did," she answered. "I guess you have to be an alien for it to work. Or you."

Up ahead Bryce could see his friends tiring, even Jason, the athlete. Spending days in cramped tunnels and living on the green juice had taken its toll. Bryce even felt his own energy lagging under Amanda's weight. Luckily, the fork was just ahead.

Suddenly Bryce heard a blast, and then a shock jolted through his leg. He fell to the ground, Amanda spilling off his back. He tried to stand up, but his muscles refused to work, and he collapsed again.

His mind became foggy. He could hear the voices and noise around him, but it felt like part of a dream.

Even in his confused state, he knew that he needed to get to his feet and fast. The hoverboards circled fifty feet above them, firing occasional blasts, seemingly content to have trapped them. The guards behind them on the path were closing in.

"Are you able to walk?" Jamal asked. "Because they're here." He pointed toward the path. At least a dozen guards marched in their direction.

His mind clearing, Bryce rose to his feet. His right leg

ached, and in the moonlight, he could make out a hole in his Specials suit and a black burn on his calf. It hurt to put weight on it. He couldn't imagine having to walk on it. Or, worse, run. "Let's go," Bryce said through gritted teeth. He grabbed Amanda's hand—he wouldn't be able to carry her with a bad leg.

"Good thing they only got you in the leg," Jason said. "I thought you were a goner."

"Not yet," he said. "Jason, try a shot on those guards coming at us. Aim for the center. You might be able to take out more than one."

The guards were over a hundred feet away, but the basketball player had remarkable accuracy. Jason squinted as he sized up the advancing guards and let loose with a bomb. Bryce lost it in the darkness as it sailed, but it must have been a true shot. Three guards collapsed, and the others scattered, confused by the attack on their fallen comrades.

"Go," Bryce shouted.

Each step sent stabs of pain up Bryce's leg. Jamal and Merry took the lead. Cherie and Reese held on to Amanda, with Bryce and Jason taking the rear, throwing flower bombs and blasting at the trailing guards.

The pain in his leg had subsided a bit, but the muscles in his leg refused to function normally. Running was awkward, his good leg pulling along his lame one. He wondered if he would be able to make it to town. He couldn't be the one to slow his friends down. If he needed to, he would stop so his friends could go on.

The blueskin guards behind them regrouped, advanced, and began firing shots at them. The aliens had learned something—instead of bunching together, they fanned out, making them harder to pick off in groups. But the guards hung back oddly, content to let loose the occasional volley of blaster shot to keep Bryce and the others moving. The hoverboards did the same, not engaging them directly, but almost pushing them forward, herding them.

A thought clicked in Bryce's mind.

The blueskins almost want us to move forward. Toward the three Imjac guards with the heavy blasters.

He realized it too late. Blaster fire crackled through the air, this time coming from in front of them. Of course. The guards at the fork must have regrouped and were now attacking them. They were surrounded.

"Get off the road!" Bryce yelled, pulling Amanda aside. The others followed, taking cover in the low brush. They were pinned down, guards on each side of them and the hoverboards above.

"We've got to take these blueskins out," Bryce said after a blast whizzed by his head.

"I can hit the guards on the ground," Jason said.

The guards were closing in, and the shots were gaining accuracy.

"I'll give you cover." Bryce turned on his back and fired at the hoverboards, which pulled back.

"On it," Jason responded. He rose to his knees and began zinging bombs at the pack of guards. Merry and Jamal joined him. In a few throws, four more guards hit the dirt, and the others fell back. The guards at the fork remained a problem, though. Their guns blasted away with lethal force, tearing up the cover around Bryce and the others. Dirt, rocks, and shredded shrubbery rained down on them. Soon, there wouldn't be anything to hide behind. And those guards were too far away to hit with flower bombs.

"What do we do about those guys?" Jamal asked.

Bryce didn't have an answer. No one did. Jason heaved a bomb in their direction, but it fell far short. The hoverboards returned, shooting at them from above. So they dug further into the brush to avoid the alien fire.

Bryce shot occasionally at the hoverboards, but otherwise kept his head down. They were trapped. The blasts were coming nearer and nearer. He put his arm around Amanda's shoulders.

"I guess this is it," he said to her softly. "We tried."

Suddenly, the fire lessened from the fork. Instead of three guns firing, there were now two. Then one. Then there was no fire at all.

"Why have they stopped?" Merry asked.

Bryce lifted his head. "I don't know. But let's not wait around to find out." He squeezed a few shots at the hoverboards and at the guards behind them. "Go!"

They rose as one and sprinted down the path. When they reached the fork, three dead blueskins lay on the ground. Behind them, with a satisfied grin on his face, stood James.

"You saved us!" Merry said.

"It was the least I could do. They were so occupied with you guys, they didn't bother to look behind them."

Bryce looked at the small boy with admiration. "You did great, James!"

The path to the town was open. But the hoverboards continued to dog them from the sky, firing at them and tracking their movements as several guards trailed them on the ground. As long as they were in the open, escape would be impossible. It was all Bryce could do to keep them back with blaster shots.

As the road branched toward the town, Bryce noticed a thickly forested area to the left of the path. "Over there." He pointed.

Merry looked at him quizzically. "But the town is this way," she countered.

"Yes, but if we can't shake the troops or the hoverboards, the town can't save us."

"He's right," Jamal said. "They'll find us for sure. We

can lose them in the forest."

Bryce found a gap in the brush that must have been an animal trail. "C'mon, this way!"

The others followed. In the back of Bryce's mind, he wondered if he'd just led them into more danger. The forest could lead to a dead end, and then the blueskins would have them trapped. And at this point, it wasn't likely that the aliens would forgive and forget.

Yet Bryce knew under the canopy, the hoverboards would be vulnerable. They would have to fly low and slow, leaving them open to flower bombs or blaster shots. Eluding the blueskin troops would be easier too. They would have darkness and cover.

Thick-trunked trees grew close together, blocking out the moonlight. It took a minute for Bryce to adjust to the darkness. Would the lack of light be an advantage for them or for the blueskins? He didn't know how well the aliens could see in the dark.

Low-lying brush caught their legs and slowed their escape. More than once, Bryce stumbled, causing his injured leg to rage with pain.

They had gone about one hundred feet into the forest, when Bryce turned around and signaled for them to stop.

"We should split up," Bryce said. "Cherie, can you and Reese take Amanda that way?" He pointed toward the town. "When you reach the edge of the trees, wait for us." Cherie nodded and took Amanda's hand.

"Wait, we'll need some flower bombs," Reese said.

Jamal transferred a handful.

Cherie turned to Jamal. "Be careful, brother."

"Always," he replied.

Cherie and Reese led Amanda by the arms toward town.

"What are the rest of us going to do?" Jamal asked.

"We're going to set a trap."

CHAPTER
TWENTY-ONE

THE TRAP WAS SET, but would the blueskins fall for it?

Bryce sat on a thick branch overlooking the path that led through the forest. His feet dangled off each side, twenty feet off the ground. Jamal and James were perched on a branch near him, and Merry and Jason positioned themselves in a tree on the other side of the path. They had divided the leftover flower bombs among them. Bryce only had a few left. They would be no match for a large group of troops. Bryce had the blaster if they ran out of bombs, but the alien weapons didn't work for the others. Not that he wanted to get into a shootout—that was almost certainly a losing battle.

His eyes and ears strained for any hint of blueskins on foot. He could hear the hoverboards whirring aimlessly through the skies above them. That part of the plan had worked. The hoverboards lost track of them under the thick canopy.

Finally, he saw the guards marching down the path. Just as he had hoped, a dozen guards moved in a tight formation. Perfect.

Keep coming, blueskins. Keep coming.

Bryce grabbed Jamal's arm. "Wait until they're almost right below us."

Jamal nodded and held his hand up to signal the others. They had to time this right. Too early, and they might take out a few guards, but give away their position to the others. It would turn into a blaster fight, and they would be outgunned. Too late, and one of the guards might decide to look up. They would be sitting ducks.

The blueskins continued charging down the path. They were fifty feet away and still holding their tight formation. Then thirty feet. Then twenty.

Bryce cocked his arm and released toward the center of the group. He hit his mark directly in the head, a cloud of toxic dust exploding on contact. The alien fell to the ground, clutching at its face. The others threw bombs, and more aliens fell. The remaining blueskin guards turned and ran.

"That's right!" Jason yelled after them. "Go back to your stupid spaceship!"

"And go back to your planet while you're at it!" Jamal added.

They dropped down from the trees. Bryce felt a jolt of pain in his injured leg as he landed. His leg didn't feel like any sprain he had before. It felt paralyzed, as if the muscles had forgotten to work. He wasn't sure how much more running he could do before it gave out.

"Oh, yeah! Now I'm ready to kick some alien butt!" Jason said.

"Be careful what you wish for," Jamal replied.

"I think we should go," James said, pointing in the direction of the town.

The others nodded and started to move.

Suddenly a hum sounded in the distance.

"Hold on!" Bryce said. "Do you hear that?"

"I don't hear anything, bro," Jason said.

"I do," Jamal said. "It sounds like one of their ships. One of their fighters."

The droning intensified.

"It's coming this way," Bryce said. "Run!"

The roar of the ship was right above them. Two immense blasts ripped the canopy away from above them, sending branches, limbs, and leaves raining down on them. Bryce felt himself flying through the air. He landed roughly at the base of a tree and covered his face as he was pelted with debris. He might have blacked out, but he wasn't sure. He lay there for a second, gathering his senses, before he lifted himself from the ground and shook off the branches and leaves. Merry, James, and Jason were also on their feet. But Jamal was nowhere to be found.

"Jamal!" Bryce called. "Jamal, where are you?"

"Over here," said a faint voice.

Bryce followed the voice and found Jamal with a large tree limb lying across his chest, pinning him to the ground. Jamal's eyes were closed, a grimace of pain painted on his face.

"Hold still, Jamal. I'll get this off you." Bryce bent his knees and tried to lift the branch by himself, but with his injured leg, it was too heavy. "Guys, can you help?" he called to the others. "Jamal is stuck."

The others rushed over, and working together, they lifted the branch off Jamal's chest. He lay there for a moment without moving.

Please be okay.

"Are you going to make it?" Jason asked.

"Yeah, I think so," Jamal said, opening his eyes. "Just taking inventory."

Bryce and Merry helped Jamal to his feet. "Can you walk?" Bryce asked.

"I had better," he said. "The blueskins are coming." He pointed to the sky. The hoverboards zig-zagged in their direction. The canopy that had been their cover was now gone.

"We need to get moving," Bryce said.

"But where?" Jason said.

"Anywhere but here." Bryce started toward the nearest cover, which led to the path to town. He didn't want to give the blueskins any idea where they might be heading. His leg ached with every step, but to stop was to die. The others were faster than he was, so he moved to the side of the exposed forest, where he would be less of a target.

With their cover gone, the hoverboards dogged their movements, shining down through the now-exposed forest with their lights. Bryce turned and fired off two shots, and the boards slowed and circled back for a moment, but then returned. The ship's blasts had cleared the forest for hundreds of feet in front of them. They were exposed every step of the way.

"Hold up!" Bryce shouted.

The others stopped.

"We need to take them out," Bryce said.

"Why?" Jamal asked.

"If we keep running toward town, they'll just track us. We need to lead them away from the town. Let's take them deeper into the forest, away from town. Then we can circle back when we've lost them."

The others nodded at his logic. Still hobbling on one foot, he turned and led them back to the forest. Soon they were back under thick canopy again.

"Won't they just blast the trees again to expose us?" Merry asked.

Bryce nodded. "You're right, they probably will. But I've got an idea."

They gathered around, and he explained his plan.

"It might work," Jamal said. "Or it might get us killed. The problem is that I can't think of a better idea."

"Let's do it!" Jason exhorted.

Merry and James nodded.

They climbed up a particularly large tree as high as they could, pulling each other up until the branches began to bend under their weight. Positioned for the attack, they heard the hoverboards flying above them, their lights peeking through the canopy and bouncing off the forest floor.

"Let them get close," Bryce said. He gripped the blaster in one hand, hoping for a clear shot. He could see a small window through the leaves. If he shot too early, the hoverboards would know where they were and call in the fighter again. He began to shake the branches above their heads. The idea was to draw the hoverboards nearer without exposing themselves.

The whirring came closer until the hoverboards were right above them, moving in tight circles.

"I've got a shot," Jason said, and loosed a flower bomb through the tree. Jamal followed with his own. They heard an alien scream, and one of the hoverboards crashed through the trees, its rider hitting the ground beside it, unmoving.

"I hit it!" Jason said, pounding his chest.

"No, I did," Jamal argued.

The remaining hoverboard blasted through the canopy, sending branches and debris down on them. Bryce held the aim of the blaster steady through the gap in the trees. Finally, a shape flashed through the opening in the canopy, and Bryce fired. He hit the bottom of the board and saw a shower of sparks. The board crashed through the leaves and branches directly above him. Bryce closed his eyes and covered his head with his arms to protect himself.

He heard a crash and saw the hoverboard lying on the ground below. But where was the driver?

"Bryce, look out!" Merry screamed.

Bryce looked up. The alien's legs and torso had been caught in the branches just above him, but his arms were free, and he lashed out at Bryce, who lost his balance. He felt himself falling out of the tree. Reaching out with both hands, Bryce grasped the underside of the limb and swung his legs up. His bad leg crashed into the branch, sending a shockwave of pain that nearly caused him to lose his grip. The alien continued to thrash at him, snapping at Bryce with his mouthful of sharp teeth. Bryce scrambled down the limb, away from the alien jaws.

With a surge, the blueskin freed himself from the branches and lunged. He grabbed Bryce's arms with an iron grip and pulled his face toward his snapping jaws.

Thunk!

A flower bomb exploded in the blueskin's face. He roared and clawed at his face, raking ineffectually as the powder did its work. Then he fell to the ground, dead.

Bryce pulled himself up on the branch again and looked at Merry.

"Thanks," he said. "I owe you one."

"Consider us even." She smiled.

Bryce motioned to the others and climbed down the tree trunk.

He stood under the canopy and caught his breath. Bryce felt exhausted, like he could lie down and sleep for a week.

"I guess that's it," Jason said. "Let's head to town."

Bryce searched around and listened. No movement. No sound. No sign of life anywhere. Maybe they had lost the blueskins.

He was about to suggest they go find the others when the loudest roar yet echoed in the distance. The sound of another fighter coming their way.

"Run!" Bryce yelled.

They bolted toward the open area of the forest. Two steps into the clearing, the forest exploded behind him, knocking him off his feet. Bryce tumbled and slammed into the ground face-first. A jumble of tree branches and leaves landed on top of him. He lifted his head slowly off the ground, his ears ringing from the blast. He turned over and pushed the debris off of him.

Bryce surveyed the scene. Jason, James, and Jamal were on their feet looking dazed. But where was Merry?

Then he saw her, twenty feet ahead of him, nearly covered with branches—just her red hair poked out beneath the debris.

"Help!" Merry cried.

Bryce and the others ran over. They raked away the branches with their hands. Thankfully, the fighter hadn't come back yet.

"Stop," Merry said. "Be careful. There's something stabbing my leg."

The thick branch jutted out from the side of her leg. Blood from the wound pooled on the ground.

"I'm going to take the branch out," Bryce said. "On the count of three. One..." And he pulled the branch out.

"Ahh!" Merry screamed. "I thought you said three!"

"It's better that way. You weren't thinking about it. Can you sit up?"

"I'll try." She turned on her haunches and examined the wound. It was bleeding slowly and steadily.

"Yuck!" Jason said.

Jamal smacked him in the arm. "That's not helpful. Can you walk, Merry?"

"I'm going to need to, right?" She rose to her feet, then let out a groan. "Ah, it hurts."

"We'll help you." James said, grabbing one of her arms and draping it around his shoulders.

They walked in the direction of the town with Jason leading the way.

"I hope that the fighter ship doesn't come back," Merry said.

"Me too," Bryce said. Truth be told, he hoped that they wouldn't see any aliens at all. They were nearly out of flower bombs. They would be easily overmatched by any alien force.

The canopy thinned as they approached the town. Bryce stopped. "Let's wait for a minute."

Jason looked at him quizzically. "Why? We're so close."

"We need to make sure that we weren't followed."

Merry seemed to acknowledge his point. "Let's not wait too long."

They stood in the center of the path for a moment, looking for movement in the shadows. The forest was still; the small creatures that normally inhabited a forest having long burrowed underground or run away after the alien blasts. The silence was like a break after a torrential storm.

They waited several minutes, but the aliens didn't come.

"I guess we're okay now," Merry said.

"We did it." Jamal smiled with relief. "We really did it."

"Yeah, bro," Jason said, fist bumping Jamal. "We're going be home soon."

Bryce said nothing. Where was Red Scar?

They walked in silence, sticking to the shadows at the edge of the devastated forest. Bryce realized that he had dealt with the pain from his injured leg before because of the adrenaline running through his veins. Each step now felt like treading on needles. Luckily, the town was less than a mile away.

They trudged ahead. Slowly, Bryce began to fall behind. First it was fifty feet, then a hundred.

Jamal and Jason looked back.

"Are you coming?" Jamal asked.

"I'll catch up," Bryce said. "I just need a minute."

The boys nodded and continued walking.

Finally, the pain got so bad he didn't think he could take another step. A walking stick might help. Bryce left the path and searched through the brush. It took a few minutes to find a sturdy stick that could handle his weight. When he returned to the trail, the others were almost out of sight. Holding the alien blaster in one hand and the branch in the other, he set out to follow them.

Just then, Red Scar, ten blueskin guards, and Cai Lun emerged from the darkness, cutting him off from his friends.

"I'm sorry, Bryce," the interpreter said. "Your escape ends here."

CHAPTER
TWENTY-TWO

Bryce and the aliens stood twenty feet apart. The blueskin guards had their weapons at their sides for now—more proof of their arrogance. The crimson mark on Red Scar's face was conspicuous even in the meager light, and his eyes reflected extreme malice. He held his massive blaster across his chest, daring Bryce to move.

Red Scar uttered something in his alien tongue.

Cai Lun translated, "The great Imjac leader says you have caused enough trouble, tunnel trash. Drop your weapon and accept your fate. You will die here." There was something in the interpreter's eyes that Bryce couldn't place. Resignation, maybe?

Bryce considered for a few seconds and obliged, his weapon and his walking stick clattering to the ground.

Red Scar aimed his savage-looking weapon toward Bryce, and his soldiers followed suit.

Red Scar spoke again.

"Before you die, the great leader would first like to know how you discovered the yellow material would be harmful to the Imjac?" Cai Lun obediently translated.

"Tell him that I'll show him."

Cai Lun's eyebrows rose with surprise as Bryce dropped to his knees and sidearm-tossed a bomb in the direction of the aliens. He rolled off to the side but looked up in time to see one of the guards fall to the floor in agony. His bad leg nearly gave out as he rose, but he pushed through the pain. He didn't have time to celebrate his success, though—a bolt from Red Scar's gun sizzled past his head, cracking into a tree behind him. But his flower bomb had done the trick, as the remaining guards scattered into the cover of the forest. All except for Red Scar.

Bryce picked up his blaster and ran for cover. Blasts followed his movement, destroying the foliage in his wake.

Good, follow me and stay away from my friends.

He led them deeper into the forest, with the aliens loudly thrashing behind him. Branches whipped at him, and vines snagged his feet. Exhausted and with his leg giving out, he hid, crouching with his back to a tree.

He held his last remaining flower bomb in one hand and the alien blaster in the other. In the dim light, he couldn't see where the aliens had gone, but he could hear them closing in. He peered around the tree. A shot rang out over his head. From the sound of it, Bryce could tell it was one of the guard's guns, not Red Scar's huge blaster. A few small branches tumbled onto his head. Then more shots struck the tree, bits and pieces of it shredding with each blast. A large branch came down, smashing Bryce on his shoulder, nearly knocking him to the floor. The tree was quickly losing its bulk.

They're not waiting for me to come out—they're just going to blast my cover away.

Finally, a shot from Red Scar's blaster split the tree in two just above Bryce's head. Bryce had to run. Another tree with a thicker trunk stood ten feet away. Bryce shot off two quick blasts and scampered behind it. He could feel the heat of the returning blaster shots as they whizzed by him.

The blueskins focused their shots on the new tree. Luckily, it was much thicker and provided better cover. But Bryce was stuck—he needed to find a way to get around them or lose them in the forest. He couldn't stay behind this tree forever. Eventually, it would fall, like the other.

One hundred feet in front of him, the forest's canopy thickened, drowning out all of light from the night sky. If he could make it there, he might be able to lose them. That would be more than enough time to get away. He dropped to the ground and crawled on his hands and knees, keeping in line with the large tree. He moved quickly; if the aliens saw him in the open he would be an easy target. But the blasts continued striking the tree. They hadn't seen him yet. When he had crawled twenty feet, he rose and sprinted into the darkness.

The shots at the tree stopped, and he could hear the blueskins moving through the brush behind him. Bryce pushed himself as fast as he could, but his leg throbbed with every step. The blueskins' steady gait kept pace with him.

Bryce veered left and right then left again, but the aliens stayed doggedly on his trail. Branches and twigs snagged his ankles and lashed his legs. Soon he became completely disoriented in the woods. His energy dwindled beyond what he thought was possible, and he wasn't sure how long he could keep going. He needed a way to stop the chase.

He had one bomb left and had to make it count. Up ahead he spotted a tree with thick, low-lying branches in a small clearing. He scrambled up the bottom limb, twice falling, as his painful leg would no longer support his weight. He sat up, pulling his body as close to the trunk as possible.

Red Scar and the surviving guards trampled out of the woods, with Cai Lun behind them. They paused at the clearing, looking for his trail. They stepped closer to the tree and began to talk in their alien tongue. Bryce held his breath, afraid to be given away.

When the aliens were directly below him, he dropped his final bomb. It landed on Red Scar's head, creating a massive cloud of yellow dust. The large alien lurched back and screamed in agony. Two nearby guards fell to their knees and then collapsed on the ground. The remaining guards retreated into the forest.

Bryce frantically jumped out of the tree, falling the last ten feet and landing awkwardly on his injured leg. He let out a squeal of pain but forced himself to his feet. He began to scamper back into the forest toward the town.

He made it to the clearing when heard the loud crack, followed by a jolt of pain in his shoulder. It must have been a glancing blow, but it sent him tumbling to the ground, where he collapsed in a heap.

The pain paralyzed him at first but began to slowly diminish. He rolled on his back and looked up. Thirty feet away, Red Scar stood with his smoking blaster at his hip. How had the yellow powder not affected Red Scar like the others? Did his immense size protect him? Bryce would never know.

The remaining alien guards quickly fell in behind their leader.

Bryce reached for his blaster, but he realized he had lost it when he was shot. He tried to scramble to his feet, but his legs fell from under him. He collapsed on his back and awaited his fate.

Red Scar advanced, then stopped twenty feet away, a sickening look of satisfaction on his face. He leveled his blaster at Bryce. Bryce looked at the sky.

Mom, Dad, I guess the blueskins are going to get me too.

Well, he wouldn't give them the satisfaction of seeing him afraid.

"If you're going to shoot me, go ahead and do it," he yelled at Red Scar.

Red Scar gave him a quizzical look, then seemed to shrug as if what Bryce said didn't matter. He raised the gun and took aim.

Cai Lun appeared from out of the forest and rushed over to Red Scar. He said something in the Imjac tongue, and the alien answered.

"Bryce, I asked if I could say a few final words to you."

"Yeah, what are they?" Bryce said angrily.

"I want you to know that I feel horrible for my role here. I did nothing by choice—the blueskins hold my wife and daughter hostage in China. They said if I didn't come here to interpret that they would kill them."

"Why are you telling me this?"

"Because I've made a choice. I will not help them any longer. Listen carefully. When I say so, turn over and cover your ears for your own safety."

"What?"

And then he saw it. Cai Lun held one of the mining bombs in his hands. Red Scar noticed it too, and a new emotion registered on the giant alien's face: terror.

"Now, Bryce, now!"

Bryce turned on his stomach and covered his head. Then the world went black.

———

Bryce opened his eyes to find his friends standing in a circle over him, looks of concern on their faces.

"Are you okay, bro?" Jason said. It sounded like he was talking under water—even though Bryce had covered his ears, the blast must have affected his hearing.

Bryce sat up slowly and looked himself over. All limbs were attached, no bleeding anywhere. The only thing wrong, other than his hearing, was that his suit was covered with blue slime.

He wiped some of the slime off his suit. "What is this stuff all over me?"

"Do you really want to know?" Jamal said, a small smile on his face.

"Yeah."

"Alien guts. The blast turned the blueskins into alien smoothie."

Merry made a face. "That is disgusting! Bryce, do you think you'll be able to walk? We should get out of here. There could be more aliens coming."

"I just saw an alien ship land near the Mothership," Jamal explained. "Let's hope it's not those extra guards."

Bryce slowly rose to his feet. All that was left of the blueskins and Cai Lun was a large indentation in the ground.

"How did they blow up?" Jason asked. "We were almost to the town when we heard the explosion. Weapon malfunction?"

Bryce just shook his head sadly. "No, it was Cai Lun. He did it. He sacrificed himself for me. For us."

"Cai Lun? The interpreter? I always thought he was one of the bad guys," James said.

"No," Bryce said. "He was forced to do what he did. They had his wife and daughter as hostages." He suddenly thought of his cousin. "Where's Amanda?"

"Over here," Cherie said, waving from the edge of the group. Amanda stood placidly next to her, a glazed expression on her face.

Bryce waved at Amanda, who stared at him blankly. *Still not back.*

"We better find someplace to hide in town. It won't take them long to start searching for us again," James said, extending an arm to help Bryce to his feet.

———

They reached the main street of the town in a few minutes. It was eerily silent, considering the devastation that had taken place nearby. It was likely the people had learned to hide from the blueskins when they heard trouble.

"Where do we go?" Jason asked.

Bryce scanned the street. "There, that's the house." Bryce pointed to the building that he and Merry had noticed on the scouting trip.

Bryce grabbed Amanda's hand and led her, while the others helped Jamal and Merry. Bryce's leg raged, but he could only imagine what Jamal was going through. The thin boy looked close to passing out from the pain.

Hopefully, help was close.

The front door had been red at some point, but the paint had chipped over time and faded into a light pink. Bryce turned back to the others, who looked at him expectantly.

He rapped on the door and waited. There was no answer, so he pressed his ear to the door. He couldn't hear any movement inside through the solid wood.

"Are you sure this is the one?" Merry asked.

"I'm sure," Bryce said. "This is where we saw the light." He knocked again, louder this time.

The door opened a crack, and Bryce found himself staring at a girl who appeared to be about four years old. She had dark hair and large brown eyes. She stared at Bryce and the others with surprise.

"*Mamá,*" the girl said. "*Hay gente aquí.*"

Suddenly her mother stood beside her, a taller version of the little girl.

"*Lucita, ven aca,*" she scolded and then stopped when she saw them. She hesitated a moment, and Bryce could tell that she was going through options in her mind. Bryce knew the easiest one was to slam the door in their faces and lock it. If she aided them, she put her family at risk.

"Help us," Bryce pleaded. "Help us. *Por favor.*"

"*Podemos ayudarlos, Mamá?*" the young girl asked, pulling at her mother's shirt.

The woman looked them over. Bryce saw something register on her face. Maybe sympathy. Maybe fear. Hopefully sympathy.

"*Por favor,*" Bryce pleaded. "*Por favor.*"

Then the woman opened the door wide and gestured them inside.

CHAPTER
TWENTY-THREE

BRYCE WOKE WITH A START. It took him a moment to gather his bearings in the pitch black. For a moment he thought he was back at the Imjac camp, but then he remembered. The escape. The battle with the blueskins. Cai Lun and the explosion. The town.

Stiff from sleeping against the chilly wall, he stood to stretch. Careful not to wake the others, he extended his injured leg out, working the muscles back and forth. It was still sore, but each day it felt slightly better. Soon, he hoped, it would be fully healed.

The footsteps on the floorboards above him told him it was morning. For the last week, they had been cooped up in this basement, without so much as a window. The room was small and dank, with barely enough room for all of them to lie down to rest. Still, no one complained.

The woman who rescued them was named Manuela. Although she didn't say it, Bryce could tell that she was worried. If the blueskins found them hiding in her basement, Bryce knew the aliens would show her no mercy. She and her family would pay with their lives. The woman had three children, Lucita and an older brother and sister. The brother seemed about nine years old and was fascinated with them. He frequently stared down at them from the top of the basement door until his mother called him away. The oldest sister was a year or so older than the boy and had the worried face of her mother. No father lived in the house; Bryce wondered if he had died fighting the blueskins. Maybe that was why the woman had been willing to help them.

Manuela told them that she had arranged passage for them on a fishing boat. They would leave in the night, in pairs, to the docks where a ship would be waiting. The boat would take them to Southern California. From there, they would be on their own getting home. It was far from a perfect plan, but better than no plan at all.

The door cracked open, bringing with it welcome light. Two sets of footsteps sounded on the stairs, Manuela and Lucita, with breakfast on a tray. Lucita shone a flashlight on the stairs as she walked ahead of her mother, with the other hand on the railing.

Manuela placed the tray on the floor. "The boat ready tonight. You go." She smiled as she said it. Bryce wondered if she was smiling at the thought of their freedom or because she would be free of the worry harboring them caused her. Maybe both.

But they had to go. Bryce could see it in Manuela's eyes. The blueskins had already come through the town looking for them. They even searched the house. But the door to the basement was short, and Manuela and her children pushed a bookshelf in front of it, making it invisible to the naked eye.

"*Gracias*," Bryce said, and grabbed a small pastry from the tray. "For everything."

"Yeah, thanks," Jamal said, pulling himself to a seated position.

"You saved us," Cherie added. "We'd be dead without you."

The others nodded, even Amanda.

"Tonight, you be free," Manuela said, smiling. "You go home."

Bryce nodded, but he hoped it would be so simple. If only.

The day crept by. Bryce slept as much as he could, knowing that he would need to be awake and alert. At last, he heard the household quiet, the four sets of pattering footsteps pared down to just one.

The door opened.

"It's time," Manuela said.

Jason and Reese volunteered to go first. They were the healthiest of them all. If they encountered any trouble, they would run back and warn the others.

The truth was they would all be going out blind. If one group was captured, there would be no way to warn the others. They could be walking into a trap, one pair at a time.

As they gathered around the doorway to the house that night, Bryce felt jittery. It would be a long walk to the boat by the shore and much could go wrong. The blueskins were surely still looking for them.

At last, Jason and Reese waved and disappeared into the darkness. When Jason and Reese didn't return in five minutes, Merry squeezed Bryce's hand, and then she and James left as well.

Five minutes later, Cherie and Jamal rose to their feet.

"See you at the boat," Cherie said.

Jamal wearily extended a hand. "Good luck."

Bryce shook Jamal's hand. "Same to you." And when it

was finally their turn, Bryce took hold of Amanda's hand. She stared into the street vacantly.

"Thank you for everything," he said to Manuela. And then he thanked the three children. Lucita had tears in her eyes.

"Be safe," Manuela said.

The streets were dark and deserted. The gloomy gray sky would normally have been a depressing sight, but after over a week in a dank room, the briny air refreshed him. They strode down the street, Bryce leading the way, Amanda obediently following. The strength in Bryce's leg hadn't returned yet, but the pain was mostly gone.

Soon they cleared the town. The path to the sea lay in front of them.

Several small boats were tied to the dock. Bryce stopped and looked around.

"Over here," a voice called.

Bryce turned and saw a short, paunchy man with a dark mustache standing in the awning of a decaying hut.

The others stood inside. Bryce could see the hope in their faces; he felt the same. But at the same time, a feeling of unfinished business loomed large.

"We're getting on a boat," he said to Amanda.

"Boat," she repeated.

Good, she understood.

"Let's go now," the man said, leading them to the dock.

Later, as they crossed the channel to the neighboring island, Bryce stared back at the mountain of Islas del Diablo. It seemed to stretch into the sky. The power of the blueskins lay in its core, but so did the material to defeat them. He thought of the hundreds of kids who still toiled at the mountain, and the thousands more who would replace them. All to give power to a brutal alien race.

In his heart, Bryce knew his fight against the aliens wasn't done.

———

A week later, a truck pulled to a stop at the end of a long driveway. Bryce climbed from the bed, then helped Amanda down. He rapped on the tailgate and yelled a thanks to the driver, who beeped his horn twice and zoomed off. Bryce took a moment to take it all in. It was late afternoon, the winter sun casting long shadows through the trees. There was a chill in the air, but Bryce barely felt it.

As they passed under the Hubbard Dairy sign, he looked up at the house. The farm looked unchanged and brand new to him at the same time.

Someone sat in shadow on the front porch of the farmhouse. As Bryce and Amanda started up the driveway, the person got up and went to the railing of the porch. It was Aunt Sammie. She stared at them for a moment in disbelief.

"Amanda? Bryce? Is that you?"

Bryce held a hand up. "We're here, Aunt Sammie!"

Amanda grinned. "Mom."

Aunt Sammie let out a jubilant shriek, then opened the door to the house and yelled inside, "Kyle, they're home. They're home!"

Aunt Sammie raced down the porch stairs, stumbling a bit, then toward them, arms spread wide. Uncle Kyle was right on her tail.

They met halfway up the driveway, in a group hug that felt like it lasted for hours.

"I can't believe it," Aunt Sammie said finally. "You're home!"

"Yep, we're home." Bryce said, and he felt it in his bones.

ACKNOWLEDGMENTS

I could not have finished this book without the help of others. Thanks to my editor Lauren Ruiz, who found typos and made key suggestions to improve the story. Two fantastic English teachers, Bonnie French and Donna Sorensen, provided great feedback and gave me the confidence to keep going. Autumn Birt created the cover and helped get the book ready to print. Most of all, I'd like to thank my wife, Seiko, who put up with me while I tapped away on my keyboard when there were a million things to do around the house.

ABOUT THE AUTHOR

L. J. Monahan lives in Northern California with his wife, two sons, and a crazy dog named Luna.

Thanks for reading. If you enjoyed this book, please consider leaving an honest review on your favorite store.